Who in the world are you, Jack Wolf?

Giving up the idea of sleep, Terry lay on her side with her head pillowed on her arm and watched him, there in his little island of light. Watched the way the corded muscles of his forearms moved below the rolled-up sleeves of his flannel work shirt as he shuffled and dealt cards with the practiced grace of an expert. Watched laughter carve engaging parentheses in his cheeks and etch a fan of creases at the corners of his eyes, without melting the ice in their depths.

Jack Wolf, who are you? she wondered, lying troubled and wide-awake. Who are you, and what in the world do you want with me?

There, in the safe cocoon of her sleeping bag, she was suddenly awash with goose bumps, as if she were standing in a chilly Baja wind, naked, raked by a pair of vivid blue eyes. Eyes with a curiously intent and feral gleam . . .

Dear Reader,

When two people fall in love, the world is suddenly new and exciting, and it's that same excitement we bring to you in Silhouette Intimate Moments. These are stories with scope and grandeur. The characters lead lives we all dream of, and everything they do reflects the wonder of being in love.

Longer and more sensuous than most romances, Silhouette Intimate Moments novels take you away from everyday life and let you share the magic of love. Adventure, glamour, drama, even suspense—these are the passwords that let you into a world where love has a power beyond the ordinary, where the best authors in the field today create stories of love and commitment that will stay with you always.

In coming months, look for novels by your favorite authors: Kathleen Eagle, Marilyn Pappano, Emilie Richards, Judith Duncan and Justine Davis, to name only a few. And whenever—and wherever—you buy books, look for all the Silhouette Intimate Moments, love stories with that extra something, books written especially for you by today's top authors.

Leslie J. Wainger
Senior Editor and Editorial Coordinator

KATHLEEN CREIGHTON

Wolf and the Angel

SILHOUETTE·INTIMATE·MOMENTS®

Published by Silhouette Books New York

America's Publisher of Contemporary Romance

To Lisi, my daughter, whom I often bewilder and
sometimes disappoint, thank you for loving me anyway,
and for teaching me poker.

ACKNOWLEDGMENTS

Special thanks to Lee Brown, for taking me up in a small
plane for the very first time, and to Gary, for answering all
sorts of questions I'd have been afraid to ask anyone else.

SILHOUETTE BOOKS
300 East 42nd St., New York, N.Y. 10017

WOLF AND THE ANGEL

ISBN: 0-373-07417-4

First Silhouette Books printing February 1992

KATHLEEN CREIGHTON

has roots deep in the California soil and still lives in the valley where her mother and grandmother were born. As a child, she enjoyed listening to old timers' tales, and her fascination with the past only deepened as she grew older. Today, she says she is interested in everything—art, music, gardening, zoology, anthropology and history, but people are at the top of her list. She also has a lifelong passion for writing, and now combines her two loves in romance novels.

A Note From The Author:

Dear Reader,

In 1961, two female pilots made an emergency landing on an isolated mesa in Baja California, Mexico. People from the nearby village sheltered them and found fuel for their plane so that they could continue on their way. To show their gratitude for the townspeople's kindness, Polly Ross and Ailene Mellott decided to organize an airlift of food and toys. A doctor named Dale Hoyt, who was also a pilot with the Civil Air Patrol, joined the project, and after the food and toys had been distributed, asked if anyone wanted to see a doctor. He treated twenty-two people before he ran out of supplies, but from that first visit an organization known as the Flying Samaritans was born. Today, the Flying Sams are a well-organized group of professionals with more than a dozen chapters in California, Arizona and Tijuana, dedicated to bringing health care to people in isolated places.

While *Wolf and the Angel* was inspired in part by the organization known as the Flying Samaritans, the people, places and procedures described in the story are pure fiction. They are not intended to be an accurate portrayal of the activities of the Flying Sams, and should not be interpreted as such.

Chapter 1

He'd been in worse joints. Two years driving eighteen-wheelers and another three bustin' his butt on the two-bit rodeo circuit had made Wolf an authority on joints. There was one on the outskirts of every town in the San Joaquin Valley, and some in the Mojave Desert that pretty much *were* the town. This one he'd probably rate about five on a scale of one to ten—one being don't walk in unarmed, drink with your eyes open and always play with your back to the wall. At least it had cold beer, clean cards and a waitress with yes in her eyes, which was about all he ever asked of a place.

But then again, this was Tijuana. In Tijuana, everything had a price, and Jack Wolf had learned the hard way never to trust anyone, man, woman or town, that could be bought.

"The game is stud, two up, three down, nothing wild," the dealer intoned. His voice was as silky and deceptive as hundred-proof tequila in a strawberry margarita. "Ante up, gentlemen. Mr. Wolf, are you in?"

"I'm in." Wolf tossed a chip into the center of the table and leaned back, pulling hard on his cigarette. From behind a screen of smoke he watched the dealer's small, beringed hands dole out cards, twice around the table, once facedown, once turned up.

The face-up card in front of Wolf was a red deuce; the dealer's was a ten of spades. Wolf took another drag on his cigarette and lazily tipped the ash before picking up his second card. Deuce of clubs. He made damn sure his eyes didn't flicker, and when it came his turn, matched the bet without comment.

The next card was dealt facedown. Wolf let his card lie until the last second while he studied the dealer, one eye squinted against the curl of smoke wafting up from the end of his cigarette. Not a big man, he thought, but that was deceptive; he had a massive chest and thick neck, a look of power. And a face, Wolf noted sourly, with all the animation of a Mayan effigy. He wasn't going to get any help there.

Not that it mattered, he already knew quite a bit about Juan Navarro. Such as the fact that, along with his associates in certain South American countries, the man controlled a sizable percentage of the illegal goods that passed regularly through the U.S.-Mexican border. The Drug Enforcement Agency knew it, too, but couldn't prove a thing, which was why there were a whole bunch of federal agents who would give an arm or a leg to be sitting where Jack Wolf was right now, preferably wired for sound.

None of which mattered much to Jack Wolf. What did matter was that Señor Navarro had something Jack wanted. Badly.

That, and a notorious weakness for cards.

Wolf's third card was the king of hearts. The Suicide King. It crossed his mind as he methodically added chips to the pile on the table that if he were superstitious he'd probably consider that an omen of some kind.

The fourth round of cards whispered onto the green tabletop. A second red deuce slid over and partly obscured the one already lying faceup in front of Wolf. The dealer's eyes flicked at him with cold curiosity, like the tongue of a snake, as he placed the king of spades with precision beside his own ten. From the man on Wolf's right, obviously one of Navarro's bodyguards, came the soft hiss of an exhalation.

To Wolf, the atmosphere in the bar seemed to shift, like a picture slipping just a little out of focus. In his perception the light around the card table dimmed and the American rock music issuing from a portable radio behind the bar faded, becoming no more obtrusive than the rhythmic swish of the ceiling fan above his head. He could *smell* the game now—a smell unlike any other in the world. The smell of cigarettes and *cerveza,* sweat and adrenaline, and an indefinable aura of money, greed and deception.

The waitress came and was waved away. The only sounds now were the clack of chips, the faint swish and smack of the cards. Wolf's last card skated toward him across the table, borne on a thin cushion of air. He pinned it casually with a forefinger and turned up a corner, then placed the two cards in his hand facedown on top of it, tapped them once and leaned back, quietly smoking.

The man on his right made a disgusted sound and folded. The man on his left coughed, shifted indecisively and tossed some chips into the center of the table. Wolf noted that he had begun to sweat, and curved his lips in a thin, sickle smile. A so-so hand, he thought, and no real stomach for gambling. The man would fold on the next round.

Juan Navarro's eyes zeroed in on Wolf—flat, black, dispassionate as bullets. Wolf avoided them by taking a long pull from his bottle of *cerveza.* Knowing Navarro was taking careful note of every swallow, he allowed a few careless drops to drip down his chin, then wiped them off with the back of his hand. It never hurt to have an opponent think you were drunker than you really were.

Navarro's lips formed a meager smile. "Mr. Wolf?"

Wolf sat forward, set the bottle down with a clunk and tossed in enough chips to cover the bet. Then he passed a considering hand through the modest pile that remained— he'd been winning steadily but not spectacularly—and separated out a ten dollar chip. "Raise," he grunted as he added it to the pile.

"I'll see that—" the dealer's voice was a soft murmur of confidence "—and raise."

As expected, the man on the dealer's right threw down his cards and lit a cigarette, muttering to himself in Spanish. The other bodyguard was now watching the proceedings through slitted eyes, arms folded on his barrel chest. The shape of the bulge under his left arm was unmistakable.

Here we go, Wolf thought, time to make it interesting. His heartbeat quickened.

It was the hand he'd been waiting for all night, and the moment he'd been working toward for weeks. There were only two hands Navarro could possibly have that would beat his. Wolf didn't know what the mathematical odds were that Navarro might be holding either a straight flush or four tens, but he figured they were good enough to stake his life on. He took another swig of *cerveza*.

"Looks like it's just you and me," he said, smiling his sickle smile. "See . . . and raise." He let his words slur just a little.

"Indeed," Navarro murmured absently as he counted chips into the growing pot.

"I guess we could just go on all night like this," Wolf commented affably as he lit another cigarette.

Navarro shrugged, looking bored. "You could always call."

Wolf exhaled and drawled, "Yeah, I could. Or raise the stakes."

The dealer leaned back in his chair. His chest jerked several times and a sound came from it—laughter, apparently—dry and dangerous as blowing sand. When the paroxysm had passed he touched a fingertip delicately to the corner of one eye and inquired with polite curiosity, "What sort of raise did you have in mind, Mr. Wolf?"

Wolf shrugged, planted his cigarette between his lips and stuck his hand inside his shirt. "Relax," he growled as the two guard dogs snapped to attention, and withdrew his hand along with a fat white envelope. The guards relaxed only slightly. Wolf gave them each a smug look as he placed the envelope on top of the pile of chips.

"There you go," he murmured through a cloud of smoke. "I'll see your bet, and raise you what's in that envelope."

For the space of a dozen heartbeats Juan Navarro sat still. Then, his manner casual, almost negligent, he picked up the envelope and ran one finger inside it, separating the contents.

The bar grew silent. The ceiling fan stopped turning. From the corner of his eye Wolf caught a small movement as the guard on his right pushed his hand deeper into his armpit, closer to his gun.

Navarro lifted his eyes from the document he'd been reading and spoke softly. "What game are you playing, Mr. Wolf?"

For the first time that evening Wolf allowed himself to meet that flat, black gaze. Copying the dealer's quiet tone he replied, "If you know my name, you know the game."

"A very dangerous game."

Wolf shrugged. "It's always dangerous when the stakes are high."

"Perhaps higher than you can afford." As the dealer's fingers moved caressingly back and forth across the envelope, a sapphire ring on one of them caught the light and winked once, twice. "The information in this envelope is indeed worth a great deal of money. Of course, it is also worth your life. Only a DEA insider could have access to such detailed information."

"That's right," Wolf snapped, suddenly dropping all pretense. "And you know damn well which DEA agent it came from."

"Ah yes, DEA Agent Frank Wolf. Your brother. A tragic business..." Navarro shrugged an apology, though his expression didn't change perceptibly. "Nevertheless, I'm afraid I can't afford to take chances. I am a gambler, Mr. Wolf, not a fool. You understand." He tapped the cards before him on the table. "Win or lose, you must know that you are a dead man."

Wolf shook his head and leaned forward, ignoring ominous rustlings from his flanks. "I don't think so, Navarro." He kept it low, intense. "And if you'll send the Blues Brothers here out for coffee, I'll tell you how this hand is going to be played so we both come up winners. Come on..." He relaxed suddenly and held up both hands. "Hey, you might as well call. What have you got to lose?"

Navarro stared at him unblinking, one finger still stroking the envelope, back and forth. Wolf waited for uncounted moments.

Then the dealer's head jerked twice. Muttering their disappointment, the guards scraped back their chairs and went to take up positions against the wall, where, Wolf was certain, they'd make sure to keep him in a reasonably clear line of fire.

"Yeah, that's better," he drawled. He sat back, picked up his beer bottle and drained it.

Navarro's chest shook silently. "In this country there is a word for people like you," he remarked as he beckoned to the waitress.

"Oh yeah? What's that?"

"*Loco.*"

Wolf just snorted.

When the waitress had come and gone, Navarro picked up his glass of tequila and inspected it through half-closed eyes. "Tell me, Mr. Wolf. If you are not crazy, why are you so certain I will not kill you?"

"Two things." Wolf made a sizable dent in the fresh bottle of *cerveza* before going on. "For one, we both want the same thing."

"Oh?" If Navarro was surprised, he didn't show it. "And what is that?"

"The men who killed my brother."

Navarro sighed and shook his head. "But in any war there must be casualties, Mr. Wolf. And in this particular war, I regret to say, your brother and I were not on the same side. I understand why you should want revenge on the men who killed him, but why should I?"

Wolf's fingers tightened on the neck of the *cerveza* bottle. He fought the rage and spoke softly, in a voice as cold and deadly as a sidewinder's warning. "Because they went too far, isn't that right, Señor Navarro? They got carried away... not only killed the DEA man, but killed his family, too. His wife and his little girl. They weren't supposed to do that, were they? Really stirred things up, made it hot for everybody, and now the crackdown is hitting where it hurts. Isn't it, Navarro? Right in the profits. The way I hear it, even the company that hired the hit wants those guys dead, because the DEA is pulling out all the stops on this one. They want those guys badly, and if the DEA gets to them first and they start spilling what they know, it's bad news for your side. Hey—how'm I doing so far?"

Navarro sipped tequila, then pressed his lips tightly together. It was more expression than Wolf had seen in his face all night, a sign, possibly, of extreme agitation. But all he said was, "I understand your position. Even... a certain desire for revenge. But since the fate of your brother's killers seems to be, shall we say, an inevitability, why not let things take their natural course?"

Wolf's swallow of *cerveza* went down like battery acid.
"Because," he said softly, "I want them. Personally."

"Revenge can be very costly."

Wolf nodded. His lips twisted painfully. "I'll pay the
price with what's in that envelope. That's straight from my
brother's files, which his killers failed to locate, by the way.
Ironic, isn't it?" He washed a bitter chuckle down with more
cerveza and leaned back in his chair. "I figure whoever has
it gets an advantage on his competition worth ten to twenty
million, maybe double that. High stakes even for you,
Navarro."

"What stakes?" The dealer's chest bucked, again be-
traying amusement. "Mr. Wolf, you are forgetting, I can
still kill you and keep the envelope. Do you have another
reason why I should not?"

Wolf grinned suddenly, showing teeth. "Because you're
a gambler, Señor Navarro. There's nothing you love more
than a good game of cards—except maybe money." He
leaned forward and softly played his trump card. "And because there happen to be three more envelopes just like that
one, which right now are safely in the keeping of an attor-
ney I know. But in the event of my untimely demise or sudden and unexplained disappearance, they'll be mailed to
your competitors in Bogota, Quito, and Lima. And there
goes your advantage." He casually snapped his fingers.
"The way I figure it, killing me, while it might eliminate one
very small problem, is going to wind up costing you,
oh...twenty million dollars, give or take a few million."

To Wolf's surprise Juan Navarro began to laugh again,
with a sound like windblown sand. Finally, still quivering
with it, he took a pen from his shirt pocket, drew a paper
napkin toward him and scribbled a name on it.

"The names of the murderers of your brother's family,
and the last place they were seen," he said as he folded the
napkin once and placed it on the pile of chips on top of the

envelope. "Mr. Wolf, I believe that meets your last bet. I call."

Wolf listened to the thunder of his own heartbeat while he watched the dealer turn over his cards. Two kings and the ace of spades.

He let his breath out slowly. "Sorry, Navarro. Four deuces beats three kings." He turned over his two deuces, then picked up the folded napkin and the white envelope. Navarro's hands jerked spasmodically. Wolf held his up, stopping the dealer halfway out of his chair.

"Ah, ah—" he murmured, showing his teeth, "remember the three envelopes."

He tucked the napkin into his shirt pocket, and casually held a corner of the envelope to the end of his cigarette. As he puffed it to a red glow and watched a small flame flower, he murmured conversationally, "You know, if your competition ever got hold of one of these, it'd probably put you out of business. Something to think about."

Navarro watched the flames eat into the envelope, his face suffused and darkening but still impassive. When Wolf had ground the ashes into powder under the sole of his boot, he spoke one word in whispered Spanish: *"Loco."*

"Yeah," Wolf drawled, "so they tell me."

He watched in moody, heavy-lidded silence while Navarro jerked his watchdogs' chains and headed for the exit, making the poor guys run in order to get there ahead of him. Wolf almost felt sorry for them.

Once they were gone, he allowed himself one short, grim chuckle. Then he drained his bottle of *cerveza*, took the napkin out of his pocket and smoothed it out on the tabletop beside the forgotten pile of poker chips.

Bernardo Cruz and his brother Billy. At last, the names of the men who'd killed Frank, Barb and Carrie Elizabeth. And the name of a place called *El Refugio de los Angeles*. Angels' Refuge. A beautiful name for a godforsaken place.

No. His lips twisted in response to a spasm of unbearable pain as he touched the chain that hung around his neck. There were two rings on the chain, one a man's gold wedding ring, the other a child's ring with a tiny rose-pink heart. They lay hidden inside his shirt, against his skin, a constant burning reminder. *No.* The men he was looking for weren't angels—they were pure evil. There would be no refuge for them, no refuge anywhere on this earth, as long as Jack Wolf had life in his body. No matter where they went, no matter what it took, he would find them.

Wolf beckoned to the waitress and ordered two more bottles of the strong Mexican beer. She gave him a look as she set them down in front of him, half-inviting, though maybe a little less certain about it, now, half-measuring, wondering how much he'd had to drink and trying to decide whether he was likely to cause problems. She didn't know there wasn't enough *cerveza* in all of Tijuana to make Wolf drunk. Not enough beer in the whole damn world to put out the fire inside of him, or dull its pain.

Hell no, alcohol wouldn't do the job, but something else would. Sometimes. For a little while.

When the waitress came back with his change, Wolf looked straight up into her eyes and smiled.

It was always the smell that came to him first.

He didn't even know if you were supposed to be able to smell in dreams. Maybe it was only the memory of that particular smell, and the feelings of horror and dread that came with it. The smell of violent death.

He'd be standing on the doorstep, knocking, everything so quiet and normal, sun shining, sprinklers going, birds singing. But there was that smell. So he'd call and put out his hand to open the door. The knob would be sticky; his hand would come away red. He'd push the door open and walk in, and the smell would leap at him, grab him by the throat, choke him. And then he'd be running through rooms, calling and calling, calling for Barb and Carrie, calling Frank, his voice echoing louder and louder, his heartbeat thundering faster and harder. Then he'd be opening doors, and there was blood everywhere, everything he touched sticky with it, until finally there was only one door left to open. He never wanted to open it. He knew what he'd see beyond it, and he didn't want to see. His mind, his whole being screamed in protest; his heartbeat bludgeoned him, his breath burned like acid in his throat.

But he knew he had to open the door. *He had to.* Every nerve in his body fought him as he reached out his hand, every movement an agony, his fingers shaking.

Wolf sat up in bed, ice-cold and drenched with sweat. The woman beside him stirred and murmured a sleepy question in Spanish.

"It's nothing," he answered her, his voice guttural, the words slurred. "Just a dream. Go back to sleep."

He sat for a while, his shoulders slumped, breathing slowly and deeply, until the shaking stopped. Then he lay down, stiff as a post, staring into the darkness. Afraid to close his eyes.

The next time the woman stirred he drew her into his arms and pulled her over him, covering himself with her body, tangling his hands in her hair. Her warmth poured into him, heating his chilled body. Her long coarse hair slipped through his fingers like water, cleansing them. Her woman's scent filled his nostrils, gradually eclipsing the other. Her mouth and hands moved expertly over his skin, slowly but surely driving away the last remnants of the dream.

"Of course we understand, David. These things happen. Don't worry. Go to bed, drink plenty of liquids—" Terry broke off to listen for a moment, nodding her head and laughing. "Yes, right. Take two aspirin and call me in the morning. Listen, just take care of yourself, okay? We'll find someone. Don't worry."

Dr. Teresa Duncan pressed the disconnect button and handed the cellular phone back to the burly gray-haired man leaning with both arms on the open door of a black Chevy van.

"Well, that was Dr. Garcia," she said, exhaling in exasperation. "Temp of a hundred and two, can't even get out of bed, much less fly a plane."

Dr. Carl Wahlberg digested the news, then said, "Who else is there? Can we get somebody else?"

Terry turned to look down the long row of hangars, shading her eyes with her hand against the intensity of the November sun. At that hour on a Thursday morning the airport was a busy place. Several of the hangar doors were open, people bustling around, and from somewhere nearby came the whine of a power drill.

Two doors down, a rather scruffy-looking individual in jeans and a bomber jacket was involved in conversation with the owner of a blue-and-white Cessna, a businessman Terry knew slightly, mostly just to say hello to. When he saw Terry looking his way, the businessman—she couldn't remember his name—waved and nodded. The guy in the bomber jacket looked, too, then lit a cigarette and went on looking, frankly observing. She turned back to Carl.

"We could find a pilot, maybe. David said to go ahead and take his plane—he's sending Linette over with the keys. But a Spanish-speaking pilot who also happens to be a dentist?" She gave a snort of disappointment and looked at her watch. "Look, you and the others had better go on without me. We can't let all those people down. Meanwhile, I'll make some phone calls, try to round up someone to take Dr. Garcia's place. If I can, I'll catch up with you later."

Carl pondered the situation, chewing his lip. "Why don't you just come with us? We have an extra seat."

Terry shook her head. "There's Ingrid, too, don't forget. We were supposed to pick her up in San Diego. And even if one of us stayed behind, you wouldn't have that extra seat in case someone needs to be transported. No, it's best if you go on ahead. I'm sure I'll be able to find someone—although it would be easier if it wasn't a three-day weekend.''

It was Dr. Wahlberg's turn to check his watch. Then he gave the door of his van a decisive slap and hoisted his bulk into the driver's seat. ''Well, okay, if that's what you want to do. We'll see you down there, then—I hope. Hate to leave it like this, but we've got to roll if we're going to make all our stops.''

''I know,'' Terry assured him with a grin of confidence. ''Better the rest of you get to the clinic on time, at least. Don't worry, I'll be right behind you.''

The doctor nodded and waved. Terry stood in the November sun and watched his van roll away down the long avenue between hangars.

The owner of the blue-and-white Cessna watched the van, too, then jerked his head in its direction and said, ''Now that's who you should be talking to, Jack, if you want to get to the real interior of Baja.''

''Oh yeah?'' said Wolf absently, still studying the tall, redheaded woman. She was wearing light tan slacks and a plain white T-shirt, and had her hair tied down at the back of her neck with something utilitarian, like a rubber band. He decided she looked the athletic type—angular and long-legged—and too small-breasted to be his type. ''Why is that?''

''Ever hear of the Flying Samaritans? Flying Sams, they call them. Bunch of doctors and nurses who fly down to Baja about once a month to take care of the people down there—you know, the ones that live so far from anything they'd have no medical care at all, if it weren't for the Sams. You want to talk about remote? Those guys land on airstrips you couldn't pay me to put my plane down on. Dr. Wahlberg—that's the guy who just left—told me once they came in and found the only landing strip in a hundred miles plowed and planted in pinto beans!''

"Yeah?'' said Wolf. He jerked his head in the direction of the red-haired woman, who at that moment was shading her eyes with her hand and gazing indecisively into the distance. He noticed that the sun gave her hair a kind of reddish halo effect where it shone through the cloud of escaped curls around her face. "Who's the lady? She one of them— the Good Samaritans?''

"Her? Oh yeah, she's one of the regulars—doctor, I think. Let's see . . . *Duncan,* that's her name. Dr. Duncan— can't forget that, can you? Can't think of her first name, though. Tracy, maybe. Or Tony. Something like that. One of those names you can't tell if it's male or female.'' The businessman chuckled dryly. "She's not the kind of person you get on a first-name basis with right off the bat, if you know what I mean.''

Wolf chuckled in a comradely way, but his mind wasn't on it. He wasn't interested in getting on a first-name basis with the doctor. Flat-chested do-gooders *definitely* weren't his type. What he was interested in was the fact that she kept pacing a little way down the row and then turning back, as if she couldn't make up her mind whether to go or stay.

"Wonder what she's doing,'' he said thoughtfully.

"Huh.'' The businessman, an old friend of Wolf's from his trucking days, gave the doctor another glance and shrugged. "I don't know, they're usually all long gone by now. Looks like she's waiting for somebody.''

"She looks stood up,'' said Wolf.

His heartbeat quickened; he felt a surge of grim exultation. It seemed a pretty damn good bet that the lady with a problem might just be the solution to his.

Chapter 2

"Excuse me."

The unexpected masculine voice gave Terry a nasty start. She turned to look for the speaker and sighed inwardly when she saw the man in the brown bomber jacket strolling toward her, thumbs hooked in the belt loops of his jeans, teeth showing white in an unshaven face. She recognized the type, the over-confident grin, that certain almost-swagger in his walk.

Since she didn't have either the time or patience to deal with a man on the make at the moment, she wasted no time on subtlety. She injected her voice with frost and snapped, "Yes?"

The man gave one of those self-deprecating shrugs that are meant to be just the opposite and drawled, "I don't know, you looked like you had a problem. I thought maybe I could help."

Terry subjected him to a dismissive once-over, squinting against the sun. "I doubt it—unless you happen to be a dentist who speaks Spanish and flies."

"That sounds like some kind of riddle." The man chuckled, then held out his hands as if to say, Look, here I am—the answer to all your prayers. "Hey—two out of three ain't bad."

"Oh yeah, sure," Terry began, then gave the guy a second, longer look and ventured, "Which two?"

"Let's put it this way." He rubbed the bridge of his nose with a work-hardened forefinger; the grin slipped awry in a way even Terry had to admit was engaging. Sort of. "I don't think you'd want me poking around in your mouth . . . with sharp metal objects."

That did it. Any thoughts Terry might have entertained of changing her mind about the man evaporated. That tiny little pause, ever so subtly suggesting a double entendre . . . she really didn't need this. Not this morning.

Barely suppressing a shudder, she murmured politely, "I'm sure you're right. Now if you'll excuse me, I really do—"

"Have a problem. That's obvious. That's why I'm offering my services." A lean brown hand touched her arm. The voice became softer, deeper and slightly scratchy. "Listen, my Spanish is only fair, but I'm a damn good pilot."

In spite of her better judgment Terry hesitated. Something made her give the man another look, made her search his dark, unshaven face and finally meet his direct—and curiously intent—blue gaze. She saw nothing there to reassure her, nothing to make her trust his sincerity. In fact, she felt an odd uneasiness, a peculiar *quickening* inside, as if all her senses and instincts had just been turned up a notch.

The man, however, was apparently encouraged by her hesitation. He gave her a big friendly smile and looked as if he wanted to stick out his hand, but thought better of it. "My name's Jack, by the way. Jack Wolf. I'm a friend of Lee's—the blue-and-white Cessna over there."

He nodded to the businessman whose name she hadn't been able to remember. The businessman favored them both with a jovial smile and wave in return. The man who called himself Jack Wolf turned back to Terry, oozing charm—and that sincerity she'd been looking for—from every pore.

"You know, he's been telling me what you people are doing down there in Baja, and I just wanted to let you know, I think it's great. In fact, I've always thought about it— wondered what those people do, you know? For doctors, I mean."

"You have, have you?" Terry said acidly.

Careful, Wolf cautioned himself silently, don't lay it on too thick. This lady's no fool.

Abruptly changing his tactic, he answered the doctor's cynical gaze with an offhanded shrug. "Well, yeah, as a matter of fact I spend quite a bit of time down there my-self—fishing, a little hunting—and it's occurred to me more than a time or two that if anything happened—you know, if I got hurt or sick or anything—I'd be up a creek, with the nearest doctor a couple hundred miles of bad road away."

He hooked one thumb in a belt loop, gave a casual wave and turned away. "Hey, listen, I didn't have anything pressing this weekend, and what you guys are doing sounded like fun, so I just thought maybe you could use another hand. But if you've got it covered . . ."

He could almost hear the battle raging inside her, the fight between the woman part of her that didn't trust him any farther than she could throw him, and the doctor part of her that needed him and knew it. But he never for a minute doubted what the outcome would be. Saints and do-gooders were all pretty much the same when it came to priorities.

Even so, she actually let him take three steps. "So—" she said in a loud, hoarse voice, then paused to clear her throat as if the words were hanging up there. "You say you're a pilot. Do you have a license?"

Wolf slowly turned. "Right here," he said, patting his hip pocket.

"Current?"

"Renewed last summer."

She stood there struggling with it for a while longer, chewing on her lower lip. For no particular reason Wolf suddenly noticed that, while the rest of her features were rather angular—prominent cheekbones, bold chin, arrogant, high-bridged nose—she had a very full mouth, with nice, soft lips. Definitely not the kind of mouth usually associated with saints.

"It can be tricky, flying in Baja," she said finally.

"Not so much flying as landing," Wolf remarked with a grimace. "Where you going? I hope not Colnett—geez, they've got these little tiny cactuses there that can play hell with your tires. And the airstrip at Punta San Carlos is apt to be half under water at high tide. Personally, I think that's better than trying to land on one that's been plowed under, but—"

"Dos Caminos," she said on an exhalation, a capitulation of sorts. "And then Santa Luisa."

Wolf put on his poker face and managed not to flinch. And all he said aloud was, "Not bad. Santa Luisa's a little narrow. How big is your plane?"

She must have told him, but he didn't hear her. He didn't give a rip how big her plane was, he'd have set a 747 down on that runway if she'd asked him to. It was better than he'd dared hope for, so good he figured it must have been Fate— or Luck, a lady he was always glad to have on his side. Here he'd been prepared to hijack the damn plane, or steal it if he had to, to get within striking distance of El Refugio de los Angeles, and now Fate was about to hook him up with somebody who could set him down within twenty miles of the place. And a medical team, yet. He couldn't have come up with a better smoke screen if he'd tried. Even if those two murdering Cruz brothers were watching their backsides— and with hit men on both sides of the drug war after them they were bound to be—the last place they'd expect retribution to come from would be a bunch of doctors and do-gooders.

"We're a volunteer group, I wouldn't be able to pay you," Terry said doubtfully, wondering whether she was trying to recruit the man or warn him away. She just wished she could make up her mind, one way or the other.

By all appearances—and disregarding *his*—the man named Wolf seemed like a godsend. Almost *too* good to be true, if he really knew Baja as well as he seemed to, and could manage even basic Spanish. For some reason she didn't doubt his ability to fly a plane; there was something, an aura of competence about the man that made her believe he could do pretty much anything he set his mind to.

But she didn't trust him. Oh no. Not any farther than she could fly that plane.

On the other hand, Terry was honest enough to admit that part of her reservations might be due to his rather casual approach to personal grooming, although she didn't like to think of herself as the sort to judge a person by superficialities. And anyway, she'd seen rougher-looking faces than Jack Wolf's smoldering at her from the covers of upscale men's magazines. Now that a quarter-inch of beard stubble seemed to be the current "in" look, she supposed she couldn't really hold it against him.

Nor could she fault his physical conditioning. She had to admire—from a scientific point of view, of course—the lean, streamlined look of his body, the taut, economical way he moved. Rather like a racing greyhound, she thought, or a wild predator in his prime.

Wolf.

Again that odd little quickening of unease prickled the skin on the nape of her neck.

"Well . . . if I can get in a little hunting, maybe some fishing while I'm down there, that's payment enough for me," the man named Wolf drawled, still smiling.

And Terry thought suddenly, I know what it is—it's his eyes.

The smile didn't reach them. An intense and unusually vivid blue, they burned at her from out of deeply shadowed sockets like something wild and elusive roaming the shadows just beyond the firelight.

She opened her mouth to say something, but before she could get a word out a red BMW came barreling up and jerked to a gravel-crunching stop beside them. And although she was conscious at the time of having been interrupted before she could say something important, looking back on it later Terry couldn't remember whether what she'd meant to say was yes, or no.

The BMW's door opened even before it had stopped rolling. Terry recognized Linette Garcia, both the car and the driving style. Linette jumped out, keys in hand, words spilling from her in a breathless, French-accented jumble that was her way even when she wasn't rushed.

"Oh, hi, Terry—I'm so sorry to keep you waiting, I know you have to get going—David is so *sorry* he can't go with you, but I told him he would be crazy to try, and he would just make everybody else sick, too. He called all his partners, but the ones who are not on call already have plans, because of the long weekend—you know, family things—and anyway, I don't think any of them knows how to fly an airplane...." She paused, apparently in order to concentrate on fitting the proper key into the lock, then heaved the hangar door open and turned her perpetually flustered smile on Terry. "So you would have to find a pilot anyway. But... have you found someone already? Is this your new pilot? But that is marvelous! *Fantastique!*" Her smile, transferred to the man standing silently behind Terry, grew radiant.

Again Terry opened her mouth, but before she could either confirm or deny his right to do so, Jack Wolf strolled past her and into the hangar. Blithely unaware of undercurrents, Linette followed, chattering enthusiastically.

"It is a nice plane, isn't she? So sleek, so elegant... Is this the first time you will go with the Sams? You will have a wonderful time, believe me, it is a fantastic experience, just fantastic."

Terry stood in the hangar doorway and watched the man in the brown bomber jacket walk around the red-and-white Cessna Centurian, trailing his fingers across the underside of a wing, squinting critically at the landing gear, moving with that cocksure grace she found so annoying and yet so fascinating.

Fascinating? Well, yes, Terry was honest enough to admit, and even, in an odd sort of way, *seductive*.

She moved on into the hangar, folding her arms across her chest in a posture of instinctive feminine defense.

Wolf, who had opened the door to the plane and was poking around inside the cockpit, barely glanced at her. Instead, having apparently found what he was looking for, he began with quiet purpose to do something to the undersides of the wings, first one, then the other. It was a process Terry had seen David Garcia repeat many times, and it irritated her unreasonably that she didn't know what it was for, and even more so that she'd never before thought to ask.

"What are you doing?" she asked now, her voice sharp with suspicion.

"Just checking the fuel lines for condensation," Wolf informed her, waiting until he'd finished and grinning with that particular masculine arrogance.

"Of course," she muttered grudgingly.

"We don't want any unscheduled landings, do we?"

There was a long silence, during which even Linette's chatter faded into the hum of background noise.

I don't know why, Terry thought, but I still don't trust him. And then, almost in panic: but damn it, I need him. *I need him.*

What was more important, there were some sick children in Baja California who needed *her,* and this man could get her there. She was being unnecessarily paranoid. After all, Lee-of-the-blue-and-white-Cessna was a friend of his, and Lee was a reputable member of the business community, even if she hadn't been able to remember his name. What did it matter if Jack Wolf had reasons of his own—and she didn't for one minute believe those reasons were as altruistic as he claimed—for wanting to help her? It was none of her business. It simply didn't matter, as long as he got her to the clinic as planned. Anything else she could handle; she'd dealt with men like Jack Wolf before.

She let out a breath she hadn't known she was holding and said dryly, "No, we certainly don't want any unscheduled landings. The scheduled ones will be quite exciting enough, thanks."

He tilted his head slightly and narrowed his eyes. "That mean I'm hired?"

Terry muttered, half to herself, "I don't think I have much choice," then relented and held out her hand. "All right, Mr. Wolf, you're hired. Welcome to the Flying Sams. But it's not a vacation, so don't expect it to be a picnic. Sometimes it can be gut-wrenching. And you'll be expected to help out wherever you can."

He nodded and solemnly shook on it.

When Terry touched Jack's hand two things happened. Two important things, although she didn't realize how important at the time. And because the two things happened at exactly the same moment, they effectively swamped her senses and short-circuited her usually acute powers of observation—which was the only explanation she could think of for failing to give either the attention it deserved.

First, her hand. When she felt that hard-callused palm come against hers, for an instant there was a peculiar and shocking sense of intimacy, as if he'd touched her somewhere much more personal, and with erotic intent. She felt a rush of warmth, even embarrassment, and, to her extreme disquiet, a fleeting but powerful desire to hold on.

But as unsettling as those sensations were, she was distracted from them by a fascinating phenomenon she had heard about but never seen before. The instant Jack touched her hand his face changed, just suddenly lost all expression. It was as if he'd turned to wax, right before her eyes. Odd, when she'd have expected a victorious grin, or at least a glint of triumph in those intent blue eyes.

Then, just as abruptly, he nodded and let go of her hand. "That all you've got?" he asked, jerking his head toward the nylon duffel bag she'd left sitting on the ground outside the hangar.

"Uh...yeah, just personal stuff," Terry murmured, pushing back stray wisps of hair from her forehead, something she only did when she was flustered.

Annoyed with herself for the momentary loss of composure, she pulled herself together and explained that most of the medical supplies were waiting for them at Brown Field in San Diego, along with Ingrid, the nurse who would be assisting her this trip. She told Jack that they would be refueling there as well, so that the tanks would be as full as possible when they crossed into Baja. "Because down there," she concluded, "you never know whether there's going to be gas at your stop or not."

Jack just looked at her with one eyebrow arched—that typically male, slightly patronizing look that said, "I *know,* lady, I *know*"—but absorbed the information without comment. He was all business now, Terry noted as she watched him stow her bag in the cockpit. His face was tight with concentration, his movements spare and efficient. A totally different person, in fact, from the one who'd been laying on the charm with a trowel only a few minutes ago.

She wondered which was the real Jack Wolf, and whether she felt easier about this one, or less so.

While Jack was towing the Cessna out of the hangar, Terry made arrangements with Linette for returning her husband's keys, said her goodbyes and watched the red BMW roll away. Then she climbed into the cockpit, closed and latched her door and window and fastened her seat belt…did all the things she'd done so many times before she didn't give them a second thought anymore. But today she did them with a strange kind of awareness that could almost be called a premonition, if she believed in such things, a fatalistic realization that she was putting her life into the hands of a complete stranger, and that she might be making the biggest mistake of her life.

Perhaps, she thought, that was why her eyes kept coming back to the man. Why she covertly watched him as he took off his jacket and climbed into the pilot's seat, as he adjusted the radio headphones, checked dials and flicked switches. She couldn't help noticing that the muscles in his arms and shoulders looked smooth and hard, the tendons in his wrists and hands whipcord strong and well-defined. His eyes were narrowed, focused on the controls, and beneath the shadow of beard stubble on his jaws a small muscle tightened, then released.

He turned on the ignition. The plane's engine fired, coughed and settled down to a steady racket that shook the little Cessna like a restless wind. He looked over at Terry and asked, "All set?"

She nodded, and the plane began to roll.

As she listened to the familiar but unintelligible mumble of preflight dialogue between pilot and control tower, Terry looked down and found that her arms were covered with goose bumps.

Wolf had very little use for saints. Having spent most of his life in the shadow of one—namely, his late brother Frank—he was of the opinion that they were all pretty much a royal pain in the butt, and impossible to live up to. He'd long ago given up trying.

He didn't really think Dr. Terry Duncan was a saint—she didn't smile enough, for one thing, and she was too damn bossy—but she was close enough to it to make a confirmed sinner like him nervous. It was a shame, too, because she wasn't a bad-looking woman if you liked them tall, rangy, redheaded and smart. Personally, he liked his women softer and sweeter, with not too much on their minds besides pleasing him. And from what he'd been able to observe on this trip so far, two things were pretty obvious. One, Dr. Duncan had a great deal on her mind. And two, pleasing a man wasn't ever apt to be high on her list of priorities.

Those impressions had been formed and solidified on the trip from Van Nuys to San Diego, partly from her silence and the way she kept looking at him like he'd just shown up on her doorstep claiming to be the telephone repairman when she hadn't called one. But mostly it was plain old gut instinct, a certain kind of tension in her that told him her barricades were up, her doors bolted and her windows shuttered.

Ordinarily he'd have considered that a challenge, and in fact there had been a second or two there in the hangar when he'd taken her hand... Just for a moment there'd been a flash of something—a thought, a mental picture, the kind that usually only came to him when he'd had enough tequila to take the edge off and was making eye contact with a pretty woman across the table, knowing her mind was running along the same track as his.

There were a lot of reasons why he'd slammed the lid on it in a hurry. For one thing it had caught him by surprise. He figured his instincts must have short-circuited or something, because they were sure way off-base on this one. And for another, if he was trying to get the woman to trust him, it wasn't going to help matters if she knew he'd been thinking about how those long legs of hers might feel wrapped around him.

But mostly it was because he didn't want any distractions, not that kind, and not right now. He had a rendezvous in a place called Angels' Refuge, a job to do, a score to settle. And he wasn't about to let anything or anybody get in his way.

He'd been prepared to endure a long silent flight to Dos Caminos—figured it was worth a few hours cooped up in an airplane with a woman who treated him like a bad smell, as long as it got him where he wanted to go—but after San Diego it wasn't too bad. They'd taken on fuel and medical supplies and a nurse named Ingrid, an ex-army "lifer" who'd seen action in both Korea and Vietnam. Ingrid had frizzy brown hair, a craggy, compassionate face, and brown eyes that didn't miss a trick.

Since Ingrid didn't seem to have the same reservations about him that Dr. Duncan did, she took the seat next to his while the doc moved to the back. Which was okay with Wolf. For some reason Ingrid reminded Wolf of his third-grade teacher, Miss Letitia Latimer, the only teacher he'd ever had who'd never compared him with his brother Frank.

He discovered that Ingrid liked to talk, which was also okay with him, since she had some interesting stories to tell and it made the time go faster. He also discovered that unlike a lot of people who'd been there, she didn't seem to mind talking about Vietnam.

"My brother was in Vietnam," Wolf volunteered, surprising the heck out of himself.

"Oh yeah?" Ingrid gave him a narrow-eyed look and said in her blunt, crusty way, "Not you, though, you're too young."

Wolf snorted. After a moment he surprised himself again. "He was wounded during the Tet Offensive. Shoot, maybe he came through your unit. You might have taken care of him."

"Might have, I took care of a lot of 'em . . ." She sighed and shook her head. It was a while before she asked, "Where's your brother now? He come out of it okay?"

He didn't know why he'd mentioned it in the first place. He was sorry he had. He thought about lying, thought about shrugging it off, putting an end to the subject, but he couldn't, not with his third-grade teacher's eyes drilling holes in him. So he coughed and squirmed a little and finally told the truth.

"He's dead."

Ingrid shook her head, balled up her fist and brought it down with controlled anger on her thigh. "Ah . . . damn. I'm sorry. Where'd it happen?"

"Not in Vietnam. He managed to come through that with flying colors—medals, the whole bit." He kept his eyes on the wild blue yonder and tried a grin, the twisted, ironic kind he often used to cover up pain. His fingertips brushed the front of his shirt, briefly nudging the warm metal against his skin. "Nah . . . he died just six months ago. In Texas."

When he said that, Wolf heard a rustling of interest from the back seat. Ingrid said "I'm sorry," and let it drop, but even with his eyes front Wolf could feel the redhead's eyes on the back of his neck. For the rest of the flight he could feel her watching him off and on. He wasn't sure why. Trying to figure him out, he supposed.

Well, good luck, Doc, he thought with a dark, inner smile. She was welcome to try.

So far as he knew, no one on God's green earth had ever been able to figure out Jack Wolf, including Jack Wolf.

"What do you think of him?" Terry whispered to Ingrid as they waited for the gun-toting Federales to finish checking out the plane.

Ingrid was busy repacking a box that had already been inspected and didn't bother to look up. "What do I think of who?"

"Our new pilot."

"Jack?" Ingrid shrugged and went on rearranging medical supplies. "Well, he's a passable pilot, anyway. Nice-looking."

Nice-looking? It wasn't exactly the term she'd have picked to describe Jack Wolf, Terry thought, studying him covertly and critically while she slathered her face and arms with sunscreen. Of course, at the moment the only parts of him she could see were his torso and backside, his head and upper body having disappeared under the hood of the decrepit pickup truck that was waiting to transport them to the clinic in Dos Caminos. And yes, she conceded that he was attractive. But "nice" had nothing to do with it.

"I don't know," she said, keeping her voice hushed, "don't you think there's something a little odd about him?"

"Like what?"

Terry was tucking her hair up into the floppy brimmed cloth hat she always wore to protect her skin from the Baja sun. She paused in the middle of what she was doing, frowning. "Well, I don't think he seems much like the volunteer type, for one thing."

"Yeah, I think he probably has his own reasons for being here," Ingrid said dryly, obviously not much perturbed by the fact.

"Doesn't that bother you?" Terry persisted. She felt vaguely and unreasonably frustrated.

"Nope." Ingrid, who had a touch of arthritis in her knees, struggled to her feet with a loud groan. "The fact that there's more to Mr. Wolf than meets the eye makes him interesting, but it doesn't *bother* me." She glanced at Terry as she dusted off her slacks, one eye squinted shut against the desert glare. "It sure does bother you, though. Why is that, I wonder?"

Terry had known Ingrid long enough to know exactly what she was hinting at. She could see the teasing gleam in her eye. She tried to douse it by saying austerely, "I don't think there's any mystery about it at all. I just don't trust him."

"Hah!" said Ingrid. "He's just more man than you're used to having around, that's all."

"Now wait a minute," Terry began. "If that's a reference to Robert—"

"Oops, there's the 'all clear,'" Ingrid interrupted cheerily. It appeared the Federales had finally finished their inspection. "Let's get this stuff loaded. I don't know about you, but I'd like to find out how that little Rojas baby is doing—the one with the heart defect, what was her name?"

"Estrella," Terry said, letting out the breath she'd already hauled in in preparation for a huffy defense of her ex-husband. "Yeah, me too. I didn't tell you—I've just about got things set up to take her back to the States for surgery. Now if I can just convince her parents to let her go..."

There were such things as priorities, she reminded herself as she picked up a box and started across the hard-packed dirt airstrip. And worrying about Jack Wolf's motives and arguing with Ingrid about her sex life—dismal though it might be—were *way* down on the list.

That crack about Robert had struck a nerve, though. It must have, because she wasn't ready to let go of it yet. Darn it, she thought, nursing the familiar twinge of pain, Robert had been a good husband! And she'd been happy with him, or at least, contented. All right, so it had never been the kind of relationship with a lot of fireworks and passion—that stuff wasn't all it was cracked up to be, anyway. In Terry's opinion it was mostly just exhausting and nerve-racking, and with med school and internship, she hadn't had the energy for it.

Robert had been the perfect husband—patient, gentle, considerate. Nothing that had gone wrong between them was his fault. He'd wanted children, a large family, like the one he'd grown up in. She couldn't blame him for that—a man like Robert *should* have kids. And she didn't blame him for finally getting tired of waiting for her to stop taking care of other people's kids long enough to give him some of his own. She really did understand. It was too bad she just wasn't cut out to be a mother, because someday Robert Duncan was going to make some lucky child a wonderful, wonderful father.

"Can I give you a hand with that?"

With her thoughts full of her failed marriage, Terry was in no mood to be confronted by a hundred and seventy pounds or so of raw masculinity. She pulled up like a startled racehorse, hauled her eyes away from the sculpted, white T-shirted chest and said coldly, "I have this one, thank you. I suggest you go and get one of those others on the ground over there."

"Yes, ma'am," Jack said, and muttered something under his breath.

Terry glanced suspiciously at him, but his expression was bland. She went on her way feeling vaguely puzzled and resentful, as if there were something going on she should know about but didn't.

Still, she was able to shrug off the formless discontent as she climbed into the back of the old pickup truck, and in a matter of minutes had forgotten it completely. For this was Baja. And there was nothing in her life that had more meaning, more importance than the work she did here. It wasn't that all those well-baby checkups, ear infections and respiratory viruses that trooped through her office day in and day out, and the truly sick children that always got to her emotions even when she knew she shouldn't let them weren't important to her, too. But she knew that if she could find a way to afford it, she'd leave them all behind in a minute for a chance to work full-time in a clinic like the one just beyond the next cactus-covered hill.

In that frame of mind she began to feel a little ashamed of herself for the way she'd been treating the newest member of the team. She reminded herself that without him she wouldn't have been able to make this trip at all. It really wouldn't hurt her to give the man the benefit of the doubt. She could even try to be friendly.

With that resolve in mind, and ignoring a sideways look and a half-hidden smile from Ingrid, she scooted across the bed of the pickup truck and settled down next to Jack.

"Well," she said brightly as the truck lurched forward in a cloud of dust and exhaust fumes, "what do you think of the Flying Sams so far?"

Jack shrugged and took a pack of cigarettes out of his pocket. "Haven't seen much."

Terry eyed the lighter flame with distaste, but went on trying to make friendly conversation in spite of it. "Dos Caminos isn't much of a town," she said, trying a polite cough, which Jack ignored. "There probably aren't more than thirty or forty people left in the whole place by now. Most of those came during the construction of the trans-Baja highway. This was an equipment and maintainance depot then. God knows why they're still here. Some of them still work for the road crews, I guess. The rest manage to make a living raising vegetables, or beans. Everybody seems to grow beans."

"And goats," Ingrid said dryly, as the pickup lurched to a bone-crunching halt to avoid a half dozen or so of the animals that happened to be meandering unhurriedly down the middle of the dirt road. "For goodness' sake, don't forget the goats."

Terry laughed. "How could I? They've been known to come wandering through the clinic in the middle of exams!" She waited for Jack to join in the laughter, even politely, but he just went on smoking and watching her in disconcerting silence through a curl of cigarette smoke.

"Of course," Terry continued doggedly, taking a deep breath, "the main problem is always water. Their only source is a spring that runs dry every so often, usually without any warning. When that happens, water has to be trucked in. You should be here then, it's a real adventure. El Refugio would probably have been a better place for a clinic, it's got a much more reliable spring and twice as many people, but—"

"El Refugio?" Not surprisingly, Jack's voice sounded hoarse, as if it had rusted. "Where is that?"

"Just south of here. The terrain is too rugged for an airstrip, so the people there have to come either here or to the clinic in Santa Luisa. It's kind of a shame, actually. It's really a pretty little town, a real oasis, you know? With palm trees—"

"You've been there?" Jack's question seemed no more than curious, but once again Terry felt an odd unease, a sense of something watchful beyond the curl of smoke.

"Yeah, several times." She wanted to say more, to find out if she'd imagined that sudden quickening of interest, but just then the truck wheezed to a stop in front of the clinic, a corrugated tin building that had once housed the heavy equipment used by the road builders.

The conversation ended there, and Terry was left with a nagging sense of something unfinished.

Since Terry's last visit to the clinic, someone had built plywood partitions to replace the curtain dividers in the examining rooms. There was an almost overpowering smell of fresh paint, but as inconveniences went, they'd had to put up with a lot worse.

As she made her way through the crush of people in the waiting area, Dr. Wahlberg poked his head around one of the partitions.

"Ah—Terry. Glad you made it. As you can see, it's standing room only. Let me know as soon as you're set up—" He stopped when he saw Ingrid and Wolf right be-

hind her. "Ingrid, good to see you! This your new pilot?"
He came forward, hand outstretched, beaming; Carl Wahlberg was never happier than when welcoming a newcomer
to the Flying Sams. "A rookie, huh? That's great, just
great. What's your speciality, Doctor?"

Jack's voice was bland, his smile sardonic as he shifted
the boxes of supplies he was carrying and shook Carl's
hand. "Just plain Jack. And my speciality would have to be
machines, I guess. Sorry."

"Hey—that's okay. We have a few of those that need
patching up, too, believe me. Listen, after you get those
supplies unloaded maybe you could take a look at our water
pump." Carl made a clicking sound with his tongue and
added straight-faced and with a droll twinkle in his eyes,
"It's been sounding a bit under the weather, if you ask me.
Pressure's way down."

Jack chuckled to show he'd got the joke and said, "Sure,
be glad to."

Carl clapped him on the shoulder. "Welcome to the Flying Sams, Jack. Ingrid, you want to show him where to stow
this stuff? I've saved examination rooms three and four for
you guys... right through here."

Terry watched Jack deftly sidestep a toddler with a sagging cloth diaper and a runny nose, and follow Ingrid
through a gap in the partitions. She was wondering how in
the world the man had managed so easily to win over both
Ingrid and Dr. Wahlberg. Couldn't anyone else in the world
see that there was something just... *wrong* about the guy?

She caught Carl's arm as he was about to duck back behind the partition and asked in a low voice, "Has the Rojas
baby been in yet?"

"That's your little heart patient, isn't it?" Carl shook his
head. "You know, I haven't seen her. The parents, either,
come to think of it. Were you able to arrange for the surgery like you wanted?"

Terry nodded. "It's all set. Dr. Ito's going to do it. Now all I have to do is get the parents to let me take her back with me. That's why I'd hoped they'd be here. Oh well, I'm sure they'll show up. Meanwhile, I'd better get started—looks like a full schedule."

"Wait a minute—" Carl was scanning the crowded waiting area. "Isn't that one of the Rojas baby's relatives? Over there, the girl in the red blouse. Isn't she a cousin, or an aunt or something? Why don't you ask her?"

"I think you're right," Terry said briskly, "and I will. Right now, in fact."

Terry made her way slowly through the throng, smiling at a few familiar faces, murmuring words of reassurance to a child with tear tracks on her cheeks, pausing to inspect a black eye and administer a nose-tweak to its proud owner, a seven-year-old boy with a gap in his grin. A low murmur of sound followed her; even the children's voices were hushed in the presence of the flying doctors from North America. Shy hands reached out to her as she passed, as if some comfort could be derived from just her touch.

How good it is to be here, she thought suddenly, her heart swelling with emotion. This was what she was meant to do. These people needed her. This was where she belonged.

The girl in the red blouse looked startled when Terry greeted her. Terry gave her a reassuring smile and asked in clumsy Spanish if she was the aunt of Estrella Rojas. The girl looked at the floor and murmured a barely audible *"Sí."*

"¿Donde está Estrella?" Terry pressed eagerly. *"¿Como está ella?"*

The girl's only response was a quick headshake, and then a small, unhappy sniff.

Terry's heart began to beat faster. She caught the teenager's arm and repeated with more urgency, *"¿Como está Estrella? ¡Dígame!"*

The girl turned her frightened, tear-filled eyes on Terry and tried to pull away. *"Pobrecita..."* she whispered, shaking her head. *"Pobrecita..."*

"Hey, you're scaring her to death, Doc," said a soft, ironic voice in her ear. "Let go of her. I'll handle it."

Terry never knew what made her obey that arrogant command. She was numb, she supposed, because the answer to her question was so tragically obvious. All she could do was stand there cold and helpless while Jack Wolf led the weeping girl away to a quiet corner and spoke to her in gentle Spanish.

In a few minutes he was back, his face utterly barren of emotion. Terry looked at him with hot, angry eyes, rejecting his words before he'd even spoken them.

"The baby's dead." Jack confirmed it in a flat, inexorable voice. "The girl says she died two days ago. They buried her this morning."

Chapter 3

One of the things Wolf liked about Baja was that if you wanted to get away from people it was easy to do. The trouble was, while he did want to get away from people, he didn't necessarily want to be *alone*, which was a dichotomy that always left him feeling restless and edgy. Tonight it made him regard the sun's spectacular plunge into the distant Pacific almost with resentment. As far as he was concerned, such beauty was false advertising, and he was long past being taken in by it.

So he turned his back on it, literally, lit a cigarette and leaned against the fender of an abandoned car body, ignoring the sandy scufflings made by its permanent residents as they adjusted to his presence. Below him in the valley the sun had already set, mercifully veiling the scattered houses of Dos Caminos, its goat sheds and bean fields and abandoned cars, in purple shadows. There were a lot of cars, Wolf noted. Baja exacted a heavy toll from both men and machinery.

Most of the houses were dark, except for the clinic—which was still lit up like a used car lot—and the cinder block building next to it, that did triple duty as town meeting hall, school and Catholic church. That's where the townspeople were now, Wolf surmised, busy setting up cots for the visitors and cooking their evening meal. They'd made a party of it; voices and laughter drifted up to him along with the smells of pinto beans and chili peppers and some kind of meat, which under the circumstances he figured was probably goat.

The head doc, Wahlberg, had made a point of inviting Wolf to dinner, but although the smells were inviting, the company didn't appeal to him. In fact, it was just about the last place he wanted to be tonight. He'd had all he could take of people with long faces and teary eyes sniffling into hankies when they thought nobody was looking. And he was damn tired of getting looks from people who couldn't understand why he wasn't as broken up about that little baby's death as they were. Well, *hell.* Sure, it was tough. *Life* was tough. But what they didn't know was that Wolf had no tears left to shed. And that the only emotion left alive in him was a deep and burning passion for revenge.

He heard a sound that hadn't come from inside the old car and froze with his cigarette halfway to his lips. Instinct made him lower the cigarette and cup the glowing end with his hand. He had more than one good reason for wanting to see who was coming before they had a chance to see him. But even when he knew who it was coming up the hill, following the same goat path he'd taken, he didn't advertise his presence. He wasn't sure why. Something kept him where he was, motionless in the shadows.

The last rays of the setting sun touched her floppy-brimmed cloth hat first, and then her face, giving it a lush, golden glow it didn't ordinarily have. She'd taken off the doctor's smock she'd been wearing all afternoon in the clinic, so the light washed over her bare arms and throat, and over her white cotton T-shirt.

Wolf knew from personal experience that the shirt wasn't going to be much protection against the chill of a November evening, even in Baja, and that she was going to wish she had a jacket once the sun went down. Right now, though, the breeze still carried the midday heat and pungent smell of the desert, and felt damn good, which was why he'd taken off his own shirt. The air in Baja was unlike any other—sharp in the nostrils and soft on the skin, dry and fragrant as talcum powder. And, he thought wryly, about all any of them could hope for tonight in lieu of a shower.

He watched, silent as the other anonymous denizens of the rusting car, while Dr. Duncan—the almost-saint—took off her hat and tucked it carefully into the pocket of her slacks. Facing the sun, she lifted her arms and pulled the fastening from her hair, then shook it and finger-combed it back from her face, letting it tumble free down her back in a profusion of curls that could only be natural. Her eyes were closed and her face, bathed in that rosy sunset glow, wore an expression of rapture, as if, Wolf thought, she were greeting a lover.

It seemed so incredibly *sensual*. Watching her seemed an unpardonable invasion of privacy, downright voyeuristic. But Wolf understood that that moment of sun worship was a forbidden luxury to someone of her coloring, and although his was not a particulary poetic nature, something in him found it oddly poignant. He knew that his perspective of Dr. Terry Duncan had been irrevocably altered by the vision, that it was going to be a long time before the image faded from his mind—the way she looked at this moment, arms and face uplifted, hair licking her neck and shoulders like hungry flames, back arched, breasts in surprisingly voluptuous relief, T-shirt stark white against a darkening sky—and that it would continue to touch him in ways he didn't care to examine too closely.

The bolt of carnal lust that accompanied his new awareness was much easier to fathom, and it didn't even come as a surprise, since it was only this morning's fantasy given flesh, so to speak. It had just occurred to him that, saint or not, Terry Duncan was a woman, and a much more attractive one than he'd realized. And Wolf had a feeling he was going to need a woman tonight, more than he had in a long, long time.

So he threw down his cigarette and ground it out with the toe of his boot, taking a primitive, almost visceral satisfaction in her small startled gasp.

"Who's there?"

Terry relaxed only a little when she saw who it was leaning against the old car, long legs crossed at the ankle, naked torso sculpted in golden light and purple shadows. And her feelings were definitely mixed as she muttered, "Oh— I'm sorry. I didn't know anyone was here."

A breath of wind stirred across her skin. It was warm, but for some reason goose bumps sprang up all over her arms and body. She could feel her nipples shrinking and tingling, hardening under her thin T-shirt. For the second time that day she found herself folding her arms across her chest in an age-old and for her wholly uncharacteristic gesture of self-protection.

"I like to come up here in the evening," she said, rubbing resentfully at the bumps on her upper arms. "After a day at the clinic I usually need to relax."

"Yeah," Jack drawled, "I know what you mean."

His voice was deeper than usual and had a kind of resonance, like a cat's purr, that was felt rather than heard. Terry noticed it, along with the fact that she seemed to be unusually attuned to the changing timbres of Jack's voice. She didn't know what either his tone or her awareness meant, but she found both extremely disquieting.

"I usually need a wind-down at the end of the day, myself," Jack continued blandly. "This seemed like a good place for it. Sorry if I took your spot."

Terry gave him a long, suspicious look, but his face was in shadow. I'm being unfair, she scolded herself silently. He's given me no real reason to distrust or resent him. No reason at all.

In an effusion of friendliness, trying to make amends, she said hurriedly, "Oh, no, that's all right, really. I just didn't know anyone was here, that's all. You startled me. I don't mind sharing." She nodded toward the purpling haze in the distance. "You can see all the way to the Pacific from here."

"I know."

"That's Santa Luisa—where we'll be going tomorrow morning." She wondered if he was mocking her with his little half smile. The uncertainty made her give her voice an edge of warning when she added, "We'll be leaving first light."

"I'll be ready." There was a soft grunt as he pushed himself away from the fender of the old car. His boots scraped on the wind-scoured ground.

"So—" He jerked his head toward the lights of Dos Caminos. "Why aren't you down there with the others? Smells like they're puttin' on quite a spread."

Now Terry caught herself wondering about that cowboy accent, which he seemed to put on now and then almost as a disguise, the way some people wore sunglasses. Angry with herself for wondering, she dismissed the thought and turned away from him with a shrug.

"I guess I'm just not ready yet," she said distantly. "To be honest, I don't feel very much like eating." And then, because she could feel her emotions dangerously close to the surface, she threw the challenge back at him. "What about you? Why aren't *you* down there? Don't you have to eat, too?"

He gave a dry chuckle, and the gusting wind carried it away. "I eat when it suits me."

Which wasn't nearly often enough, Terry thought, goose bumps rising once again as she studied Jack Wolf in the thickening dusk. There wasn't an ounce of fat on him, not even enough to smooth out the contours of muscle and bone and sinew. His body had a ropy, rawhide quality that both fascinated and repelled her. He looked very strong, but for the life of her she couldn't imagine any refuge, any comfort in those arms. No warmth at all. Only hardness.

"It got to you that badly?" he asked suddenly, his words barely rising above the whisper of the wind. "Losing the kid?"

His question had come so unexpectedly. Terry found that she couldn't trust herself to answer without tears, so she swallowed several times, shrugged again and looked away.

"Hey, you win some and you lose some, Doc, isn't that the way it goes? I'd think you'd be used to it by now."

The callousness of his comment shocked her—not so much the words, which after all were only the truth and nothing Carl hadn't said to her already, but the way he spoke them. So harshly. So coldly. More than coldly. With an edge of bitterness that burned like dry ice.

Maybe it was that strange bitterness that made Terry gulp back her anger and say with quiet intensity, "No, I'm not used to it. I will never get used to it, at least I hope I won't. Because that baby shouldn't have died, Jack. Damn it, we have the knowledge, the technology to save her. She was born with a heart defect. She needed surgery, more complex and delicate than we can manage here. I was making the arrangements—I had made the arrangements—to take her back to the States. But it took too long. There was so much red tape.... And while people were busy pushing paper around and filling out forms, that little girl *died*."

Her voice finally broke on the last word, leaving her struggling again to hold back tears. And because she was certain a man as cold and hard as Jack would never understand her tears, she couldn't bear to let him see them. So she turned her back on him and stood there hugging herself, so full of pain and rage she wanted to scream with it.

Something touched her shoulder; it was a touch so soft, so gentle, that she couldn't believe it when she looked down and saw a man's hard, rough hand there. There were no words of sympathy or comfort with it, no empty platitudes which she wouldn't have accepted anyway. Just that and no more . . . Jack's hand on her shoulder.

Common sense told her to move away from that touch, instinct told her it wasn't to be trusted. Something else made her stand still, breath suspended, heart racing, like someone listening for sounds in the night.

The hand moved under her hair, curved and tightened over the muscles at the juncture of her neck and shoulder. How did he know? Terry wondered, marveled. How could he know the exact place that always needed rubbing at the end of a long day?

Oh, be careful, her common sense warned her. *Don't trust him*.

But her head had already begun to wilt.

She resisted him a little longer, until he growled, "Come 'ere" and his other hand found its way beneath her hair and began to work in tandem with the first, expertly kneading the rigid trapezius muscles, delicately probing the tight places in her neck and at the base of her skull. Nothing, Terry thought, had ever felt so good.

She could feel his body there, close to her back, and then closer, until somehow she was leaning against him and his warmth was seeping through her shirt and into her skin. And yes, she'd been right about him—his body *was* hard. Hard as rock. Hard as saddle leather, hard as sun-baked earth. But she'd been wrong, too, because there *was* comfort there. Comfort, and an amazing and almost overwhelming sense of safety.

It must have been that feeling of safety that made her obey the subtle pressure of his hands, moving closer when they asked her to, even turning, finally, to face him. Standing there like that, closer to him than she wanted to be but unwilling to move away, she found herself searching his face, looking for something that would explain the confusion inside her. Looking for answers to the questions she couldn't put words to, even to herself.

But if his face bore any expression at all it was lost in shadows, giving her only a silhouette against the lavender sky. A silhouette of naked shoulders and long hair blowing in the wind.

Maybe it was being in Baja again, or perhaps she was just tired, but all at once she was thinking of the people who had first populated this hostile and beautiful place, in a simpler and more savage time. In a moment of pure fantasy *he* seemed to be one of them . . . a primitive man, untamed as the land and every bit as beautiful.

The hand on her neck was so hard, so very strong. Frighteningly strong. Shouldn't I be afraid? she wondered, as shivers rippled down her back and her heartbeat quickened. But the shivers weren't from fear. The hand was gentle, too, and the feeling of safety even stronger than before. Yes, he was strong, and she could sense the ruthlessness in him. But in those earlier savage and dangerous times a strong man protected his woman.

When his lips touched hers it seemed at first a part of the fantasy. *She* seemed a part of the fantasy, a part of him, of the land, and of the wind. She felt his breath, tobacco-scented and warm, the wind tugging at her hair, the ancient ground beneath her feet. She felt his naked chest against her palm, the softness of hair on her fingertips—and something unexpected, a chain and a medallion. No, not a medallion—rings. And then his mouth, and the intriguing prickle of whiskers. His hand, moving from her neck to the side of her face, caught a windblown strand of her hair. His fingers tangled themselves in it, crushed it against her cheek. Her mouth opened.

Something exploded inside her. She felt the shock wave like a blindside punch, and a wave of heat that seemed to melt her very bones. *It's been so long.*

And with that wave came the blinding white light of total awareness. Terry's mouth, opening to meld with his, instead released a gasp of purest shock. Her hands, tingling with the urge to touch and explore, flattened against his naked chest, against the two rings that rested there, and pushed. Hard.

Jack gave a soft grunt of surprise. He put a hand to his chest and by taking one step backward managed to maintain his balance as he muttered, "What the hell was that?"

"What the hell was that? What the hell do you think you're doing?" Terry's voice was hoarse with anger.

But even then she knew the anger was more for herself than Jack. She'd been half expecting something like this; she'd distrusted the man from the beginning, hadn't she? So how could she have done such a thing as respond to him, even for an instant? And to let him feel her response! Oh God, she thought, please let me take it back. She hadn't meant it—she *hadn't.*

She swiped a hand across her mouth and found that she was shaking.

"Hey now, Doc, take it easy," Jack said, that elusive cowboy drawl more marked than ever. "Nothin' to get upset about."

"I'm not upset," Terry ground out through rigid jaws. "Just insulted."

"Insulted?" There was a mirthless bark of laughter. "Because I kissed you? Most women would feel just the opposite—in spite of what they'd say."

Terry felt the heat rising inside her, prickling her scalp and the palms of her hands. She dug her nails into her palms and managed a calm, cool tone when she replied, "Well, I must not be like most women—at least not the ones you're used to dealing with. I really don't like being kissed by strangers. I'm insulted that you thought I would.''

A cigarette lighter clicked and flared, throwing sinister shadows across Jack's face. For an instant Terry saw the tiny golden flame reflected in his eyes, then the lighter snapped shut, and the end of the cigarette glowed red and arced downward.

''Hey, look,'' he said, ''no big deal.'' His voice had a hollow quality to it, as if it came from a great distance. ''I was needing a little help chasing away some demons, and it looked to me like you were, too. I thought maybe we could help each other. Guess I was wrong. My mistake. Sorry.''

Terry rubbed at her upper arms, aware all at once that the wind had grown cold and that the desert around her was vast and empty. ''Well, you were wrong,'' she said through chattering teeth. ''About a lot of things. One, I don't have any demons to chase. And two, if I did, I still wouldn't appreciate your help.'' She drew a long breath and let it out. ''God—I hardly know you!''

''That,'' Jack said dryly, ''is something I was trying my best to remedy.''

''Look, let's get something straight. I agreed to let you come on this trip because I needed someone to fly the plane. And that's *all* I need you for.''

The cigarette flared, briefly illuminating a sardonic smile.

Terry snapped, ''Don't press your luck, Jack. You pull something like this again, and I swear to God *I'll* fly the damn plane. As far as I'm concerned, you can *walk* back to San Diego!'' She hurled the last words over her shoulder and stalked off, furious to discover that her legs were wobbly.

Well, she sure did have a redhead's temper, Wolf reflected as he listened to the diminishing crunch of her footsteps and, after one prolonged and somewhat irregular scrape, some inventive swearing. So much for sainthood.

But he found that he was grinning to himself there in the darkness, thinking about the redheaded doctor. The day's depression had left him. Suddenly he felt stimulated, full of energy, *alive*. Come to think of it, it was the way he felt once in a great while at the start of a high-stakes game, when he'd sized up his hand and his opposition, and known right then and there that the hand was his if he played it smart.

Because however much the lady might deny it, he'd felt the flare-up of response in her—all of it—the melting and the fire, the beginnings of passion and the rejection of it. And he knew that sooner or later he was going to have her in his bed—long legs, temper and all. Yeah . . . all he had to do was play his cards right.

It was pretty quiet by the time Wolf got back to the church—or the dormitory or whatever they were calling it tonight. The locals had cleaned up and gone home, except for the mayor, a skinny man with a salt-and-pepper mustache, a straw cowboy hat with silver conchos, and the improbable name of Jesús Junior Miranda.

Jesús Junior was sitting at the mess table talking with the other pilot, a pharmacist of Hispanic ancestry who still spoke the language pretty well. The others were fairly well scattered and were passing the long evening hours, each in his own way. Wahlberg was at the far end of the table writing in a notebook of some sort; the other doctor, an orthopedic surgeon from Encino who'd been nursing a bad sinus infection all day, had retired to his sleeping bag on one of the folding cots that had been set up at the back of the room.

Terry was there, too, pretending to read a paperback novel by the light of a portable Coleman lantern. Wolf was careful not to look directly at her, but he knew she was there, and that she was equally aware of him—and just as carefully not looking at him. He smiled to himself, enjoying the quickening he felt at the thought of her, the little kick of adrenaline. It was all just part of the game to him. Part of the challenge.

"Nice evening for a walk," Ingrid greeted him dryly, coming from the sacristy—or the kitchen, Wolf wasn't sure which—to waylay him as he was making his way to the table. "Here—" She nudged his elbow with a napkin-covered paper plate. "I saved you some dinner. Go sit down over there and eat it."

Wolf took the plate and lifted the napkin, getting a whiff of hot chili peppers. He looked at Ingrid and lifted an eyebrow.

"Go on—no arguments. You need some meat on those bones." She gave his forearm a squeeze. Wolf looked down at the hand on his arm—an old nurse's hand, gnarled and blue-veined, cool, strong and amazingly gentle—then back at the twinkle of laughter in those sharp eyes.

"Yes ma'am," he said meekly, thinking of Miss Letitia.

He ate the way he always ate, mostly without chewing, while Ingrid sat beside him, watching him like a hawk and muttering her disapproval of his habits. As far as Wolf was concerned, though, eating was pretty much the same as putting gas in a car. He did it only when necessary, and spent no more time on it than he had to. He polished off the plateful of food in a matter of minutes, then balled up the napkin and tossed it and the plastic utensils onto the plate. Pushing it aside, he reached for his cigarettes. Ingrid gave a little warning cough.

"It's a good thing I like you, you know that?" Wolf growled out of the side of his mouth. But he tucked the pack of cigarettes back into the pocket of the plaid flannel shirt he'd put on after Terry had left him.

Ingrid just chuckled. Wolf unbuttoned the other pocket and gave her a sly, sideways glance. "Okay, then, how about a little game of cards?"

The nurse regarded him with one eye closed. "What'd you have in mind?"

"Poker," Wolf said blandly, taking the deck of cards out of his pocket and sliding it across the table. "Is there any other kind?"

"Hah!" Ingrid picked up the deck and halved it. "My daddy always told me never to eat at a place called Mom's or play cards with a man who carries his own deck." She tapped the cards once on the tabletop and began to shuffle with a deft and experienced hand. "You know...I never did pay attention to Daddy."

"Uh-oh," Wolf muttered, "I think I'm in trouble."

Ingrid looked up from her shuffling long enough to yell across the room, "Hey, anybody for poker? We got a game going here."

The pharmacist was an immediate taker. Mayor Jesús Junior was invited to join, but excused himself and went off to his home and family. Dr. Wahlberg just waved benignly and went back to his journal. There was no response at all from the orthopedic surgeon.

"Come on, we need somebody else," Ingrid persisted. "Terry, what about you?"

"Yeah, Terry," Wolf innocently chimed in. "You up for a little game?"

"She's always good for a hand or two," Ingrid said confidently to Wolf.

"Not tonight," Terry called without looking up from her book. "I have a headache."

Wolf snorted. The pharmacist guffawed and made a ribald comment.

"Still upset about the Rojas baby. That's not like her," Ingrid said thoughtfully. She gave Wolf a narrow-eyed look as she handed him the deck. "She say anything to you about it?"

"Not a word," he muttered with a shrug, and cut the cards. "You want to deal?"

"Yeah, sure, I'll deal. Five card stud okay with everyone?"

The pharmacist nodded. "Fine with me," said Wolf. "What about stakes? You set a limit, or what?"

"Nah," said Ingrid, "we never play for money. No hard feelings that way."

Wolf gave her an incredulous look. "What do you play for, then? You got to have stakes, or what's the point?"

Ingrid shrugged. "Whatever's handy—beans, matches, tongue depressors. Charlie, you want to check the kitchen, see if there's some pinto beans in there?"

"Well, hell, that's no fun, playing without stakes," Wolf grumbled good-naturedly as the pharmacist went to look. "Sort of like playing strip poker in the dark, if you know what I mean."

Everybody laughed, even Doc Wahlberg. Everybody but Terry.

Wolf had noticed that, although she still had her nose in that book, she wasn't turning any pages. He'd also noticed she was wearing sweats and had her hair tied back again, and a pair of reading glasses were perched on the end of her nose. She sure didn't go out of her way to make herself attractive, but Wolf decided he liked that about her. A lot of women looked like a million dollars in the evening, but were a real shock to wake up to in the morning. He thought if this was the doc's worst, then he'd sure like to be around to see her at her best.

Charlie, the pharmacist-pilot, came back from the sacristy-kitchen with a double handful of pinto beans and the game got under way, but Wolf only played with half his attention on poker. The rest was on the *other* game he was playing... and the greater challenge.

Dr. Duncan. Terry. That's all she was to him—a game and a challenge, like a good hand of poker. He wasn't going to forget that he had a job to do. He touched the chains and rings that were his talismans. No, nothing and nobody was going to get in the way of that, but when it came to holding off the nightmares, he'd take his diversions anywhere he could find them. Tonight he'd have to settle for cards, but sooner or later he was going to have that stubborn redhead in his bed. He could bet on it.

Terry had given up trying to read. She hadn't really been reading anyway, just staring at paragraphs while her mind scurried here and there on its own. Finally she dog-eared the page, shut the book and placed it on the floor, folding her glasses and laying them carefully on top of the book. She turned off the lantern and lay back with a sigh, prepared to shut out the noise of the card game by an exercise of sheer will. As an intern she'd learned to sleep in hospital corridors; how tough could one lousy poker game be?

Strip poker in the dark.

The instant she closed her eyes the phrase was there in her mind, growing ever more insistent, like a ticking clock or a dripping faucet.

Damn the man. Damn his voice, which she could somehow hear above all the others, though he spoke softly and seldom. *Strip poker.* Had he said that just for her, knowing her mind would conjure images of his leather-tough body...naked, silhouetted against a darkening sky? Had he guessed that she'd still be feeling his bare chest on the palm of her hand, the warmth of it, the teasing texture of hair, the unexpectedness of those rings? Would he know she could still smell his skin, the clean-sweat masculinity of it, the surprisingly pleasant tang of tobacco?

Who in the world are you, Jack Wolf?

Giving up the idea of sleep, Terry lay on her side with her head pillowed on her arm and watched him, there in his little island of light. Watched the way the corded muscles of his forearms moved below the rolled-up sleeves of his flannel workshirt as he shuffled and dealt cards with the practiced grace of an expert. Watched laughter carve engaging parentheses in his cheeks and etch a fan of creases at the corners of his eyes, without melting the ice in their depths.

She thought of the way he'd spoken to Estrellita's aunt, how he'd soothed and calmed her fears, of the coldhearted way he'd dismissed that baby's tragic and unnecessary death. She thought of the callousness, and remembered that he'd tried to take advantage of her grief over the loss of a patient to make a clumsy pass. She remembered the unexpected gentleness of his hands. And those rings.

Jack Wolf, who are you? she wondered, lying troubled and wide-awake. Who are you, and what do you want with the Flying Sams? What in the world do you want with *me?*

Strip poker.

A familiar chuckle of triumph rose from the island of lantern light; Terry could hear it even over the collective groan of defeat. Oh, the man did know his cards, she thought wryly. In any game of poker, strip or otherwise, it wouldn't be Jack who lost his shirt.

There in the safe cocoon of her sleeping bag, she was suddenly awash with goose bumps, as if she were standing naked in a chilly Baja wind, raked by a pair of vivid blue eyes. Eyes with a curiously intent and feral gleam . . .

Chapter 4

"Oh, look, there's Jack," Ingrid said, stopping so abruptly just inside the entrance of Santa Luisa's only cantina that Terry almost ran into her. "You want to ask him to join us?"

"And ruin my appetite?" Terry retorted crossly. "No thanks."

She'd been looking forward to dinner at Pepe's Cantina all day. Pepe Gomez was a wizard with fresh-caught fish, and he always went all out when the Flying Sams came to town, especially ever since they'd seen his grandson through a bad bout of pneumonia last year. She wasn't about to let Jack Wolf spoil her dinner the way he'd wrecked her sleep the night before. Not after she'd had a particularly hard day at the clinic on top of it. She couldn't remember being this tired since her days as an intern. All she wanted now was to enjoy one of Pepe's masterpieces, maybe sip a margarita or two and go to bed early.

"Besides," she said to Ingrid, trying not to be too obvious about looking Jack's way, "it seems he already has company."

"Huh—so he has." Ingrid, it appeared, didn't share Terry's reservations about spying. "Wonder who that is."

"Don't stare," Terry hissed, then proceeded to ignore her own admonition. "They look like locals."

Pepe's Cantina was small, irregularly shaped and dimly lit. Not much more than a cabaña, it was perched haphazardly on the sand just above the high tide line, and had big screenless windows covered by shutters that could be raised and propped open with a stick during the daytime and when the weather was nice. Right now, though, with a brisk onshore wind blowing, the shutters were closed. A single ceiling fan stirred the air in smoky eddies.

The table where Jack was sitting was only a few yards away from the entrance, but with his attention focused on the two men with him, he didn't seem to have noticed the newer arrivals. For some odd reason Terry had a feeling he wouldn't be pleased to see them.

"I wouldn't think he'd know anybody here," Ingrid commented when they'd settled themselves. She didn't seem perturbed about it, just mildly curious.

"I don't think it's a friendly get-together," Terry muttered, frowning. "It looks like business. Doesn't it to you?"

"Well, if it is, it's his business and none of yours." Ingrid gave Terry one of her patented piercing looks. "So how come you're so interested in Jack's business, anyway? I thought you didn't want anything to do with the guy."

"I don't," Terry said flatly.

"Oh yeah? That why you've been watching him all day long? Seems to me like you can't keep your eyes—or your mind—off of him." There was an infuriating gleam of amusement in the nurse's shrewd brown eyes.

Under their steady gaze Terry shifted restlessly and muttered, "I don't trust him. I think he's up to something, and
I want to find out what it is. Don't you?"

Ingrid just shrugged. After a moment or two, in her own
direct way, she asked the question Terry had been carefully
avoiding, even in her own mind. "What are you afraid he's
up to—smuggling? Drugs?"

Terry didn't answer. She couldn't. The idea of anyone
using the Flying Sams for such a purpose was too terrible to
think about. But she *had* been thinking about it. It had been
keeping her from sleep, taking her concentration away from
her work, and now it was giving her a queasy feeling in the
pit of her stomach. For that alone she could kill him, but
when she thought of the damage he could do to the Sams if
he *did* try to use the organization to smuggle drugs—it was
just unthinkable. It was unforgivable. He could destroy
everything they'd worked to build here, all the good they
were trying to do.

Her stomach gnawed and knotted. She felt responsible.
She was the one who'd brought—and what an apt meta-
phor it was!—the wolf into their midst.

Then and there she vowed that whatever Jack had in
mind, he wasn't going to get away with it. If she had to,
she'd stick to the wretched man like glue for the rest of the
trip. She'd watch every move he made.

She was about to tell Ingrid what she had in mind when
Pepe spotted them. As always, he came over to their table,
grinning and wiping his hands on his apron, expressing in
flowery and passionate terms his delight at seeing them
again and his eternal gratitude for their services to his family. After describing in exquisite detail the feast he planned
to prepare for them, he personally brought them both huge
double margaritas and went off to his tiny kitchen to perform culinary miracles.

As soon as he was gone, Terry picked up her glass and
across its salt-encrusted rim focused on Jack's table. A sec-

ond later the glass clinked untasted onto the tabletop and ice-cold liquid slopped unnoticed onto her hand. She leaned forward and hissed, "There—did you see that?"

Ingrid took time for a long, judicious sip before inquiring, "See what?"

"*Money.* He just gave those men money, Ingrid. And now they're shaking hands. He's made some kind of deal with them, that's obvious. The only question is, *what?*" Terry picked up her margarita and drank absentmindedly and deeply, frowning at the back of Jack's neck. After a while she smacked her hand down on the tabletop and said, "You know what? I'm going to find out, that's what. And if it's drugs..." She gulped half of her drink.

"If it is," Ingrid said mildly, "what do you think you're going to do about it?"

Terry polished off the rest of the margarita, shoved back her chair and stood up. "That's easy," she said, stifling a hiccup. "I'm going to shoot him."

Wolf sat in a relaxed sprawl and watched the two young men from El Refugio leave the cantina. Outwardly he was relaxed; inside he was humming like a high-tension wire. Things were falling into place.

Tomorrow. By this time tomorrow, one way or the other, it would all be over.

He picked up his bottle of *cerveza* and took a long swallow, observing under cover of his eyelashes that the doc had gotten up from her table and was making her way toward him. He'd seen her come in with Ingrid, of course. He'd known she was watching him, too. He figured she'd seen just about enough to pique the hell out of her curiosity and he'd been wondering if she'd have the guts to confront him with it. He should have known better.

She didn't waste any time on polite formalities, just pulled out the chair opposite him and plunked herself down without waiting for an invitation. She looked pretty magnificent, actually, with her head up and her chin out, challenge written in every line of her body, purpose in every move she made. There was color in her cheeks, too, and a smoky look to her eyes. Wolf grinned to himself and thought about how she'd take it if he handed her that corny old line, "You know, you're beautiful when you're angry."

Instead he tipped his *cerveza* bottle toward her in a friendly way, smiled and murmured, "Well, hello there, Doc. Can I buy you a drink?"

A corkscrew strand of hair had come loose from the fastening at the back of her neck and slipped forward over her shoulder. She poked it impatiently behind her ear and said, "No, thank you," in a voice as clipped and cold as ice.

It was easy to see she had something important on her mind. First she put her elbows on the table and laced her fingers together so they covered the lower part of her face. Above them her eyes regarded him unblinkingly, smoldering like two lumps of charcoal. After a few moments of that she lowered both her eyes and her hands, gave a nervous cough and swallowed twice. Wolf rather enjoyed watching the ripples in her throat, noticing the sheen of sweat in the hollow at the base of her neck, admiring the rise and fall of her breasts beneath her shirt. When she abruptly sat back and folded her arms across her chest, he especially enjoyed knowing that it was his gaze that discomfited her so.

Part of the game, he thought, smiling to himself. *And Doc, so far you're losing.*

Wolf was a patient man. He sat and drank his beer and let her fidget, until finally she gave a small hiccup and just blurted it out in a voice that was tight and a little too loud.

"Those men. Who were they?"

He raised his eyebrows, feigning the right degree of surprise. "Couple of locals, I guess. Why?"

"What were you doing with them?"

"Talking." He took his cigarettes out of his pocket, shook one out and stuck it between his lips.

Her chin came up another notch. "You gave them money."

"That's right." He clicked on his lighter; the flame burned yellow and gold for an instant as it bit greedily into paper and tobacco.

"Why?"

"Lady," Wolf murmured as he pocketed the lighter, narrowing his eyes against the billow of new smoke, "you ask an awful lot of questions about things that aren't any of your business."

A capricious air current carried smoke into Terry's face. She didn't flinch. "It's my business," she said, her voice low and her gaze steady, "if you're planning on using the Flying Sams to smuggle drugs."

So that was it. She suspected him of trafficking in drugs. He snorted softly and shook his head at the irony in that. After a moment he touched his talisman and shifted restlessly, scraping his boots across the rough plank floor. "Nothing like that."

Terry threw back her head and followed him with an accusing stare as he slowly rose to his feet. There was fire in her eyes now, as well as in her cheeks. "Am I supposed to believe you?"

Wolf stood still for a moment, looking down at the doctor with the flame-red hair, looking into those smoky blue eyes of hers, eyes that betrayed every thought in her head, every feeling, every emotion. A little fireball of anger rocketed through him and exploded in a totally unexpected desire to kiss her.

"Lady," he growled, "you can believe whatever you want."

He picked up the *cerveza* bottle, drained the last swallow and set it back down with a thump. Then he turned and headed for the exit.

Outside the beach beckoned to him, a long, curving line stretching from the dark hulks of the fishing boats like beasts asleep on the sand to the low point where the dry creek bed met the sea. He left his boots by the cantina's front door and jogged through soft sand to the water's edge, where the beach lay silver under the light of a newly risen moon, glistening in patches left by retreating waves...a broad pathway unbroken by any footprints save his own.

It felt good to him, the cool crunch of sand beneath his feet, the salt tang of the sea in his nostrils, the thunder of surf in his ears. It felt good to run. When he was running he didn't have to think about anything but the pounding of his own heart, the pumping of his lungs and the blood surging through his muscles. In the last six months he'd done a lot of running on a lot of beaches.

He wasn't really surprised to hear the thump of footsteps behind him. He'd half expected the doc to come after him, and with those long legs of hers she wouldn't have much trouble catching up. He didn't make it easy for her, though. He didn't speed up, but he didn't slow down, either. Not until she caught him by the arm and held on to him, forcing him to stop or pull her off her feet.

"Lady," Wolf said as he turned, in a voice that was soft and steely with warning, "you are on dangerous ground."

She just stood there looking at him, breathing hard, but he didn't think it was from the running. Then she said tensely, as if she'd been crying, "All right, if it's not drugs, then what is it? Damn it, I have to know."

"Business," Wolf said distantly, closing himself off from her. Sympathy was a luxury he couldn't afford. "Personal business—and none of yours."

His arm was like his voice, Terry thought, as cold and unyielding as stone. As she let go of it she felt an odd frisson of fear, as formless and powerful as the waves that surged again and again across the sand, straining to reach them and then retreating. She hugged herself against the shivering, refused to give in to the fear and finally shouted, "Damn it, Jack! If it's anything that would hurt the Sams, it is *too* my business. I brought you into this team. Do you know what it would do to the Sams if you use them to smuggle drugs? *Do you?*"

His eyes looked beyond her; the moonlight bathed his face in silvery translucence, giving it the austerity of marble. "I told you—I'm not smuggling drugs."

His voice, his words had the ring of truth to them, but his face, his eyes, there was such ruthlessness in him! Suddenly overcome with frustration, Terry cried out, "And I'm just supposed to take your word for that? After what I saw? Look, why should I trust you, anyway? I don't know you from Adam!"

"You have to trust me," Jack pointed out flatly, no trace of emotion in his voice. "You don't have a choice. Without me you're stranded right here in Santa Luisa. Don't forget that."

She couldn't forget it. No matter how much she might bluster about flying the plane herself, she knew she wasn't capable of doing so, and neither was anyone else on the team. And there wasn't room for both Ingrid and her in Dr. Wahlberg's plane. She really didn't have a choice.

Those unpalatable facts played themselves over in her mind while she stood there curling her hands into fists and breathing like a long-distance runner. Then she uttered a soft cry and turned back blindly toward the lights of Pepe's Cantina.

But after a few steps, something made her stop and look back. What she saw stunned her.

It was just Jack, standing there in the moonlight where she'd left him, turned slightly away from her, thumbs hooked in the belt loops of his jeans. But this was a different Jack, one she'd never seen before, one she felt she *should* have seen. She, of all people.

She thought later it might have been the distance, those few steps she'd put between them, just enough space to give her a new perspective. Maybe it was the moonlight, soft-

ening rough edges, washing out shadows, letting her catch
a glimpse, just a glimpse, of the man underneath the beard
stubble, the man behind the burning eyes. She saw a lonely
man—but she'd already sensed his loneliness. This was
more. This was beyond lonely. What she saw in that moment was a man in pain.

Why hadn't she seen it before? It was right there, in the
taut, protective curve of his back and shoulders, in the stark
planes and hollows of his face, plain as day to someone
whose job it was to recognize pain and then to deal with it.
Or it should have been plain to her. Had the woman in her
been too busy disliking and distrusting the man for the
doctor in her to notice the pain? There was no real excuse
for it, and the doctor in Terry felt chastened and ashamed.

She didn't know or care whether the pain was physical or
emotional. Her healer's heart responded instinctively and
with such intensity that she had taken two steps toward him,
had actually reached out her hand to him, when something
stopped her. She felt the wall come up, a barrier between
them as inviolate as concrete. From across it came a cry, a
single word, raw and harsh as the sound of tearing cloth.

"Doc!"

She stood still and waited, while the damp salt wind stung
her cheeks and played havoc with her hair. Jack didn't
move, but fired his words in a barrage, as if he had to let go
of them all at once or change his mind.

"Look, it's not drugs, I promise you that. It's nothing
you need to worry about—you or the others. I'm looking
for someone, that's all. It doesn't concern you."

"Then why did you involve us?" Terry fired back. Her
face felt stiff. "Why didn't you just come down here on your
own and take care of this? Why did you have to use the
Sams?"

"Simple—I needed cover." His voice changed, took on
that distant, hollow tone that chilled her to her bones.

"There are reasons why I'd rather the people I'm looking for don't know I'm in the neighborhood."

"But why?" Terry whispered. She felt so cold, and more frightened than she could ever remember being in her life. "What do you want from these people? What did they do?"

"They took something from me. And now I want payment." In the moonlight she could see his lips curve in a thin, sickle smile, and that was somehow more frightening than his words. "Okay, Doc? I want payment. That's all. Just a fair price for what they stole from me."

Terry felt herself nod. Her lips were frozen, too numb to form words. But in any case, there didn't seem to be anything left to say. Finally, she just turned and headed back through the soft sand toward the light and warmth and good-food smells of Pepe's Cantina. Only with that island of safety and normalcy within arm's reach did she finally dare to turn and look back again.

Far down the beach she could still see him, running alone in the moonlight, his stride unhurried, relentless.

The lone wolf.

Terry didn't go back to the cantina. She didn't feel like eating—Jack had destroyed her appetite for even one of Pepe Gomez's famous fish dinners. She didn't feel much like confronting Ingrid and those all-seeing eyes of hers, either. Ingrid would ask questions, and she didn't know how in the world to answer them.

What she did feel was shaken and clammy, as if she'd just awakened from a nightmare too terrible to talk about or forget.

It was one of those nights when Wolf ran out of beach long before he'd outrun his demons. So he did what he always did, he turned to the sea itself. Dropping his clothes in an irregular line across the sand, he lunged furiously into the gentle surf until the waves took his footing and he sliced the swell in a shallow dive, as if the cold saltwater might finally succeed in scouring the blood from his hands and the nightmare visions from his mind.

He swam like a man pursued by demons, plunging his hands again and again into the black, moon-gilded water, powerful legs churning a frothy wake. There had been times when he'd wondered what it would be like to just keep swimming, to swim until he couldn't take another stroke, until he had no will left. Until there was nothing left to do but let go and sink without a whimper beneath the oily swell. There'd been times when he'd considered it. That he'd never gone that far was, he figured, due more to sheer stubbornness than anything else—that plus the fact that he wasn't anxious to find out what lay beyond. Better the Hell he knew . . .

So in the end, whether from cowardice or obstinance, he did what he always did. When he'd reached the edge of exhaustion he turned back to shore and reaffirmed his basic desire to live by fighting his way through the undertow, finally collapsing on the sand, gasping like a netted fish and cursing himself and the heavens with equally impotent fury.

In his lifetime Wolf figured he'd done a lot of things— more than most—that he wasn't proud of. Some had been the result of bad choices, and if he could he'd take them back. Some he'd probably do the same way over again, under the same set of circumstances. Either way he'd always taken the responsibility for what he'd done, faced the consequences head-on and found a way to live with his actions. But he didn't know about this time. He wasn't sure he was ever going to be able to live with using the doc the way he planned to do tomorrow.

Not that Wolf was above using a woman. He'd used them before, more times than he could count, in a lot of different ways and for a lot of different reasons. They'd always known going in what the score was, and more often than not the using had been mutual.

But this was different. He was going to use Terry without her knowledge and consent, in a way he'd never used a woman before. He was going to use her as a shield, hide behind her, the way a hunter hides in a blind. And while he knew it was wrong, at the same time it was so perfect he almost had to believe that Fate was on his side. And, he told himself, she didn't ever have to know. Once he got to El Refugio she'd be out of it.

But *he'd* know. For the rest of his life he'd have to live with knowing that he'd taken a doctor's dedication and a woman's compassion and used them to commit murder.

He thought about calling it off, at least her part of it. But no matter how he shuffled the cards, they came up with the same hand: without the doc he didn't have a prayer of getting into El Refugio, not without letting the Cruz brothers know he was coming. After what Terry had told him about the place he'd done some asking around. What he'd found out was that the town was at the bottom of a deep canyon, and the only way down was a zigzagging dirt track barely wide enough for a four-wheel drive. He'd also found out that the arrival of any stranger was an event—the whole damn town turned out. If he went in alone, one strange *norteamericano*, he might just as well hire a brass band.

No. He'd waited too long and worked too hard for this to turn back now just because he'd seen something in a woman's eyes that was going to haunt him for a while. It was almost over. By this time tomorrow... His fingers closed around the cool metal on his chest and he felt it warm slowly in his hand.

He lay for a long time on the beach, staring up at the sky. What he saw there weren't stars. He just kept seeing the doc's eyes, dark with compassion, glittering with an overlay of tears.

Chapter 5

Terry emerged from the clinic the next morning like a bear into springtime, squinting and muttering dire curses at the sun. She was out of sorts partly because she'd overslept, which she almost never did, and missed her sunrise swim.

Ordinarily she was out at dawn, a busy time of day in Santa Luisa. The fishermen would be loading the big circular nets they called *chinchorros,* laughing and calling softly to each other, their voices mingling with the cries of the gulls in the cool morning air. Then suddenly, as if at some unknown signal, they would all be gone, pushing their small wooden boats through the foaming surf to catch the swell, leaping in over the gunwales just before the breathtaking rise toward a lightening sky, bending hard to the oars as they headed out to sea with the water cascading from their oars in silvery sheets.

And after they had gone the beach would be deserted. The gulls would follow the fishermen, and the waves would smooth away their footprints, leaving the village to sleep a little longer in a silence broken only by the lonely piping of seabirds. Then . . . ah, *then* . . . for a little while, the beach would be hers.

Terry was jealous of that precious hour before sunrise, the only time of day when she could throw off the loathsome hats and protective clothing and sunscreens, and swim to her heart's delight, run free as a child, without fear of dire consequences. Oh, how unjust it was, that someone who loved the sunshine, who loved to be outdoors as much as she did should be cursed with flame-red hair and fair, fair skin!

But this morning she'd missed her moment. The sun was already peeking over the rocky hills to the east, sparkling like gold dust on the water. She accepted the disappointment with ill grace, pausing in the deeply recessed doorway of the rock and adobe clinic to jam her sunglasses crossly onto her face before proceeding to the outdoor "conveniences." She'd really needed that swim this morning after a night of troubling dreams. No, not dreams. Nightmares. In which, for some reason, wolves had figured frequently and prominently.

It was perhaps a good thing that the first person she ran into on the way back was Ingrid. Ingrid seemed to have a way of calming troubled souls and diffusing tensions, whether in sick and frightened children or cranky colleagues.

This morning she was already outside bustling around in the warm November sunshine, loading supplies onto the pickup. As Terry groped her way to the pickup and levered herself onto the tailgate Ingrid looked up long enough to remark, "My God, you look awful. You better watch those double margaritas."

"It wasn't the margaritas," Terry said with a grimace; she'd have been happier if it had been. "I only had one."

"Oh yeah," Ingrid said, making a big deal out of pausing to think about it, her head tilted to one side. "That's right, you left early."

She counted under her breath, jotted the number of disposable syringes on the lid of the box and closed it before craftily changing the subject. "Gee, I wonder where Jack bedded down last night. I didn't see him come in, did you?"

Terry's heart gave a bump. "I haven't the faintest idea," she said with elaborate unconcern, smothering a large, unconvincing yawn. "The last time I saw him he was jogging down the beach toward the point. Maybe he slept under the plane."

Jogging down the beach. It sounded so urban, so tame, so civilized. But Terry thought of the lone predator loping along in the moonlight—and all through her dreams—and felt her skin shrink and the fine hairs on her arms begin to rise. After that first little stumble, her heart settled down to a steady pace that was just a little too fast for a peaceful morning.

"Ingrid," she said suddenly, "Do you think I'm aloof?"

"Huh," said Ingrid. "What brought this on?"

What brought it on? *Ingrid, what would you think of me if I told you that last night I reached out to another human being, a man in pain, and ran into a brick wall . . . and that the wall was not of his making . . . but mine?*

She gripped the edge of the tailgate and rocked herself forward, shoulders defensively hunched. "Robert once told me that I keep aloof—that I don't let myself get emotionally involved with people. Do you think that's true?"

"Sure it is," Ingrid said with a shrug. "We all do. We have to. My goodness, girl, don't they teach you that in first year med school? Aloof-101—pass it or you fail as a doctor. Listen, the nurses in 'Nam made it a point never to call a patient by his name. Because if a patient had a name, that's when he stopped being the bowel resection in bed three and became a person, with hopes and dreams and a family back home. And then it hurt too much when you lost him. The trick is to learn to care about your patients, but not too deeply. You know that—it's why doctors don't treat their own kids.''

''Robert said that's why I didn't want kids,'' Terry said in a low voice, frowning at the ground. ''He said I didn't want to take the risk of *really* caring. He said... that because of some things that happened to me when I was a child, I was afraid to love someone—anyone. Especially a child. Because, he said, that's when you really learn what fear is.''

''Robert said all that, did he?'' Ingrid said dryly. ''I guess the man had more guts than I thought he did.''

''Well, do you think he was right?'' Terry's throat felt tight, her body tense, as if braced for attack.

Because it didn't matter what Ingrid answered; *she* knew it was true. That barrier that had sprung up out of nowhere when she'd reached out to Jack last night, and the fear that came after, that shaken, clammy, punched-in-the-stomach fear, she knew it had happened at the exact moment she'd first recognized his pain. The moment when she'd begun to care. Not just as a doctor, but as a woman. She'd felt herself beginning to care too much, and it had scared the wits out of her.

''Well,'' Ingrid said placidly, giving Terry a quick, shrewd glance, ''I guess you'll find out when it happens, won't you?''

Terry wanted to cry out, ''When *what* happens? Isn't that the whole point? How is anything supposed to happen if I won't let it!''

But before she could form the words Ingrid murmured, with an odd purring note in her voice, ''Oh look, here comes Jack now. I guess we must be about ready to take off. Want to give me a hand with this stuff?''

Terry nodded, but she couldn't have given anyone a hand if lives had depended on it. There was no strength at all in her limbs. Her mouth and throat had gone as dry as Baja dust.

Oh, she hadn't meant to look! She hadn't wanted to face that fear again, or the feelings and visions that had haunted her all night long. But her gaze was pulled in the direction of Ingrid's anyway, by a force stronger than she had will to resist. She looked, and felt the impact like a sonic boom.

"My, my, he looks like a bad night in Tijuana," Ingrid said, shading her eyes and taking another look. She grinned at Terry. "We used to say that when I was in nursing school. Somebody'd come in after a double shift, you know—rumpled, red-eyed, bloodstained—looking like they'd been on a three-day toot. Ah yes... those were the days."

A bad night in Tijuana, low-down, dirty and deadly. Oh yes, Terry thought, Jack was all that, and more. But there was something—she hated to admit it—*exciting* about him, something awesome, like catching an elusive wild creature for a breathtaking instant in your car headlights.

For a moment she wondered if that was what attracted her—and she *was* attracted to Jack, no matter how improbably, or how much that fact dismayed her. She wondered if that sense of danger and excitement, the very roughness that repelled her, could at the same time be a prescription for something she'd been missing. After her tumultuous youth, her own life had become so ordinary, lately the men she met so... so domesticated and buttoned-down. Could it be that difference she found so fascinating, as Ingrid said? Was it, after all, a physical thrill she was looking for? Was it just a matter of sex?

If it was, she thought with a self-derisive snort, then the next time he tried to kiss her she should probably just kiss him back and get it out of her system!

She gave Jack another look, trying the idea out in her mind. Watched him come unhurriedly toward them, plowing through the soft sand, Levi's riding low on narrow hips, shirt hooked casually on a finger and slung over one shoulder. His hair was wilder than ever, his beard darker, his naked torso as brown as any Baja native's and so lean that every muscle was starkly defined. A cigarette dangled from lips that were curved in a thin half smile, as if he knew already what she was thinking.

Terry's stomach did something that as a doctor she knew perfectly well was impossible. Oh God, she thought, I'd sooner pet a timber wolf.

Besides, she'd forgotten about the pain.

She hadn't imagined or dreamed it; it was still there, not as obviously as it had been last night, but clear enough now that she knew what to look for. She found it this time in the too-bright glitter of his eyes.

Terry never knew what she'd have said to him that morning, whether she'd have stammered like a schoolgirl or given herself away with a blush, or whether she'd have been able to meet his eyes. She was still trying to unstick her tongue from the roof of her mouth when the sounds of a commotion came from the front of the clinic—the unmistakable sounds of a child in great distress.

She and Ingrid looked at each other. Ingrid drawled, "What in the world . . . ?" Terry took off running.

She rounded the corner of the stone and adobe building to find a skinny little boy in faded black trousers and tattered white shirt squirming in Dr. Wahlberg's arms like a puppy in the embrace of a bear. Carl was muttering calming phrases in both English and Spanish, to absolutely no effect. The child just cried all the harder, eyes scrunched tightly shut and mouth wide open, tears oozing down his cheeks in muddy tracks.

Terry touched the other doctor's shoulder and said, "Here, let me try."

Carl nodded and let go of the child, who opened his eyes, took one look at Terry and launched himself howling onto her chest.

"Well, well," Terry said dryly, trying her best to keep from being strangled by a pair of scrawny, but amazingly strong little arms, "I guess it just takes a woman's touch.

Here—*hijito*—'' She patted the child's shaking back, then pried him from her neck and set him firmly on the ground.

"Now, then," she murmured soothingly, switching to Spanish as she knelt in front of him. *"¿Cómo te llamas?"*

The boy drew several great breaths and dug a fist into his eye, drawing himself up to as much height as he could muster. "Julio."

"Okay, Julio," Terry said, attempting with disastrous results to wipe away some of the tears. "Now tell me what is the matter. Where does it hurt?"

The boy began to wail again, more loudly than before. Terry promptly clamped her hand over his mouth. *"Silencio, por favor,"* she said calmly. "I am the doctor. Tell me what is the matter."

Above her hand a pair of startled brown eyes blinked at her.

"Okay?"

There was a quick nod. Terry removed her hand and the child fired off a salvo of Spanish, interspersed with snuffles and sobs. She caught the words *dolor* and *hermanita*.

"Your sister?" she prompted. "Your little sister has pain?"

"Sí," Julio sobbed, *"es muy malo."*

"Where is your sister? Can you take me to her?"

"En El Refugio. Sí, I will take you. But she is very bad . . . very bad."

"Show me," Terry said quickly, before he could begin to cry again. "Show me where your sister's pain is."

Julio let out a bloodcurdling yell and doubled over, clutching his stomach.

"Good heavens," Terry said, glancing up at Carl as Julio began to roll around on the ground, his face contorted in unspeakable agony.

"Kid's one hell of an actor," Carl said mildly.

"If you ask me, the little rascal's enjoying himself," Ingrid remarked, coming to look over Terry's shoulder.

"We have to take it seriously," Terry said, frowning. "I mean . . ."

Carl scratched his head while he eyed the writhing, wailing Julio with skepticism. Then he grimaced and said, "I know. What do you think—appendicitis?"

"How about food poisoning?" suggested Ingrid.

Terry huffed out an exasperated breath. "Maybe. Could be a lot of things. I wish we could get more out of him, but I don't think it's any use trying, do you?" She took off her sunglasses and pressed a thumb and forefinger to her eyelids. Julio's racket was making her head ache.

"You guys got a problem?"

The sunglasses flew out of Terry's hand and went skittering across the hard-baked ground.

"Sorry, Doc, didn't mean to startle you," Jack said in his thickest cowboy drawl.

"That's all right, I just didn't hear you come up," Terry said coolly, shading her eyes with her hand to look at him. He was rolling up the sleeves of his shirt, which he'd put on but hadn't buttoned, still smiling that little half smile. Terry could see a few grains of sand clinging to smooth brown skin.

"Just one *small* problem," Carl said cheerfully, shouting to make himself heard over the noise Julio was making. "As you can see."

Jack calmly finished adjusting his shirtsleeves, then leaned over, snaked out an arm and picked Julio up by the seat of his pants. "Okay," he grunted in the startled silence that ensued, "now tell me the problem."

Carl gave a bark of astonished laughter, and he and Ingrid both began to talk at once. Julio, who had regained his voice if not his feet, immediately joined them in excited Spanish.

"No problem," Terry said briskly, overriding everyone. "We'll just be taking off a little later than we planned, that's all. I have to go to El Refugio."

"El Refugio?" Jack set Julio's dusty bare feet back on the ground and gave him a cursory brushing, then planted a large, uncompromising hand on his shoulder. He frowned at Terry. "Isn't that the place you told me about? I thought you guys didn't have a clinic there."

"We don't," Carl broke in. "Usually they come here. But the boy here says his sister is ill—you caught the gist of his demonstration, I imagine. Even allowing for exaggeration, I think one of us ought to go and check—although Terry, I don't think it necessarily needs to be you. I could go, or Roland—"

"Carl, don't be silly. I'm the pediatrician, it's my field, and anyway Roland has a cold," Terry said briskly, retrieving her sunglasses and giving them a critical look and a brief swipe across her middle. "Of course I'm the one who should go. Here—give me a hand up."

But the hand that closed around hers wasn't Carl's. It was hard bone and sinew, strong as leather and warm as the hide of a healthy animal. She'd felt it against her palm once before.

Oh God, she thought, now I remember! That sense of intimacy, of stroking and of being stroked. I should have paid more attention. . . .

"Well," Ingrid said in a raspy undertone, bending down to study Julio eyeball-to-eyeball, "I don't know about you guys, but I don't trust this little imp." Julio gave her a wide, dimpled, and thoroughly irrepressible grin. Ingrid snorted. "I don't think Terry should go alone. I think I should go with her."

"Oh sure," said Carl, "then we'd have two women out there in the desert. *I'll* go."

"Now look here, Carl—" Ingrid began.

"Look, this is ridiculous," Terry interrupted testily as she snatched her hand out of Jack's grasp. She had to resist an urge to rub it against her thigh. "If you went, too, Carl, we'd have two doctors on what might be a wild-goose chase. You're needed at our next stop. Ingrid and I—"

"I'll drive 'em," said Wolf.

Everyone except Terry turned to look at him. He noticed that, for some reason, the doc seemed to be looking *any* place but at him.

He gave an offhand shrug and drawled, "Sure, why not? I'd have to wait around anyway, right? You guys go on ahead. We'll just catch up with you later."

"Well," Ingrid said after a pause, "no sense both of us going. I'm not sure we'd all fit in that pickup anyway— there's the kid, don't forget." She gave Wahlberg a dig in the ribs with her elbow. "I'll just take the spare seat in Carl's plane—if that's all right with you, Doctor? A mere *woman*—"

"Ah, come on, Ingrid..."

Wolf turned to Terry and said softly, "That all right with you, Doctor?"

For a moment or two she just looked at him. Frown lines etched the fragile skin around her eyes, unremarkable blue eyes with curling red-gold lashes. He wondered whether, under different circumstances, she darkened her eyelashes with mascara. For some reason he hoped she didn't.

"Of course," she said in a bright, clipped voice. Her eyes disappeared and he found himself looking at tiny twin images of himself instead.

That was when he realized that her eyes *were* remarkable. He'd already noticed that they mirrored her every thought and emotion; now he discovered that when she hid them behind sunglasses her face lost most of its warmth and animation, and some of its appeal. Although even without them she had a certain magnificence, like a statue of a Roman goddess—cold, aloof and untouchable.

Until you came to her mouth. For an instant, just an instant, he let himself remember the way it had felt under his, warm, generous and soft, quivering just a little, finally opening....

She hadn't missed the shift of his eyes downward to her lips. Nor did he miss their quick, involuntary parting, the way they tightened, or the nervous ripple of her throat.

"I'll need to get a few things ready," Terry said in that cool, carefully controlled voice. "While I'm doing that, why don't you go speak to Mr. Ortiz—he's the owner of that pickup truck around back. After he finishes ferrying Carl's group to their plane, I'm sure he'll be willing to negotiate the loan of it for a few more hours."

"Yes, ma'am," Wolf murmured, but the sarcasm was only halfhearted.

Doc Wahlberg and Ingrid had gone off, still bickering good-naturedly, to finish loading the pickup. Since there was no one to see him, Wolf didn't bother to veil his expression as he watched Terry go into the clinic. Just for a moment he allowed everything he felt—the bitterness and rage, the bleakness and frustration, the guilt and the resolve—to play across his features like a laser-light show. Then, suddenly aware of the scrawny shoulder beneath his hand, the round black eyes looking questions at him, he gave Julio's shoulder a squeeze and growled, "You like ice cream?"

The kid nodded with great enthusiasm. *"¡Sí, señor!"*

"Well," Wolf muttered dryly, "I'm not sure you deserve it, but let's go see what Pepe's got."

He left Julio in the shade of a palm-thatched *enramada* outside Pepe's Cantina sucking happily on a pink-and-orange stick of sweet frozen punch. The awful thing was already melting and making sticky new tracks down the kid's wrists and chin, but at least it would keep him busy long enough for Wolf to get the few things he needed out of the plane and stashed away in the pickup. His cigarettes, for one. And the canvas sports bag which contained the few things he was never without; namely, a change of clothes, a deck of cards and a .38-caliber Smith & Wesson snubnosed special.

It was his brother's gun. The police detectives assigned to the Wolf murders hadn't found it, and neither had the DEA investigators who'd come later. Both assumed the killers had taken it, and Wolf decided there was a certain amount of irony in that. The murderers of Frank Wolf and his wife and child would have a date with that gun in only a few short hours. Until then it would stay where it was, safely wrapped in a beach towel at the bottom of a blue Dallas Cowboys athletic bag.

"It shouldn't be too much longer." Terry pointed across a vast sea of gray-green cholla cactus interspersed with the weird, twisting spires of boojum trees to where a spine of rocky mountains stood in bold relief against a flat blue sky. "See over there, where the road disappears behind those rocks? That's where we start down into the canyon."

Jack grunted as the ancient pickup clunked violently into a rut and out again, and muttered under his breath, "This isn't a road, it's a penance."

Terry stole a sideways glance at him over Julio's head but didn't say anything. Jack's mood had grown steadily worse as the trip had worn on and the hour advanced toward noon. Now the tension in the cab was so thick it was almost visible. Even in profile she could see the cold glitter of his eyes, like sunlight glancing off polished steel.

Terry found that silent anger hard to deal with, harder even than last night's pain and this morning's unsettling revelations. Both of those had aroused unwelcome fears and uncertainties in her, but at least they were grown-up fears, a woman's fears. For some reason this new mood of Jack's was opening up old wounds, awakening long-dormant memories of a little girl who'd lived in constant fear of such anger. Anger from the men who'd come and gone so unpredictably, the ones her mother called "uncles." Fear that she was somehow responsible for their anger and their leaving, that she'd done something wrong, and that someday it would be she who was sent away. She'd tried so hard to be good, each time thinking that if she were good enough, maybe this one would stay. And even though she knew better now, that it had had nothing to do with her, anger still made her feel nervous and vaguely apprehensive.

Julio tugged at her elbow and lifted up a neat turkey-tail fan of cards for her inspection. Jack had given him the deck to play with, but only, Terry suspected, after the poor child had been subjected to a thorough scrubbing in cold saltwater. When the two had finally rejoined Terry at the truck, Julio had been suspiciously clean—if somewhat chastened—and had smelled unmistakably seaweedy.

"Okay, let's see what you've got. Not much in that hand, I'm afraid. Just a pair of threes." Terry pulled out the two cards and placed them on Julio's knee. "Here, you keep these. These are good—*bueno*. These others we throw away—"

Julio let out a squall of protest and grabbed for one of the cards—the jack of diamonds. Terry sighed. She'd been occupying herself on the long trip by teaching Julio to play poker, and except for this irrational fondness for face cards, he seemed to be picking it up quickly.

"No," she said patiently, "you don't want that one. That's a jack, see? It's no good—*malo*. What we want to do is see if we can get some more of these—*tres*. Understand?"

She threw a glance at Jack as she made the crack about his namesake card, but his eyes were focused on the road ahead and she didn't think he'd even heard it, much less caught on to the double meaning.

Even with two other people in that cramped space he seemed to her at that moment to be utterly alone. Not lonely, just...alone. As if he'd gone somewhere, she thought, someplace where no one could follow. Someplace just big enough for him and the pain he carried around with him. And whatever was going on in that private hell of his, there was enough tension in his muscles to snap bones.

It occurred to Terry that she was spending a lot of time lately thinking about Jack, wondering about Jack. Worrying about Jack. But not in the way she had at the beginning, when she'd been so sure he was up to no good, and definitely not to be trusted. She still didn't trust him, still feared he was up to no good, but now, somehow, the worry was different. Suddenly, just since last night, in fact, she realized that she was more afraid *for* Jack than she was *of* him. How in the world had that happened?

"Oh, all right, keep the jack," she said crossly as Julio, looking mulish, continued to clutch the brightly colored card to his chest. "But believe me, it's not going to do you any good."

And you remember that too, lady.

But instead she was remembering something else. It had been shortly after leaving Santa Luisa, before the tension had risen to screaming pitch. Terry had been teaching Julio how to shuffle. Jack had looked over, raised one eyebrow and drawled, "Not bad. Should have joined us the other night."

That was all he said. But suddenly she hadn't been able to look at him. It was this morning all over again, her mouth dry and her skin hot, her muscles quivering with a strange weakness. Instead of answering she'd gone on shuffling the cards, over and over again, watching her hands, remembering that evening, those moments just after sunset on the plateau above Dos Caminos. Remembering *his* hands and the way he'd touched her, the surprising gentleness, the unexpected comfort, remembering the kiss. Especially the kiss.

And the worst of it was, she'd known then and she knew now exactly what the kiss had meant. *Nothing.* It had been a diversion for him and an insult to her and nothing more. But still, what she was thinking about now, as she dealt Julio his last two cards, was how she would react if Jack was to try the same diversion again. Her hands trembled a little.

And dealt Julio the jack of hearts and the jack of spades.

While an ecstatic Julio raised his arms in victory and crowed with delight over his full house, the battered pickup truck dipped over the rim of the canyon and began a wheezing, zigzag descent to the village of El Refugio de los Angeles.

Chapter 6

Wolf flexed his fingers on the steering wheel and shifted their position slightly, forcing himself to relax. Yes, every nerve and sense had to be on full alert, every reflex set on hair trigger, but he was tight...too tight.

As an exercise in self-control he squinted through the dirty windshield, deliberately pulling his focus from the twin tire tracks ahead and broadening it to include the canyon wall rising on one side of the truck in stratified layers of rust, sandstone, and purple lava rock, the dizzying drop to the valley floor on the other side, the plume of dust in his rearview mirror. He had to stay loose, he told himself. Keep his balance.

But in spite of his efforts it startled him to hear another human voice—he'd just about forgotten anyone else was in the truck.

"...a really pretty place," Terry was saying. "Kind of like a little Eden."

Eden. Wolf glanced at the clusters of orange trees that crowded the lower slopes on either side of the road, the im-

mense and majestic desert palms that lined the base of the
canyon's walls like sentinels. His mouth curved in a thin,
deadly smile. He had a strong and appreciative sense of
irony, but that was almost too much for him. He wondered
what the doc would say if he reminded her that there had
been snakes in Eden.

"Of course, the people who live here are dirt-poor," she
went on, nodding toward the barefooted children who, now
that the pickup had reached the floor of the canyon, had
come from nowhere to keep pace with them, laughing and
thumping the fenders of the old truck as they jogged along-
side. "It's because it's so isolated. They have a beautiful
place to live, but no way to make a living. The only work-
able soil is here, in the lower end of the canyon, where the
flash floods lay down a new layer every few years. They
grow vegetables and citrus—the Spanish missionaries
brought the oranges—and they do well here, but it's so remote, the farmers don't have any way to market what they
grow. It's a shame, really. I suppose what it will take is for
some rich gringo to come in here and put up a resort." She
sighed. "It will happen—it's only a matter of time, now that
the highway is finished. Baja is changing."

"Change is inevitable," Wolf grunted absently. But he
was thinking about snakes—the two-legged kind—and his
eyes and mind were busy, searching the growing crowd
around the truck. His sources had been right about the welcoming committee, at least. They were picking up people
and dogs the way a magnet picks up filings. But he knew
who he was looking for, and he'd know them when he saw
them; the descriptions Julio's uncles had given him last
night in Pepe's Cantina were etched indelibly on his brain.
Even without a description he'd know them.

He glanced over at Julio. The kid seemed to be enjoying
the heck out of the situation, bouncing up and down on the
seat, waving and climbing across the doc's lap to yell at his
friends through the window. Wolf just hoped the little ras-

cal didn't get so carried away being the center of attention that he forgot what he was supposed to do. If there was one thing he *didn't* want, it was somebody else getting hurt. But if the kid followed the plan Wolf had so painstakingly worked out with the two uncles, both he and the doctor should be safely out of the way until it was all over.

"Just pull in here," Terry said, taking a deep breath of sheer relief as she pointed to an open space in front of the tiny church of whitewashed adobe that sat nested like a setting hen on a low mesa. "The road pretty much ends here, anyway. From here the canyon gets steeper and narrower, so it's the only place to turn around. This is where the supply truck usually stops to unload—they carry everything down to Señor Lopez's store by wheelbarrow or handcart."

Jack's only response was another grunt. He pulled head-in to the steps of the church and jolted to a stop, then sat there for a minute or two as if in deep thought, glowering through the windows.

"In case you're wondering, the houses are mostly around the bend, out of sight," Terry assured him as she tucked her hair under her hat and pushed her sunglasses more firmly onto the bridge of her nose. She was still breathless, probably with the same inexplicable nervousness that made her go on chattering like a tour guide to fill the silence.

"This is just part of the original church. The Spanish missionaries had a retreat here—that's where the name comes from—El Refugio. It was just a ruin, until a few years ago when they restored part of it. Now a priest comes once every two or three months, and when he does they have a big party for all the weddings and baptisms—"

She broke off with a squawk and held on to the door she'd already opened as Jack suddenly ground gears and put the truck in reverse. The engine whined, the crowd parted and a new cloud of dust rose as he backed around and finally stopped again, this time with the front of the truck facing out the way they'd come.

"Just as well do it now as later," he muttered as he slapped the gearshift into neutral.

Terry swiveled her head and looked at him with arched eyebrows and gritted teeth. "Perhaps a word or two of warning next time?" Those who knew her well would have recognized the false smile and the too-sweet tone and been warned, but both the look and the sarcasm were lost on Jack. He gave no sign of having heard her at all, just yanked on the door handle and pushed open the door.

Terry sat still for a moment, counting silently to ten and taking deep breaths to stop the inner shivering and ease the knots of tension in her stomach. She couldn't let Jack get to her like this. She was becoming too preoccupied with his problems, too tuned-in to his moods—altogether too aware of the man, period. She was losing her focus, forgetting who she was and why she was here in the first place. She was a doctor, and somewhere in this canyon community there was a sick child who needed her. She had to be calm, relaxed. Children seemed to have a sixth sense for adult moods.

Except for Julio, of course, who was apparently oblivious to undercurrents. He'd been bouncing impatiently on the seat ever since they'd reached the floor of the canyon, and the minute Terry opened the door of the truck he all but scrambled over her in his eagerness to get out of the cab.

My goodness, she thought ruefully as she watched him go darting off through the crowd, perhaps we should have made a pit stop along the way.

And then she was surrounded by most of the inhabitants of El Refugio, and for a few minutes she was too busy to think about Jack, or keep an eye on Julio. There were dogs sniffing at her feet, small children tugging shyly at her clothes, then covering their mouths in giggly embarrassment when she smiled at them. Women in faded cotton dresses held their babies up to wave at her. Helping hands reached to take her medical bag from the back of the truck. Terry recognized a man she'd stitched up during her last visit to Santa Luisa, a farmer who'd slashed his leg with a machete while cutting palm thatch. When she spoke to him, he proudly lifted up his trouser leg to show her the healing scar.

"Where's the kid?" Jack asked, coming toward her around the back of the truck, a blue sports bag slung over one shoulder.

Terry frowned and shaded her eyes with her hand as she surveyed both the crowd and the rugged canyon walls. "I don't know. He took off the minute we stopped. Oh, I'm sure he'll come back," she added quickly as Jack began to mutter profanely under his breath. "And if he doesn't, it's no big deal. Someone can tell me where he lives. It's not that big a town, Jack."

She gently but firmly retrieved her medical bag from the man with the machete wound, thanked him graciously for his assistance and started toward the hard-packed dirt path that wound through granite boulders and yellowing cottonwoods into the village of El Refugio.

She'd only taken two steps when Jack's hand closed like a manacle on her upper arm. "Where the hell are you going?"

Terry gave a short, sharp laugh and looked down at his hand. "What do you mean, where am I going?" Then she looked up, and in spite of all her renewed resolve, sucked in air in a reflexive reaction to the impact of those blazing blue eyes. His look seared her. It was like touching a hot iron. She jerked away, burned, and huffed the breath out again in exasperation. "I'm going to do what I came to do," she snapped. "Check on a sick child. Let go of me, please—*now*."

But instead of releasing her, his grip tightened. "Are you *nuts?*" Jack's voice was low and furious and very close to her ear. "Nobody trusted that kid to begin with and now he's disappeared. Everybody was afraid it might be a hoax, or some kind of a setup, right? That's why I'm here. God-

dammit, at least let me check it out before you go walking
into something!''

"Jack," Terry ground out between tightly clenched teeth,
"use your head. It was a long trip. The kid probably had to
go to the bathroom. What do you think I'm going to walk
into? Look around you—do these people look dangerous to
you? Although they might be in a minute—to *you*—if you
don't let go of my arm. And you'd better *smile* while you do
it.''

The people of El Refugio were indeed muttering and
murmuring to each other, to Terry's great satisfaction, and
several of the men, including the one with the machete scar,
had begun to shift ominously. Jack looked around him, gave
an uneasy cough and reluctantly released his grip.

"Look...Doc—''

"Thank you," Terry said in her sweet and dangerous
voice. Inside she was trembling with a combination of anger, the aftereffects of a very bad night's sleep, and several
hours' buildup of inexplicable tension. Not to mention a
different kind of tension that was altogether *too* explain-
able, and a source of shame and chagrin to her besides. But
if Jack had for some unimaginable reason succeeded in
stirring up deep-seated and ill-timed yearnings, that was her
private burden to bear, and one she was capable of handling. She wasn't about to let it affect her work. She had way
too much personal and professional pride for that.

"Now," she went on with exaggerated patience, as if
speaking to a misbehaving child, "you've done your job.
I'm going to go and do mine. There is a grocery store and
cantina down in the village—the owner speaks English. I am
going to ask him where Julio lives. If you like, you may wait
there until I finish.''

She knew he was furious; she could feel him vibrating
with it. *"Dammit, Terry—''*

She didn't wait to hear the rest. She'd had enough of
Jack's kaleidoscopic moods to last her a lifetime. She didn't

want to be attracted to him! She didn't want to care about him! She didn't want to wonder what was bothering him, what was making him angry, or causing his pain. Damn it, it wasn't her field. She wasn't equipped to deal with it. She didn't *want* to deal with it. Jack Wolf was simply not her problem, and she wasn't going to let him become her problem.

She barked, "Out of my way, Jack," and pushed past him, leaving him swearing fruitlessly beside the truck as she stalked off down the rocky pathway, the people of El Refugio falling into a protective phalanx around her.

"Doc!"

Wolf brought his fist down on the pickup's fender with a force that threatened to dislodge it. *Damn* the woman! Damn the hardheaded, hotheaded, redheaded woman! There was just no controlling her—she was like a force of nature, a natural disaster—like a typhoon, or a volcanic eruption!

All he could do was stand there and watch her go walking right into his nightmare while he fumed and gnashed his teeth with grand futility. His nerves were coiling and twisting like live wires, which wasn't natural for him, and not the way he wanted to be. He liked to be in control, the one pulling the strings. He liked to plan things carefully. But things weren't going the way he'd planned, and for that he blamed the doc. That woman was about as easy to manipulate as a hurricane!

But, he reminded himself, calming himself down, natural disasters happened, and if that was the hand he'd been dealt, so be it. He was going to do what he'd come to do, come hell or high water. He just had to make some adjustments, that was all. He had to be sure that blasted Good Samaritan was out of his way and occupied—one way or another.

He gave a quick look around, knelt on one knee beside the pickup and unzipped his bag. Good. His hands were al-

ready steadier, his nerves quieting down. With deft and unhurried movements he unwrapped the Smith & Wesson to
check the chamber and the safety, then tucked it inside the
waistband of his Levi's in the small of his back where his
shirt would cover it. When he stood up again he was completely under control, focused once more on what he had to
do.

He calmly looped the straps of the sports bag over his
shoulder, checked the position of the gun, gave one last look
around and took off down the trail after the doc.

Most of the crowd had dispersed by the time Terry
reached Señor Lopez's grocery store and cantina. It was just
past noon; the sun was as high in the sky as it got in mid-
November, and hot. It was also siesta time in El Refugio, so
once the excitement of new arrivals was over, most of the
villagers were eager to get back to their palm-thatched
houses and their interrupted naps. Even the dogs went loping off, one by one, to look for cool places in the shade.

A few villagers wanted to linger to talk to the *norteamer-
icana* doctor, some eager to describe their complaints in
flowery detail, others too shy to do more than cough and
shuffle their feet in embarrassment. Terry told them all she
would be happy to see them, after she had taken care of
Julio's sister.

¿La hermana de Julio? When she said that, the villagers
looked at each other, murmuring questions and shrugging
their shoulders.

The significance of this wasn't lost on Terry. She thought,
Julio, you little scamp! It was beginning to look as if the
others had been right about him. There was no sick sister at
all, and it had all been a hoax, the reasons for which she
couldn't imagine.

But having come all this way, she wasn't about to leave
without seeing for herself. And besides, she had a feeling
there was something going on here, something she didn't
understand. She meant to find out what it was. Terry didn't

like being played for a fool. Shading her eyes with her hand, she turned full circle, hoping to see Julio's impish grin and bright eyes peering out from behind a hut or a cottonwood tree. No such luck. With a sigh she left the handful of villagers patiently fanning themselves in the shade and went to find Señor Lopez.

The front half of Lopez's store consisted of a wide-open veranda of rock and adobe. *Ristras* of chili peppers and bunches of garlic and onions hung like Spanish moss from its palm-thatched ceiling. Gardening tools and sacks of oranges, pinto beans and cornmeal lay propped against peeling whitewashed walls. Except for a few flies zigzagging lazily back and forth over rickety wooden tables heaped with tomatoes, squash and wilting produce, there were no signs of life.

"*¿Buenas tardes, Señor Lopez?*"

Terry crossed the veranda and peered through the open doorway into the tiny shop. It was dark inside; the shutters had all been lowered to keep out the midday heat. She took off her sunglasses and went in, stepping carefully as her eyes adjusted to the dim light. It was a precaution she'd learned from painful experience—Señor Lopez made use of all available space. In addition to the shelves of canned foods and dry goods that lined the shop's adobe walls from floor to ceiling, there was a truly remarkable collection of merchandise: cowboy hats, coils of rope, clothing on wire hangers, baskets, pots and pans, cooking utensils and kerosene lanterns, all hanging from the low ceiling beams. Being somewhat taller than most of the residents of El Refugio, Terry had bumped her head more than once.

No one was in the shop, but she could hear the tinny beat of Mexican pop music through the curtained doorway in the rear.

Well, good, she thought. At least someone's in the cantina.

"Hello," she called in English, "Señor Lopez, are you here?" Without waiting for a reply, she stepped through a slanting beam of sunlight from a crack in one of the shutters and pulled aside the curtain.

In the murky daytime darkness she could see two men sitting at one of the small wooden tables. They looked alike, good-looking in a gaunt, predatory way, with long hair, drooping moustaches, wide cheekbones and black, slightly slanting eyes. One had his hair tied back in a ponytail. They had been playing cards, though obviously not very seriously; the ponytailed one had his chair tilted precariously back on two legs, while the other was sprawled on his tailbone with one foot resting on the seat of an empty chair.

When Terry walked in there was a little flurry of movement, the soft but well-defined sounds that accompany a sudden change from somnolence to full alert. The chair settled upright with a soft bump, feet scraped the floor and cards smacked the table. Two heads swiveled toward her. Two pairs of eyes lit with a feral gleam.

Oh boy, Terry thought. *Señor Lopez, where are you!*

She could feel the eyes trailing over her body like the caress of icy fingers. Sensual, fleshy lips curved in nearly identical smiles.

"Dr. Terry! It is so good to see you!"

Relief washed through her. She hadn't known until that moment how frightened she'd been...how cold. The words "frozen with fear" had new meaning for her; she'd been momentarily paralyzed with it, like a mouse hearing the first whir of the rattlesnake's warning.

But Señor Lopez was coming from behind the bar, beaming widely enough to show his gold tooth as he always did, muscular arms outstretched in welcome. All was normal, all was right. Terry decided that the chilling prescience of danger she'd experienced a moment ago must have been her own imagination working overtime, fed by the unusual sequence of events that had begun the moment she'd first laid eyes on Jack Wolf.

Señor Lopez took Terry's arm, glanced at his two customers and led her back through the curtained doorway into the store. "We were not expecting to see you," he said, looking worried. "What brings you to El Refugio? Someone is sick?"

"I don't know," Terry said with an exasperated laugh, "that's what I'm trying to find out. I'm looking for a boy named Julio—about eight years old. Do you know him?"

The shopkeeper's eyebrows shot up. "Julio? That little one—a real *pícarito*—how do you say that? A rascal, no? Sure, I know him. Everybody knows Julio." His expression became doleful. "Ah, but it is very sad—"

Terry's heart gave a sickening lurch. Not twice in one trip, she prayed. *Please God.*

She caught the shopkeeper by the arm. "Do you know where they live? Julio brought me here to see his sister. He told me she was very sick. Do you know—is she all right? She's not—"

Señor Lopez looked startled, then confused. "No, no, no, the little one, she is fine. But the mother—Catalina—it is very sad. She died, only a few weeks ago. *En parto,* you understand? In childbirth."

Childbirth. Terry felt a familiar rage, along with a fatiguing sense of futility. Ah, God...it was so unnecessary, and the very thing she and the other Flying Samaritans were trying so hard to prevent. Why, oh why, hadn't Julio's mother come to the clinics for prenatal care?

"Can you give me directions?" she asked the shopkeeper woodenly. "I would like to see the family before I go."

Señor Lopez nodded with great enthusiasm. "*Sí*—here, I show you." He took a stub of a pencil from his shirt pocket, licked the tip of it and began to draw on the countertop. Terry bent closer.

A shadow cut through the beam of light from the shutter. Terry looked up and felt her heart perform another medical impossibility. Jack.

He stood there in the rectangle of light from the open doorway, the same silhouette she'd last seen against a soft lavender sky. Just for a moment he stood there looking around him, looking, she felt, right at *her*. Then he stepped quickly, almost furtively to one side, into the shadows.

Now what? Terry thought. My imagination again?

"... just past the two rocks, one on top of the other, so it looks like a hat—"

Terry dragged her attention back to the countertop.

"And there it is—you cannot miss it!" Señor Lopez finished his map with a flourish.

Terry thanked him effusively, picked up her bag and moved toward the door, forcing herself with every ounce of her willpower not to look for Jack in the shadows.

"Come back when you have finished with the little one," Señor Lopez called after her. "I will save you a nice cold Coca-Cola."

Terry nodded and waved goodbye.

And at that moment, all hell broke loose in the cantina. There was a thunderous explosion—then another, and another—the sounds of splintering wood and breaking glass.

Terry's stunned mind had barely registered *Gunfire!* when something—someone—came hurtling past her and out the door. She heard Señor Lopez shout. More gunshots—from outside now—and frightened screams. She turned instinctively toward the cries, only to be shoved violently back against the door frame as a second body exploded past her.

Common sense should have told her to hit the floor and stay there; instead, like a punch-drunk fighter, she struggled to keep her balance, determined to stay upright. While she stood swaying in the doorway, groping for the support of the adobe wall, she heard a sound, the faintest of sounds, like a mosquito zipping past her ear, and then a dull *thunk*, as if something had struck the heavy wooden door frame a few inches above her head.

"Dammit, Doc—get the hell out of my way!"

Something—Jack's arm?—slammed against her back and gave her a mighty shove. Air rushed from her lungs. She went flying across the veranda, hard into one of the produce tables. The next thing Terry knew she was falling, and not gracefully, crashing down in a chaotic avalanche of flailing limbs, broken furniture, straw baskets and overripe fruit.

And then for a few moments there was silence, or perhaps it only seemed like it, after the pandemonium that had gone before. Terry lay on her back with her eyes tightly closed, fighting panic and a terrifying disorientation, afraid to move, afraid to open her eyes. She didn't know what had happened, what was happening, or whether all her arms and legs were in the right places. She wondered if she might be hurt. She didn't think so, at least not seriously, but shock was a funny thing. She'd known cases where—

"Doc! Ah, geez—Terry—" Jack's voice sounded terrible. "Say something, dammit! *Doc!*"

Renewed pandemonium close at hand gave Terry the incentive to open her eyes; what she saw almost made her close them again. Jack was clawing his way toward her, hurling baskets and boards and heads of lettuce in every direction and bellowing like a wounded bear. She watched in dazed wonder from under her lashes as he picked up the last obstacle—half of the broken table—and heaved it off the veranda, then dropped to his knees beside her in the rubble.

"Ah...Doc. Dammit, Doc." He kept saying that, or something like it, over and over. And if his voice sounded awful, his face was worse. In all her years as a doctor, she'd never seen such a look on a man's face. Something twisted inside her. It was too painful to look at him.

She gave a sharp, involuntary gasp. Was that—it was. Jack's hands were touching her. Everywhere! With surprising expertise they explored her arms and legs, pushed through her hair to probe her scalp, paused to lay two fingers against the side of her neck, timing the cadence of her pulse.

"What the hell are you doing? You can see I'm alive," Terry croaked. "I'm breathing, aren't I?"

Jack glanced down at her heaving chest. His throat moved convulsively, but he only snarled, "Lie still," and slipped his hands under her shoulders. He lifted her slightly and slid his hands downward, gently probing her spine and ribs.

"What are you doing, checking for bullet holes?"

"Shut up, dammit—" Jack's hands suddenly stilled. Under the beard stubble his face had paled to a muddy gray.

"What—" Terry began, then stopped as he slowly pulled his hands out from under her and stared down at his fingers. For a split second her heart stopped. Then she choked and would probably have burst out laughing, if it hadn't been for Jack's face...Jack's eyes. The look in them chilled her soul. To her they seemed the eyes of a man staring straight into Hell.

"It's just tomatoes, Jack," she said, her voice gentler than it had any right to be, under the circumstances. "I'm not hurt."

He uttered a succinct and disgusted obscenity and wiped his hands on his pants. He turned his head away from her for a moment, as if the sight were more than he could stomach, then suddenly jerked back to her, his face darkening, anger pulsing from him in almost visible waves. "Then why the hell did you scream?"

Anger was easier to respond to than that unfathomable anguish. Terry sat up and shouted back at him, "Why did I *scream?* Why did I scream? You *pushed* me, that's why! Damn you, I could have been seriously hurt!"

"You could have been *killed,* you idiot! Don't you know enough to duck when you're being shot at? Of all the—"

"I don't make a habit of getting myself shot at, Jack!"

He made an exasperated noise and sat back on his heels, rubbing his hands on his flexed thighs as if it were the only way to keep them from wrapping around her neck. Terry opened her mouth to fire off another withering salvo. And that was when she saw the gun.

She'd never seen one like it in real life before, only in movies and TV cop shows. But she knew what kind of gun it was, and for what purpose. A gun like that had only one purpose.

After the first instinctive recoil, for a moment or two she just stared at it. Then comprehension struck. It was like a small earthquake, triggering a veritable landslide of pieces falling into place. It was all so clear now. She understood everything.

Anger ignited within her. Each new understanding fed the flame; it mushroomed, exploded into a holocaust of rage, a magnificent rage, a rage of epic proportions. She hauled in air in several great gulps, priming herself for its venting, but before she could even get a coherent word out, there was an explosion of another kind. More gunshots, this time some distance away, from the direction of the church.

With the dying echo of the first shot Jack was on his feet, the gun in his hand. He crouched low, looked, then vaulted over the broken table and took off running, zigzagging across the open ground in front of the store. The villagers, who had begun to emerge hesitantly from their hiding places, dived back under cover, screaming and crying out to the saints.

But the volley was brief—only half a dozen shots or so. In the silence that followed it, Terry struggled to her feet. Señor Lopez poked his head cautiously through the door of his shop, then came to help her.

"You are okay? You're sure you're okay?" he kept saying as he brushed futilely at the tomato stains on her shirt. He shook his head and muttered to himself in Spanish. "I *knew* those guys were no good—bad hombres, you know? I hope they are gone for good. Your friend—he is a cop?''

A cop? Terry doubted it, but it really didn't matter. Either way, what he'd done was reprehensible. Unforgivable. And when she got her hands on him she didn't know what she was going to do. Never in all her life, not even in her lonely and confused childhood, or her angry and rebellious youth, had she *ever* been so angry. It was anger so vast she could only tremble with it, breathing hard, on the verge of sobs.

''Thank you...leave it...it's okay,'' she muttered, pushing at Señor Lopez's ministering hands. She walked to the edge of the veranda on uncertain legs and drew a shaking hand across her mouth, then used both hands to smooth back the cloud of curls that had escaped their moorings.

''*Damn you... Jack.*'' It was half a whisper, half a sob.

The villagers were coming out of hiding again. Shocked and bewildered, they gathered in little knots of twos or threes, talking softly to each other and looking to her for comfort. She passed among them in a semi-daze, stopping only long enough to make certain no one had been injured. Then she pulled away from the outstretched, beseeching hands and took off after Jack at a dead run, too upset to remember or care that her hat and sunglasses were still buried somewhere underneath the rubble on the veranda.

When she got to the mesa she thought it was deserted. The little white church sat undisturbed, shimmering in the midday sun, the dusty, battered pickup truck parked in front of it like a prostrate beggar. Although something about the pickup seemed different... she couldn't quite put her finger on it.

She didn't see Jack at first, and assumed he must have gone off in pursuit of the two men. And then she did see him—or rather, she saw his feet, sticking out from under the truck—and her heart nearly leaped through the wall of her chest.

"Jack—oh God, no."

Terry would have hated to try to describe her feelings at that moment. She stood still, absolutely cemented to the spot, shaking, so full of anger she could hardly breathe, but full of other things, too, things she didn't recognize or understand. She'd wanted to kill Jack—she still did—but the thought that he might be dead terrified her. She was a doctor—but she couldn't bring herself to touch him, to look at him. She couldn't remember how to put on a bandage. Her mind was paralyzed.

While she stood there breathing in whimpers, Jack suddenly levered himself out from under the truck and stood up, brushing dirt from his Levi's and swearing like a longshoreman.

"Goddamn so-and-so's," he muttered, firing off one of the longest and most colorful strings of street epithets Terry had ever heard. "They shot the truck."

Chapter 7

Even as upset as he was, Wolf had to admire the lady. There weren't many women who could get shot at, thrown across a veranda and practically buried in ripe tomatoes and still come up fighting mad.

Although mad might be too pale a word to describe the creature standing before him with the wind stirring up yellow leaves around her feet and tossing her hair like flames. There was something almost mythical, or biblical, about her. She brought to mind images like Fire and Brimstone, Pillars of Fire, the Wrath of God. He thought wryly, if ever anyone personified Wrath...

But while he did admire the doc, he just didn't want to deal with her. Not now. She made things too complicated. She made him feel things he didn't want to feel, things he didn't have time for and couldn't afford—like guilt. And fear. The worst kind of fear, not for his own, but for someone else's, safety. When he thought about what it had done to him, hearing her scream, seeing her lying there like that—

No. He didn't need that. He wanted things kept simple, the way they had been ever since the day he'd walked into his brother's house...and headlong into the nightmare. He needed to concentrate on the essentials, the fire and fuel that kept him going—his own rage, his own burning need for revenge.

And he'd been so close to filling that need. *So close.* If it hadn't been for that blasted doctor, if she hadn't been in his line of fire, if she hadn't screamed, if he hadn't stopped to see about her— *If.*

But it was done. It was over. After all the months of searching and planning and waiting, he'd blown it. He'd missed his opportunity. At this very moment his quarry was hightailing it into the hills, while he stood here like an idiot, stranded with a useless hunk of metal and a woman mad enough to kill him. Things were just about as bad as they could get, and if he didn't do something to let off a little steam, he was going to explode.

So he swore some more and gave the truck another kick in one of its four flat tires. It didn't accomplish much, except to bruise the heck out of his toe and give him something new to swear about, but it did snap the doc out of whatever it was she'd been lost in—some kind of daze, it seemed, because she'd been standing there looking like the Devil himself had just crossed her path. Now she gave her head a little wake-up shake, kind of tossed her hair back out of her face and came toward him, stepping cautiously, as if she still thought the ground might open up under her feet.

"What do you mean, 'shot the truck'?" Her voice sounded faint and airless. "How can you shoot a truck?"

"Take a look." He folded his arms on his chest and stood aside, but she didn't even glance at the flat tires, the bullet holes in the hood, didn't seem to notice the strong smell of petroleum, or the ominous puddle under the front end. She just stood there, looking straight at *him*. Clenching and unclenching her hands as if she wanted to strangle him.

"*Who* shot the truck, Jack? Huh? Tell me that." When he didn't answer, she took a step closer. "Who were those men?" Another step. "What business did you have with them that you needed a *gun?*"

With the last word her hand shot out, and an accusing index finger nailed him right in the middle of the chest.

It caught him by surprise. He took a step backward, but there was nowhere to go; the truck was in his way.

"You *used* me, Jack. Didn't you?" She was breathing hard, hauling in air like a long-distance runner. "You used me, you used Julio, you used all of us. There isn't any sick sister, is there? You cooked it up—all of it. You used me, and you used a child, and I'll never forgive you for that, *never.* What were you going to do to those men, Jack, tell me that! What are you, some kind of *bounty hunter?*" The look of revulsion on her face would have curdled milk.

"I told you," Wolf said stonily, resisting an urge to rub the spot in the middle of his chest where her finger had stabbed him. Not that it would have helped; the place that hurt wasn't on the surface, but deep down inside. "It's a personal matter. A debt."

"A *debt?* What were you going to do, take it out in *blood?*"

"That's none of your damn business." He pushed away from the truck, pushed past her. She whirled and caught him by the arm.

"None of my business! Then what am I doing here, huh? You tell me how come I'm standing here beside a...a *dead truck,* in the middle of nowhere, *stranded*...and with a man who just tried to *shoot* somebody. I'm a *doctor,* damn you. How could you do that to me?"

She was crying. Wolf felt his anger, the sharp edges of it, anyway, eroding like adobe in the rain. He rubbed a hand roughly over his face and growled, "Come on, Doc...."

She gave her nose an inelegant swipe and turned on him like a Fury. "So, tell me, Jack—what now, huh? What do we do now?"

What now. It was a good question, and one he didn't like thinking about. Because it was occurring to him that the lady standing there glaring at him with tear-drenched and scorn-filled eyes, the lady who only a short while ago had been his biggest asset, had now become a liability. An enormous and frightening liability. A liability the magnitude of which he was only just beginning to realize. What *was* he going to do?

"Shut up," he growled. "Let me think."

Wolf figured it was a safe bet the Cruz brothers were on foot, but then, so was he. And saddled with a woman besides. It was also a pretty good bet they'd head for the coast, either to steal a fishing boat or to hitch a ride on the Trans-Baja Highway. Either way, they'd be long gone by the time he and Terry managed to find a way back to Santa Luisa and the plane. So he'd be back to square one again. Tracking them down, smoking them out, unless, of course, they were out there in the desert somewhere hiding out, biding their time, waiting for a chance to double back, sneak in and catch them unawares....

Wolf was suddenly cold, cold as ice. Nausea rose to the back of his throat and threatened to humiliate him then and there.

"Well," Terry said scathingly, raking her hair back from her forehead, "I'm certainly not going to stand here in the sun while you *think.* I'm going back to Señor Lopez's. If he can't arrange some kind of transportation for us, at least maybe he can put us up for the night. By tomorrow—"

"No!" The cry burst from him, harsh and jarring as a gravel road. "We can't stay here."

"Oh?" Terry's eyebrows shot up and her voice beamed dangerously soft. "*We* may not have a choice, Jack. *I,* personally, intend to do whatever I think—"

"Listen to me, damn you." He caught both of her arms, his grip frighteningly strong but so tightly controlled she could feel his muscles quivering. "For once...*listen to me.*"

She wasn't nearly ready to hear anything he had to say. She stood stiff and still, trembling, chest heaving, heart hammering, chin up and jaws clenched tight in stubborn, unreasoning fury. But something in his voice, something compelled her to stop resisting, just for a moment. Something made her bite back her sharp, angry retort and listen, even though she couldn't yet bring herself to look at his face.

Jack took a cautious, unsteady breath. "All right. Now." The grip on her arms eased a little, but the tension was still there in his voice. "The way I see it, those guys are on foot, just like we are. What they'll probably try to do is head for the coast. But they can't do that without provisions—at least water—and the way they took off out of here, they didn't have time to pick anything up on the way. I figure they're going to hide out in those rocks up there and wait for nightfall and then come back into town for what they need. I don't want to be here when they do."

His voice chilled her more than his words; she felt her anger dissipate and fear come rushing in to take its place. Now she wanted to look at him. Oh, she wanted to draw reassurance and courage from those hard features and burning eyes—but she couldn't. She was afraid. Not of what she might see in his face, but of the way she felt when she looked at him. God help her, even after all he'd done...

"Why? I thought that was what you wanted," she said through stiff, cold lips, staring fixedly at his chin. "You went to so much trouble to find them. You wanted them so badly you even used me, the Sams..."

She could see his teeth clench. The grip on her arms tightened momentarily. "*Yes*—I used you." His voice was ragged with strain. "The reason I used you was for the element of surprise. It was the only advantage I had, and now it's gone. Listen—" He gave her a little shake, spitting words between his teeth like bullets. "Those men are dangerous. I can't even begin to tell you how dangerous they are. They know this town and the terrain—I don't. And there are two of them. Plus, now I have to worry about—"

He broke off. Terry's eyes jerked involuntarily, meeting his in a collision that drove a sharp gasp from her lips.

"You don't have to worry about me," she said tightly. "Leave me here. You go and...and do your thing. Just leave me out of it. I can stay with Señor Lopez until—"

"Haven't you heard anything I've said?" His face was close to hers, dark, ruthless, and indescribably tortured. "Those men are killers. They kill for pleasure. Do you know what they'd do to you if they had the chance, just to get to me? *Do you? Huh?*"

She gave a sharp cry as he suddenly jerked her close and pinned her to him with one arm. His hand closed over her throat, caressed it with brief, incongruent tenderness, then tightened. His thumb forced her chin up, baring the vulnerable arch of her neck. His lips were only inches from hers, his words a guttural whisper.

"They'd put a knife to your pretty white throat, Doc. And then they'd carve pieces out of it...and out of these, too...until I handed over my gun to them. And then...they'd slit your throat...while I watched."

Terry gave a small, desperate sniff, trying so hard to hold back, trying to keep the welling sob from bursting past her tight-pressed lips—but it was impossible. She found that she was holding on to Jack's arm, an arm that felt more like iron than human flesh, holding on to it as if her life depended on it. She wanted to close her eyes, stop looking at him, shut out the pain, the horror she saw in his eyes, but that was impossible, too. She could only stare back at him, mesmerized and trembling.

There was a harsh, inarticulate cry—whose it was Wolf neither knew or cared. One minute his hand was on her throat and he was firing cruel, ugly descriptions of violence at her, and the next he was kissing her with that same violence, forcing her head back and her mouth open, bludgeoning her, punishing her, punishing himself.

It was a kiss born of rage and frustration; even in the first shocked moment Terry knew that there was no seduction in it. But it wasn't assault, either. Because suddenly she was angry again, as angry as he was. The same frustration that had just exploded through him had been burning like a red-hot ember in *her* belly, too. After the first instinctive recoil, she fought him not to escape him, but to give as good as she got.

Her head had fallen back at first, but now her neck muscles tightened. She rose up under him, pushed against his mouth, matching his savagery with her own. Teeth clashed against teeth; tongues dueled for supremacy, giving no quarter. She felt her lips break, tasted salt, and didn't care.

But Wolf felt her tender flesh give way under his, her beautiful mouth, soft lips, full and generous, ripe for kissing. And he hesitated, feeling the pain in his heart and the fire in his belly meld into one white-hot brand that seared him to his soul. He uttered a sound, a single harsh cry—a paean to his own loneliness and longing—and catching a handful of her hair, tangled his fingers in it and held her still, held her until she stopped fighting him. Held her until he felt her lips soften and swell in the heat of his mouth. Until her tongue stopped fighting his and began to mate with it instead. Until her breath stopped coming in desperate whimpers and became a low, hungry moan.

Where had it come from, this terrible need? Terry didn't know, but she thought now that it must have been there for a long time, buried deep inside her, maybe even all her life. Whatever it was, it terrified her because she couldn't control it. Even with all her education and training, she didn't understand it, didn't even know what to call it. It couldn't be love. Oh God, no—she'd loved Robert, and it had been nothing like this! Love was gentle and nurturing, like sweet spring rains. Not like this—this was a tempest, a typhoon, wreaking nothing but havoc and destruction, sound and fury!

But oh, how she reveled in the fury. Her spirit soared with it, spiraled to wild, dizzying heights. And why, she thought, if there was no nourishment in the tempest, why was her body suddenly tingling, why did she feel hot and swollen, full to bursting, why could she feel the energy coursing through every vein? As if, for the first time in her life, she were finally, truly, *alive*.

Wolf disentangled his fingers from her hair and slid his hands downward, hesitated long enough to rub them questingly back and forth over the barriers of belt and waistband, then, in one swift movement, grasped her buttocks and pulled her hard against him. Her gasp of pain-pleasure merged with his as he lifted her, rubbing her against him in a graphic demonstration of what he wanted—what he *needed*—which was to rip away the barriers and plunge himself deep inside her, pull her arms and legs around him and lose himself in the warmth, the scent, the softness of her body.

The need had been there, he realized, almost since the very first moment, that brief moment of insight beside the airplane hangar in Van Nuys, when he'd seen, as a kind of vision, what had to happen between them—as unlikely as it had seemed—between himself and this rangy, red-haired doctor with the single-mindedness of a saint and the temperament of Mount Vesuvius. It had seemed so unlikely that he'd tried to ignore it, and that had been his mistake. Because he'd underestimated the power of the need. It had the power to make him forget who he was, where he'd come from and the path he'd chosen to take. And he couldn't let that happen. He had to stop this. *Now*. He knew he did.

He just didn't know if he could.

"Señor . . . señora, por favor—"

Wolf wouldn't have to worry about ending it after all, it seemed. Terry tore her mouth from his with a small, sharp sound like the cry of an animal in pain. His good sense told him he was glad.

But his body, and another part of him, a part he thought he'd lost a long time ago, felt a wrenching sense of loss. A little like an amputation.

Terry whirled around, one hand clamped across her mouth, adrenaline surging through her muscles. Trembling with the shock of it, she shook her head to clear away the passion fog, trying to make sense of the interruption, trying to bring into focus the cause of it.

She blinked and saw a slight, slender man with hollow cheeks and mournful eyes standing in the sun a few yards away, cradling a small, blanket-wrapped bundle in one arm. He was all dressed up in his Sunday best, in brown slacks that were too long for him and a white shirt buttoned up to his chin, and his hair had been subdued with water and combed neatly back. He looked apologetic, even a little embarrassed for having interrupted such a moment, but there was dignity, too, in the way he stood there silently waiting, pride in the way he held his body, determination in his dark, unwavering gaze.

Terry cleared her throat and said encouragingly in Spanish, "Yes, may I help you?"

"*¿Señora . . . la doctora?*"

"*Sí, es verdad*—I am the doctor."

He came forward, and as he did, Terry noticed a pair of bright brown eyes peering cautiously out from behind his legs.

There was a muffled snort from Jack. Terry gave a short little laugh of astonishment and dropped to one knee. "Julio?"

With wholly uncharacteristic shyness, Julio hung back, clinging to his father's hand. Terry gave his hair a forgiving ruffle and stood up, holding out her hand. "You must be Julio's father."

The man hesitated, then shifted the bundle and awkwardly shook hands as he muttered, "*Sí...Ramón Yberra.*"

"And this," Terry said softly, suddenly remembering everything Señor Lopez had told her, "must be Julio's sister. *¿La hermanita?*" Julio's father nodded. "*¿Por favor?*" Terry held out her arms. After a moment's hesitation, he carefully handed over his precious bundle.

It was almost alarmingly weightless. "How old?" Terry asked as she nestled the tiny baby into the cradle of her left arm.

"*Tres semanas, señora.*"

Three weeks. Terry pulled back a corner of the blanket and looked down at the sleeping baby. She saw an amazing shock of straight black hair, stubby black eyelashes and squashed infant nose. One tiny, perfect hand curled on one tiny dimpled cheek.

"*Pobrecita...*" she whispered, touching the baby's chin with the tip of her finger.

"Her name is Angelita," the father said, then added something Terry didn't understand. She looked questioningly at Jack.

"He says her mother named her," he murmured, without any inflection at all. "Before she died."

Terry nodded, and went back to gazing in utter fascination at the sleeping child. *Poor little angel.*

What in the world is the matter with me? she wondered dazedly, as the tiny face suddenly blurred and danced through a shimmer of tears. She'd held hundreds of babies—maybe thousands—but she'd never felt this, this *aching* inside. What was this lump in her throat, this feeling that her chest was too crowded and that if she didn't do something about it she was going to explode? She didn't know exactly what she felt like, but it sure wasn't aloof. Or objective, either. In fact, she didn't feel much like a doctor at all. She just felt like a woman. And something more.

There was a sudden, slight movement behind her. Jack was only reaching for his cigarettes, but Terry's nerves jumped and fluttered. Aftershocks of the recent cataclysm vibrated through her muscles.

"You just have bad timing, little one," she whispered. Oh, she knew what the problem was. In the last couple of days her emotions had been battered by one thing and another, and after what had just happened she was probably awash in female hormones to boot. So it was no wonder her feminine instincts were wide-awake and humming along in high gear. Maternal ones included.

"Yes..." she crooned softly. "So it's no wonder I'm a sucker right now for a sweet little angel like you. But I'm a doctor, you see. And doctors just aren't allowed to fall in love with their patients. So... let's see what we've got here...."

She peeled back the blanket and quickly assessed tiny arms and legs for muscle and skin tone, monitored the rise and fall of the tiny chest, felt the trip-hammer beat of the tiny heart.

"I don't think she's gaining properly," she said under her breath. "Señor Yberra—" She frowned, searching for the Spanish words. "Does Angelita have—Jack, what's the word for appetite?"

"*¡Ah, apetito!*" said Angelita's father, breaking into a smile. "*Sí, su apetito es muy saludable.*"

"That's it," Jack drawled as he took a drag on his cigarette. "He says she has a healthy one."

"No kidding, thanks a bunch," Terry said in a dry undertone. But Señor Yberra was going on, too rapidly for her to follow. She gave Jack an urgent nudge and muttered, "What's he saying now? Darn it, help me out here."

"He says..." There was a pause while he pulled on his cigarette. "Says her mother is dead and Angelita doesn't like the goat's milk. She gets hungry, she cries, he feeds her the goat's milk and...it comes back up. Makes her sick.'' There was a pause. Jack dropped the cigarette on the ground and stepped on it, grinding it carefully into the dirt. His face was like his voice, utterly without expression. ''He says he's afraid she's going to die, too.''

''Ask him if he's tried to give her anything else,'' Terry said in a low voice, at the same time offering the worried father a smile of encouragement. While she waited for the exchange, she found herself gently rocking the baby with her body, an unconscious motion that seemed so natural she thought it must be instinctive. How odd, she thought, I don't remember ever doing that before.

Jack turned back to her with a dispassionate shrug. ''No, just *aqua dulce*—water with honey in it. She does okay with that.''

''Well...'' Terry murmured, gently tickling the baby's stomach, ''sounds like we may have a little lactose intolerance here...is that right, sweetheart? Your little tummy can't handle milk, is that it?'' To her chagrin, she heard herself *cooing*. Which was deplorably unprofessional, she reminded herself, and made herself stop it.

''Well.'' She cleared her throat briskly. ''I should have some soy formula in my bag. We'll try that and see how she takes it. If that seems to do the trick I'll have to arrange somehow to get him a supply. Tell him that, will you, Jack?'' She went back to fussing over the blankets, folding and tucking them around the soundly sleeping infant. ''Tell him she needs a special formula, but she should be fine once she starts gaining some weight. Yes... aren't you just a little angel? You're going to be just fine....'' Oh Lord, there she was, cooing again.

She knew it was time to hand the child back over to her father, but for some reason it was hard to part with the tiny bundle. It was such a sweet, comforting burden.

"Doc," Jack said in an odd, gravelly voice, "we've got a problem here."

Terry tore her besotted gaze from the baby long enough to glance at him. "What do you mean?"

"You're not going to believe this." His face was a fascinating study, a field where impassivity dueled valiantly against an overwhelming battery of emotions. Temporarily, at least, emotion was the victor. He gave an incredulous laugh and croaked, "He wants you to keep the kid!"

Terry laughed, too. "What? Oh come on, you must not have understood him—or he didn't understand you. Tell him she's not sick enough to take to a hospital. All she needs is the special formula. Tell him."

Jack shook his head. "I did—I told him that. He says it's not just the milk, but that his wife is dead and he can't take care of a baby alone. He has to work hard to feed himself and Julio, and he can't work and take care of a baby, too. His neighbors help, he says, but they already have too many mouths to feed. He says—" He paused to shake his head, this time in disbelief. "He says he's heard there are rich Americans who want babies, and he wants you to take her back with you to America and find her a good home. Oh—" His lips twisted in a thin, sardonic smile. "And he wants you to have her baptized as soon as possible. He says the priest isn't due back here until next week."

"You're kidding," Terry said faintly. As she stared down at the sleeping baby, something swelled inside her chest until she felt as if she had no room for breath. "Oh, I can't believe he really wants to give her up—not permanently." Her voice was hushed, airless, the words too rapid. "Does he realize—"

"That's what he wants," Jack said harshly. "And look at him. He realizes."

Almost fearfully, with pounding heart and nerve-flutters dancing through her stomach, Terry looked at Julio's father.

There was something implacable about the slightly built man who stood in the bright sunshine amid gently scudding cottonwood leaves. He seemed unmovable, Terry thought, as if he'd grown there. One work-worn hand rested on Julio, who was clinging to him with both arms, face pressed tightly against his father's thigh. The other hand, hanging empty at his side, was curled into a tight, white-knuckled fist. He still held himself proudly, as straight and tall as ever, but his shoulders had a hunched, defensive look.

Moisture glistened on Señor Yberra's gaunt cheeks as he began to speak again.

"He says he'll sign the necessary papers," Jack translated grimly. "He says it's better to give her to someone who will take care of her than to let her die here with him."

"Oh God," Terry whispered. "I've never run into something like this before. Jack, what am I going to do?"

He looked at her as if she'd just sprouted a second head. "What are you talking about? There's no choice here. We're not taking that baby with us, no way! And that's *final.*"

If there was anything Terry hated, it was an ultimatum. "We?" she said in her softest, most dangerous voice. "It's my decision to make, Jack. Not yours. And don't you forget it."

Jack swore explosively and raised both arms in a classic gesture of masculine frustration with the implacability of woman.

When Terry turned reflexively, instinctively shielding the baby from him with her body, he said disgustedly, "Ah, geez, Doc," and swore some more, softly this time, under his breath. After a moment or two of heavy breathing, he reached out, touched her shoulder, than raked his hand distractedly through his hair.

"Look...Doc. Don't be bullheaded—this isn't the time for it. Be reasonable, here. I mean—geez, we're on foot, we've got killers out there, God knows where. Bad enough

I've got to worry about protecting you, and now you want to take a *baby* along? You can't be serious!''

"Oh? And who appointed *you* my protector?'' Terry shot back in cold fury. "I'm quite capable of protecting myself, thank you. In fact, I never needed protecting until I met you!''

But she hesitated, chewing on her lip while she gazed down at the tiny face in its nest of blankets, at the shock of silky black hair, the rosebud mouth making sucking motions even in sleep. Pride was one thing, but Jack was right. It looked as if they were going to be walking back to Santa Luisa. It would be a long, arduous hike, twenty miles or so over rugged mountain and desert terrain. Plus, if they left this afternoon, as Jack seemed bound and determined to do, they'd be sleeping outdoors tonight. It was foolish to even think about taking a baby along. It was crazy. Out of the question.

"All right...okay,'' she said in a hoarse, hurried whisper, reluctantly surrendering. "Tell him if he's serious about this we'll come back for the baby. Tell him—let's see...I'll have to find a way.... Look, I'll leave him some formula, and we'll come back next week. Maybe by then—''

"Too late,'' Jack rasped.

For Señor Yberra was speaking again, his quiet voice and the slow shaking of his head delivering a message that was as immutable as the wind.

"He's says he's made up his mind,'' Jack growled, turning to Terry with frustration burning bright in his eyes. "He says—''

"I know,'' Terry whispered, "I heard him.''

She is in your hands now. Yours...and God's.

Señor Yberra lifted his hand in a poignant little wave, then turned, took Julio firmly by the hand and slowly walked away. His head and shoulders were bowed, as if he carried an unbearable burden.

He had gone only a few steps when Julio suddenly jerked his hand from his father's grasp and came running back. He stopped short in front of Terry and looked up at her, his eyes round and bright and swimming with tears. She hesitated, then knelt and drew back the blankets. She held her breath, aching, while the little boy leaned over and with unwonted tenderness, kissed his baby sister on the cheek.

A sob trembled through Terry's chest. She fought so hard to hold it back. It was unprofessional. She wasn't supposed to let her emotions get involved. She wasn't supposed to hurt like this!

She fought it as she watched Julio go running back to bury his face in his father's side. She fought it as the father picked his son up in his arms, and for the long moment that they stood holding on to each other in mutual desolation. But when they had gone, leaving behind a few scurrying leaves and a vast stillness, it got away from her and burst forth—a shuddering gust of tears too long suppressed.

"Don't you say a word, Jack," she sobbed, turning the torrent on the only person available. "I'm not leaving this baby behind. I'm *not*. I'm a doctor, dammit. My job is to save lives, and you tried to use me to take lives, and I'm not going to forgive you for that—*ever*. I won't leave this child here at risk—I can't. I just lost one—I'm not going to lose this one, do you understand me? You can do whatever you want to, but I'm not leaving here without this baby!"

That's the way it was with a bad streak, Wolf thought. Just when you thought sure things couldn't get any worse, they did.

He stood there staring impassively down into the doc's furious, tear-wet face, feeling more helpless than he'd ever felt in his life. When had he been appointed her protector? When had he started to give a damn what happened to her? And *why?* She sure as hell didn't look like much—hair all over the place, nose and eyes bright-red and running like faucets. And she'd caused him nothing but trouble, stirring up his dormant conscience, refusing to cooperate with his carefully laid plans, getting in his line of fire and making him think she'd been·injured so he'd wasted his time worrying about her when he should have been chasing down his brother's killers. And now, when he had to worry about getting her safely back to Santa Luisa—with the Cruz boys out there, God only knew where—she was going to saddle him with a *baby!*

If there was one thing Wolf had learned, it was that when Luck turned her back on you there was no point in fighting her. When that happened, it was best just to pull out of the game and wait for her to smile your way again.

"Okay, Doc," he said with a sigh. "You win. Come on, get up from there." He held out his hand, and after a moment's hesitation and a considering sniff, she took it.

"Guess we'll have to go see your friend Lopez about some provisions," he muttered gruffly as he pulled her to her feet. He managed to evade her tear-drenched eyes by squinting up at the sky. "And then, before it gets any later, is it all right with you, *Doña Teresa,* if we get the hell out of here?"

Chapter 8

"You sure you don't want me to carry her for a while?" Wolf asked Terry. It was the fourth or fifth time she'd stopped to squint up at the canyon rim, which had been retreating before them like a rainbow for the last hour or so.

He didn't know why he bothered; it wasn't going to get him anything but another one of her blistering glares. He was beginning to be very sorry her sunglasses had gotten broken in the melee on Señor Lopez's veranda. The reproach in those show-everything eyes of hers was beginning to get on his nerves.

Her foot scraped on a gravelly patch and Wolf shot out a hand to steady her, clamping his jaws down on a pithy comment on the subject of feminist pride. He kept a tight grip on her elbow until they'd made it the last few yards to the rim of the canyon, all but boosting her up and over the roughest places, even though he knew she didn't like having him touch her.

Well, hell, she was furious with him, and he didn't really blame her. Although he was pretty sure the reason she didn't

want him touching her had nothing to do with that baby she
was being so protective of, or for that matter, getting shot
at and stranded. He had an idea that what she was really
protecting with all those bristles and thorns was something
else entirely, something she didn't want to have to look at
too closely. The lady did have a lot of pride, way *too* much
as far as he was concerned.

When they reached the top, she pulled away from him and
stumbled over to a slab of volcanic rock. "We have to stop,"
she said as she sank down on it and dumped her backpack,
glaring at Wolf as if she expected him to argue. "The baby's
waking up. I need to feed her."

Wolf just grunted, "Watch out for scorpions," and
reached for his cigarettes.

While he tapped one out and lit it, he checked out the
surrounding terrain, which at that elevation included scrub
juniper and pine trees—entirely too many hiding places for
his liking. But although it was quiet, it wasn't *too* quiet, and
he took that as a good sign. Some kind of bird was singing
away up in a nearby pine tree, and a little blue-bellied lizard went strolling unhurriedly across the face of the rocks,
pausing to give him a long yellow stare before slipping into
a crack.

They hadn't done badly, considering. He figured the
worst part of the trip—that climb out of the canyon—was
behind them now. From here on, it would generally be
downhill to the coast. It had been rougher than he'd antic-
ipated, since they couldn't risk taking the road and walking
into an ambush, but the doc hadn't uttered one word of
complaint. Though he'd never admit it to her, Wolf's ad-
miration for the lady was growing by leaps and bounds.

He caught himself watching her as she took a bottle out
of her pack and peeled the plastic cover off the nipple, then
bent intently over the blanket-wrapped bundle in the crook
of her arm. She'd partly turned away from him; he couldn't
see either her face or the baby's, but he could hear cooing

murmurs and soft, unidentifiable sounds. A sudden, sharp restlessness seized him.

"I'll do that if you want a break," he heard himself say in a voice that surprised him with its hoarseness.

It seemed to surprise her, too. She looked up at him with something in her eyes he couldn't read, something that was snuffed out like a candle in the wind when she saw the cigarette in his hand. "And have you blow smoke in her face?" she said scathingly. "Over my dead body!"

Indefinably wounded, Wolf took a long, deliberate drag and retaliated. "Yeah, well in case you've forgotten, *Doña Teresa*, that's a real possibility."

She kind of cocked her head as if she were playing that over in her mind. Finally she countered with, "Tell me, Jack, are you *always* sarcastic?"

Her voice was silky and sweet, but since he'd seen the flash of temper in her eyes, the way Wolf figured it, *she* was the one being sarcastic. So he took another pull on his cigarette and drawled, "I don't know, Doc, are you always so bossy and bullheaded?" Then he went stalking off to find a place where he could smoke and not feel guilty about it. At least it was one way to get in the last word.

He found himself another rock a short distance away, downwind, and leaned against it while he puffed resentfully on his cigarette and stared holes in the doctor's back.

Damn the woman. He wasn't exactly sure when it had happened, but at some point he seemed to have lost control of the situation. He didn't like that. Plus, he'd just childishly lost his temper over practically nothing, and he liked that even less. And he could lay the blame for both of those things squarely on that blasted red head of the doc's, which at the moment just happened to be picking up the last rays of the setting sun so that it looked like it had caught fire.

Well, all right, so he knew she wasn't really responsible for the way things had turned out. Any more than she was to blame for the fact that his nerves were jumping and

Wolf and the Angel

twitching like fleas on hot sand. The fact was, he had no-body to blame but himself. He'd let her get to him, and it had been a long time since *anything* had gotten to him, much less a woman. And it was beginning to scare the hell out of him.

Like the way he felt right now, looking at the doc—*that* scared the hell out of him. Because as ticked off as he was at her, as fed up as he was with her arrogant attitude and bossy bullheadedness, what he was feeling was a powerful desire to kiss her. More than that, actually. He'd already kissed her a couple of times, under vastly different circumstances, and what he felt like doing now was breaking some new ground.

It was a feeling he'd been having quite a lot lately, and at the damnedest times. For instance, while she sat there on her rock like a grand duchess on her throne, with her body covered from shoulder to knee in one of Señor Lopez's serapes, the sun going down in flames behind her, all he could think of was the way she'd looked with her head thrown back and her breasts pushing against the fabric of a thin white T-shirt, bathing in the rosy wash of another sunset.

But that was just lust, he told himself, and at least he could understand that—the silvery knife-thrust in his belly, the fire in his loins, the upsurge in his heart rate and breathing. It wasn't anything he hadn't felt before, although maybe not as strongly. It was the other stuff that scared him, that made him feel jumpy and restless and out of sorts. Like for instance the way he felt watching that baby's head with that shock of straight black hair kind of bobbing around on the doc's shoulder, getting all mixed up with her red-gold curls....

Damn. He thought he'd lost the ability to feel like that. He didn't *want* to feel like that, ever again. It hurt too much.

He uttered a single sibilant word in self-disgust and pushed away from his rock, crushing his cigarette under the toe of his boot, crushing his fear the same way. Burying it the way he'd once buried his dread of the monster in his closet—under an avalanche of sheer bravado.

"Time we found someplace to spend the night," he announced, picking up Terry's backpack and swinging it over his shoulder. She turned and looked at him as if he'd surprised her again, although he knew good and well she'd heard his footsteps crunching on the gravelly ground. He gave her a wicked smile and a mocking little bow. "*If* that meets with your approval, of course, *Doña Teresa.*"

She didn't say anything for a minute or two, just went on patting the baby's back and looking at him in a way she had that always made him feel vaguely ashamed of himself. Then in a soft, curious voice she said, "Why do you call me that?" She paused to shift the baby to the crook of her arm, and continued almost conversationally, "Oh, I know you mean to be sarcastic, but do you realize that's practically the only time you ever call me by my name?"

"Ah, come on," Wolf muttered. But he'd had a sudden flash of memory—someone saying to him, once upon a time, *She's not the sort of person you get on a first-name basis with right off the bat.*

"It's true, you know." She tried a smile, but it was obvious her heart wasn't in it. "You always call me Doc."

"Well, hell," he said, shifting his shoulders irritably. He could see in her eyes that he'd somehow hurt her, and was wondering why she gave a damn what he called her, wondering what in the hell was responsible for this pensive mood of hers. "You aren't exactly the kind of person you get on a first-name basis with right off the bat," he plagiarized, then thought, Good job, Jack—that's thinking on your feet!

She looked quickly down at the baby in her arms, then back at him, her chin a couple of notches higher than before. It was hard to tell in that sunset light, but he thought her cheeks seemed more colored, her eyes brighter than usual. "Are you saying that I'm aloof?"

Wolf gave a sharp bark of laughter. "*Aloof?* Are you kidding?" Then all he could do was look at her, because memory had just hit him like a punch in the stomach. The salty-sweet taste of her mouth, crushed in the heat of passion...

And now he *knew* she was turning pink. Because he could see everything in her eyes that she was thinking, and he knew that what she was thinking about at that moment was the same thing he was thinking about. The thing they'd both been trying *not* to think about. The thing she'd been protecting and that they'd both been tiptoeing around all afternoon as if it were a sleeping rhinoceros. He wondered when someone was going to get brave enough to mention it.

"Aloof?" He said again, and snorted. "God, no. Just arrogant."

Her mouth popped open as if she planned to argue the point, but Wolf had had enough. It was hard enough being around her when she was mad at him. He wasn't sure what he'd do if she softened up on him. He said through his teeth, "Come on, damn it. It'll be dark in a minute."

To his surprise, she closed her mouth without saying a word and slid down off the rock.

They walked a ways in silence. It was easy going there on the summit of the ridge, fairly level and carpeted with new grass and pine needles and strewn with cones. They walked side by side, which was something they hadn't done before, Terry watching where she put her feet and leaving it to Jack to keep an eye out for a good place to shelter for the night.

It was funny, she thought, how easy it had been to abdicate that responsibility. So easy that it seemed almost an instinctive thing. Funny, when she had always been so self-reliant. With Robert, it had been she who'd taken care of the basics of shelter and security, she who had bought the townhouse, the cars, the insurance policies. She who, since the divorce, had prided herself on needing no one.

What, she wondered, had become of her anger? The truth was, at this moment she was very glad to have Jack there beside her; his strong, lean body was a reassuring presence in the growing dusk. Terry hated to admit being afraid of anything—anything but her own feelings, anyway—but she was afraid now. Afraid of the vastness of the mountains and desert, afraid of the dark and the threat of unimaginable violence that lurked in it somewhere. Afraid of the awesome responsibility for the tiny scrap of life sleeping in her arms. And while she knew perfectly well that it was Jack who was mostly responsible for the mess she was in, and that he deserved every bit of the anger she'd thrown at him today, on another level of awareness entirely she knew that he was the one who would get her out of it. That, when it came right down to it, he would take care of her, and the baby.

She stole a sideways look at him from under a windblown strand of her hair, noticing the way the wind picked up his hair in wings as they walked. He wasn't naked to the waist now. Like her, he was wearing a blanket poncho borrowed from Señor Lopez, but for some reason she was suddenly thinking of that first night in Dos Caminos, those strange moments of regression to an earlier, simpler and more savage time. A strong man, she'd thought then. A protector.

It's unbelievable, but . . . I feel *safe* with him.

The thought set loose an avalanche of conflicting and bewildering emotions, which tumbled around and around inside of her looking for a way out. The best she could manage, finally, was a question, thrown up out of the turbulence in her mind without preamble or forethought.

"You really don't like me much, do you?"

Wolf threw her a quick, hard look, then shifted his shoulders, that restlessness again, as if he had an itchy spot he couldn't scratch. "Liking's got nothing to do with it," he said gruffly. They tramped on, four steps, five. "People like me just don't have a whole lot in common with people like you."

He heard her haul in a breath, a long one, not quite steady. "What do you mean, people like me?"

He shrugged. "Aw hell, Doc, it's a classic fairy-tale scenario. Bad boy, good girl... But that's what it is, you know—just a fairy tale. The truth is, the two never do mix— oil and water, that's us. See, people like you are always tryin' to reform people like me. And I've got no particular wish to be reformed. Doc, what the hell—"

He broke off because suddenly she wasn't there; she'd stopped dead in her tracks a few paces back.

"Is that really how you see me?" she asked faintly, shaking her head as if she needed to clear away fog. "A 'good girl'?" She gave a soft, breathy laugh. "That's funny, you know. Really funny."

He waited for her to tell him why, but she just tossed back her hair, gave the baby a little hitch and came on.

"Just shows how much you know me," she remarked flippantly when she caught up with him. The Doc at her most arrogant and sarcastic.

To hide his frustration Wolf lit up another cigarette, muttering around it, "Yeah, well, like I said, Doc—you're not easy to get to know." It was hard to remember, now, that not too long ago he hadn't wanted to know anything about her, not even her name.

"I don't think that's true," she said lightly. "I've never had any trouble making friends."

"Is that right?" Wolf snorted. "Yeah, well, making friends and letting them *know* you—that's two different things."

He left her thinking about that one over while he checked out a crevice between two big boulders. After he'd rejected it as a possible shelter—too many approaches—he turned back to find her staring at him as if he were some kind of puzzling case she was trying to diagnose.

"You know, you're a fine one to talk, Jack." He thought she sounded a little out of breath. "I've never seen anyone as good at hiding things as you are. You have this way...sometimes your face just goes blank. Your eyes, too."

Wolf laughed softly. "I'm a card player, Doc—a gambler. That *way* I have, as you call it, that poker face is one reason I'm good at it."

"Yes, but you do it even when you're not playing poker. And you do other things, too—like your sarcasm, and that cowboy drawl—" Wolf made a sharp, disdainful sound. "You *do*. You turn it on and off, Jack. And you always seem to turn it on when something comes up that you don't want to talk about."

He didn't say anything while he took a drag on his cigarette, turning away from her and cupping his hand around it to shield the baby from the smoke. He wondered if she'd notice that in the process he'd also managed to shield his face from her, and if she did, whether she'd call him on it. He had a feeling she would notice; apparently not much got by her. It surprised him more than he cared to admit that she had already figured out so much about him. He'd have to be more careful from now on.

"Yeah, I do that," he said, using his deepest drawl just to make a point, "but that's because I choose to. Maybe it's because I don't want to let anybody know what I'm thinkin', not because I can't. If I decide to let you know how I feel, Doc, I promise you, you're gonna know...."

He let the words trail off as he stuck his cigarette between his lips and used both hands to pull himself up onto a ledge. A little farther up he'd spotted a depression in the rocks, too shallow to be called a cave, but deep enough to put something solid overhead and against their backs. He also liked the fact that it was up high, and that anyone approaching would have to come across open ground.

He jumped down from the ledge with a soft grunt, dusted his hands and removed the cigarette from his mouth, jabbing a forefinger in the doc's direction. "And anyway, we aren't talking about me. We're talking about *you*, lady, and I don't think you'd even know how to let anybody close enough to find out what makes you tick. Here—you think you can climb up there?"

The light was going fast, but he could still see her face well enough to know he'd scored a direct hit. He could see her struggling with it, knew she wanted to argue with him about it and hated like hell to have to put it aside to deal with more immediate concerns, such as food, shelter and safety. He wondered if she'd guess that he'd deliberately distracted her, hoping to keep that analytical mind of hers from figuring out what he was up to.

Of course, he wasn't all that sure himself what he was up to. He found that he wanted to goad her into opening herself up to him; the question was, why? It frustrated the hell out of him that he could read her like a book and still not be able to figure her out. He told himself he wanted to crack her just because she was so bent on keeping him out—he never had been able to resist a challenge. He told himself he didn't really care what made her tick, that it was all just part of the game.

But it was a dangerous game he was playing, in more ways than one. He wasn't sure yet what the stakes were, or whether or not he was in to stay, but he couldn't bring himself to play it safe and fold, either. He'd played the game enough to know that the heady feeling—that old adrenaline rush—could sometimes lead to a hard, painful fall. And as far as danger went, the doc represented a whole new variety. He was beginning to wonder what kinds of surprises she might have up her sleeve.

And right about then she played one of them.

"Sure, I can get up there," she said. "Here—hold the baby."

It took him completely by surprise. He fumbled his cigarette, dropped it like a guilty schoolboy and croaked,

ACCEPT FOUR BRAND-NEW

YOURS

We'd like to send you four free Silhouette novels, worth more than $13.00, to introduce you to the benefits of the Silhouette Reader Service. We hope your free books will convince you to subscribe, but that's up to you. Accepting them places you under no obligation to buy anything, but we hope you'll want to continue with the Reader Service.

So unless we hear from you, once a month we'll send you four additional Silhouette Intimate Moments® novels to read and enjoy. If you choose to keep them, you'll pay just $2.96* per volume—a saving of 33¢ each off the cover price. There is no charge for postage and handling. There are no hidden extras! And you may cancel at any time, for any reason, just by sending us a note or a shipping statement marked "cancel." You can even return any shipment to us at our expense. Either way, the free books and gifts are yours to keep!

ALSO FREE!
VICTORIAN PICTURE FRAME

This lovely Victorian pewter-finish miniature is perfect for displaying a treasured photograph—and it's yours *absolutely free*—when you accept our no-risk offer.

Perfect for a treasured Photograph

Plus a FREE mystery gift! follow instructions at right.

WE EVEN PROVIDE FREE POSTAGE!

It costs you *nothing* to send for your free books — we've paid the postage on the attached reply card. And we'll pick up the postage on your shipment of free books and gifts, and also on any subsequent shipments of books, should you choose to become a subscriber. Unlike many book clubs, we charge *nothing* for postage and handling!

"Now, wait—" But she'd already dumped the baby into his arms and was pulling herself up onto the ledge.

For a minute or two Wolf just stood there holding the bundle, his mind a complete blank. Then he thought, she's so light. Hardly weighs anything at all. Memories crowded in, memories of Carrie Elizabeth, and the very first time he'd held her. Her christening. In a panic he pushed them back.

The bundle moved and emitted a sound—a sort of squeaking noise. Wolf's heart stopped. When it started again he cautiously pulled back a corner of the blanket. One tiny arm came shooting out, fist all doubled up like it was taking a swing at him. He could feel the little body in his arms arch and squirm.

"Doc," he whispered hoarsely, "for God's sake, hurry. I think she's waking up."

Terry peered down at him from the ledge. Her eyes were way too bright to give her solemn expression any credibility at all. Damn her, she was enjoying this. "Don't look so terrified, Jack," she said serenely. "You've been wanting to hold her all afternoon."

Had he? No, he couldn't have. Okay, he'd asked if he could carry the kid a couple of times, but he couldn't for the life of him figure out why. He must have been out of his mind. He wasn't ready for this. He couldn't handle it.

The baby was making faces, an incredible array of them. Wolf stared down at her in unwilling fascination. He seemed to be having trouble breathing; his heart was taking up most of the room in his chest, beating like a jackhammer.

He couldn't stand it any longer. "Here," he growled, "you take her. I don't know what to do with her." He held the bundle at arm's length, as he might have a ticking bomb.

"Oh, for heaven's sake," Terry scolded, switching to some kind of sickening sweet baby talk as he handed the baby up to her. "Big Bad Wolf is afraid of a sweet little girl like you? Come here, angel...."

Muttering savagely under his breath, Wolf turned his back on her and lit another cigarette with unsteady hands. Her amused voice floated down to him.

"My goodness, Jack. And you say *I'm* aloof?"

Wolf hauled smoke into his lungs and stared furiously into the darkness. He hadn't meant to respond at all, but he couldn't resist saying, "Arrogant. I said arrogant."

"Oh really? I don't suppose you'd care to tell me what the difference is?"

Damn it, he'd lost control of the game again; it seemed to be like a tennis match, one minute in his court, the next minute in hers.

He turned and looked up at her. It wasn't quite dark yet, so he could see her clearly, sitting cross-legged in the sheltered alcove like the Queen of Sheba on her throne. He gave a bark of laughter. "You want to know what the difference is? I'll tell you—look here, this is a perfect example. You don't distance yourself from people, Doc—you just put yourself a little bit above them. And then you sit there making judgments and pinning labels on people. Hell, that's what you are—you're judgmental."

"I am not!" She didn't sound amused anymore. His game again. "I don't do that. I never label people—"

"The *hell* you don't. You've had me boxed and labeled since day one." Wolf threw out his arms, baring his chest and the imaginary letters written there. "CAUTION!" he intoned. "UNKNOWN SUBSTANCE—POSSIBLY DANGEROUS—KEEP AT ARM'S LENGTH."

Terry snorted. "That's ridiculous."

"Is it? Haven't you been judging me ever since? Hell, judge *and* jury! I get an urge to kiss you in the twilight, and I'm a jerk makin' a pass. You see me doing business with some locals, and right away assume I'm tradin' in drugs. I go after a couple of killers, and already you've got me all pegged as a mercenary, *right*, Doc?"

"Do you blame me, Jack? How could I not make judgments? I was there, remember? You used a team of doctors—you used *me*—to get down here to Baja just so you could *kill* someone! Can you deny that? You used a *child*, damn it. You used Julio—in a sense you even used this baby. If that's not the most cold-blooded, ruthless—"

"*Guilty*," Jack snarled, hurling his cigarette to the ground. "Guilty as charged."

He came up over the rocks with the fluid power of a springing predator, reprising the creature of Terry's troubled dreams so startlingly that she couldn't hold back a gasp. Cold, she'd called him, and ruthless, too. Like the timber wolf.

For a moment he crouched there in front of the shelter, one hand braced on the rocky overhang, his face dark and lean, teeth bared in a savage smile. Then he laughed, a low sound without a trace of humor.

"Yeah, Doc, that's me—guilty as sin. So where does that leave you, huh? How does it make you feel, knowing you're about to spend the night alone with a cold-blooded killer? Boy, it really looks like you're stuck between a rock and a hard place, doesn't it?"

"Shut up, Jack," Terry muttered, repressing a shiver.

He shook his head and tsk'd softly. "Hell of a way to talk to a killer, Doc."

"Look—" She took a deep breath. "I don't know how I feel. You told me you had a reason for wanting to find those two men, you said they owed you something. But you meant to kill them all along, didn't you? You would have, if I hadn't been in the way. So if you're not a killer yet, it's only by accident. And you still mean to kill them when you catch up with them, don't you?"

"That's right." The cold, flat way he said it sent another shiver up her spine.

She realized that she was rocking the cradled baby in her arms, rocking her body slowly back and forth, and that it

made her feel calmer, somehow. Stronger. "I'm trying not
to judge," she said tightly. "But it's not fair of you to ac-
cuse me as if I was in the wrong for doing so. I'm not the one
who's doing something wrong, here, Jack. How can you
ridicule me for being afraid of you? I *should* be afraid.
Anyone in their right mind would be afraid!"

"Yeah, you're probably right about that," Jack said as
he settled himself beside her with a soft grunt. "So tell me,
Doc—how come you're not?"

She held the baby closer and couldn't answer, cursing the
man in silent fury, angry with him for hitting so unerringly
on the source of her confusion. Why *wasn't* she afraid? Why
was she still so attracted to a man she thought of as a predator, a man who, if not cold-blooded, was certainly ruthless and probably amoral besides? So attracted that just
having him near her in the dark like this made her feel hot
and weak, and full of shivers.

"Hey, Doc, are you cold?"

"Why?" she snapped, her vulnerability making her hostile.

"Come on, I can feel you shivering clear over here."

"I guess I am, a little," she lied. "Can't we build a fire?"

"Don't want to risk it, not unless it gets a whole lot colder
than it is right now." She felt him shift, moving closer; his
hand brushed almost furtively past her arm, touched the
baby's blankets and then withdrew. He gave a little cough
and said gruffly, "How is she? Do you think she'll be warm
enough?"

"I think so." Her voice jerked with her shivers. "If I keep
her next to me, inside my poncho. My body heat should
keep her warm."

"Yeah, we might just have to do that, too, you and I."
His chuckle whispered through the darkness and rippled
across her nerves like a breeze over new grass. "Now that's
a delicious irony, isn't it, Doc? It puts you in a hell of a position, doesn't it? Whether to stay over there and freeze to

death, or come and get warm in the arms of a cold-blooded—''

"Stop it, Jack." Her voice was sharp and fragile; her neck and jaw muscles ached with tension.

There was a curiously electric little pause, as if both were listening intently to the other's silence. Then Jack said softly, "Hey…Doc."

There were rustlings, scufflings, and his warmth closed in around her. His hands tugged on her poncho, lifted and re-settled it so that the baby was inside it, next to her body. His arms crisscrossed her waist.

He gave her a shake and murmured deep in his throat, "You're stiff as a post. Come on—relax. Lean back. What are you afraid I'm going to do—try something right here, right now, with a couple of killers roaming around out there lookin' for us? Hey—I may be frustrated, but I ain't crazy!"

Terry gave a surprised gasp of laughter.

Jack purred, "Yeah, that's better," and shifted his legs to make room for her.

She settled back into the warm cradle of his body with a nervous chuckle and then a sigh that was both an accep-tance and a surrender, of sorts. She knew that what she was doing was foolish and dangerous; that was the acceptance. The fact that she was doing it anyway was the surrender. She was no naive child. She knew that in spite of Jack's reas-surances, what she was doing was setting in motion a series of inevitable events that would eventually lead to an inevi-table conclusion—like knocking over a domino.

Or maybe…maybe, she thought, this was only one in a series of inevitable events that had already been set in mo-tion a long time ago—three days ago, to be exact—in an airplane hangar in Van Nuys. Just another domino.

His body was as hard as she remembered. Even through the wool poncho she could feel its sinewy, unyielding strength. For an instant, before she could shut it out, her mind gave her a full sensory impression of what it would be like to have that body pressing down on hers. She saw it so clearly, her milk-white skin stark against his dusky tan. Her small, almost virginal nipples grazing his hair-roughened masculine chest, hardening to pink buds with the shock of that first exquisite contact. She heard her own gasp of pleasure-pain, and then a sigh of pure joy as his weight came slowly, slowly down, first nesting, then gently pillowing, and finally crushing her breasts beneath unyielding muscle. She felt every sensation of that sweet erotic dance, her belly's feathery trembling as it met the mysterious intimacy of his hair, the delicious warmth, the all-over kiss of two bodies meeting for the very first time.

Her stomach writhed and twisted with such violence that she felt almost seasick. She put her head back against Jack's shoulder, closed her eyes and groaned softly.

"Hey, what's the matter?" She could feel his warm breath on her temple, the rasp of his beard against her ear.

"Nothing," she murmured, her words slurred, drunken. "Just...can't believe this is happening. Can't believe I'm here, like this...with you."

She felt rather than heard his chuckle. "Yeah, I know what you mean." His arms suddenly tightened, pulling her even more securely into their encircling warmth.

Terry sat very still, almost afraid to move, listening to Jack's breathing, the baby's soft snores, the unsynchronized rhythms of their heartbeats. She could hear the faint rush of wind, the far-off yipping bark of a coyote.

"Are you hungry?" she asked suddenly, turning her head to look up at him in the darkness. "There are some granola bars, and some more of those burrito things Señor Lopez fixed us."

She felt him shake his head. "If I eat I'm afraid I'll get sleepy. You go ahead and eat if you want to. I think I'll wait till morning."

Terry thought about it. She *was* hungry, but couldn't bring herself to move from that warm, safe nest in Jack's arms. "I'm not all that hungry yet," she lied. "Next time the baby needs to be fed . . . I'll eat something then."

"It's gonna be a long night," Jack said. His voice was gruff and soft. "Why don't you get some sleep?"

"What about you?" Terry whispered. "Are you going to sleep, too?"

Another head shake. "No, I don't think so. Think I'd better keep my eyes open. Just in case."

A delicious warmth crept through her. She hadn't thought it possible that she would ever find the prospect of being cared for and protected so enjoyable. Even . . . erotic.

She cleard her throat and protested, "No . . . I wouldn't feel right. I can't just go off to sleep and leave you to keep watch all alone."

Jack's chuckle brushed her temple. "Don't worry about it—hell, I'm used to it. I used to drive a truck, used to pull those long, cross-country hauls, you know?"

Terry murmured sleepily, "Oh yeah? Well, I've had some pretty long hauls myself, back when I was an intern. God, it was awful. . . ." She stirred restlessly, then tilted her head to ask, "How did you stay awake?"

Jack snorted. "Anyway I could. Drank a lot of coffee . . ."

"Yeah, we did, too. And on quiet nights we played cards in the doctor's lounge. Gin rummy, poker . . . we made up games, too. I remember we had this silly version of poker where everybody had to put one card on his forehead—you couldn't see your own card, but everybody else could."

Jack drawled, "We used to call that Indian poker. Don't ask me why." He shifted as if he'd suddenly grown uncomfortable, and for some reason Terry's heartbeat accelerated.

"Too bad we can't play cards now," she said, unable to keep a certain telltale breathiness out of her voice. Please God, she thought, don't let me start to tremble. I don't want him to know.

"Yep," Jack drawled, "you can't play cards in the dark." Terry gave a husky, shivering laugh. He gave her a little squeeze and said, "What's so funny?"

"I was just remembering something you said that first night, in Dos Caminos, when you were all playing cards. You made a remark about playing strip poker in the dark. I don't know, for some reason it stayed with me."

"Yeah?" His tone was amused and knowing, but for some reason that didn't annoy her.

She pushed on, making rapid, almost desperate conversation. "Yeah, it's funny, because I only thought about the strip part of it—the pointlessness, you know? It never even occurred to me that you can't play any kind of poker in the dark."

"No..." Jack said slowly, "but there are other kinds of games you can play." Terry could hear a new note of alertness in his voice, feel a new kind of tension in his body. She waited, and after a long pause he said unexpectedly, "How 'bout matching?"

"Matching?" She laughed nervously, feeling confused. "You mean where we each put down a card? But you'd have to see for that, too."

"No, no—not with cards, you use fingers—like this, see?" He took one of her hands in his warm grasp, leaving the other arm to cradle the soundly sleeping baby, an insignificant weight against her breasts. "Hand to hand, so you can't cheat. Let's say I bet that I'll match you, odds or evens. We count one, two, three, if you put up two fingers and I put up three—or one or five—I lose. If I put up two or four, I win."

"Okay," Terry said, breathless again with the same indefinable excitement she felt in him. "Win what? What are the stakes?"

"Well, you were so fascinated by the idea of playing strip poker in the dark..."

"Come on, Jack—"

"Relax, Doc." He chuckled and his arms tightened, holding her still. She was suddenly conscious of his hands, which until now had been an indistinguishable part of the circle of warmth that surrounded her. She felt them open, felt the heat from his palms soaking through her shirt. "Appealing as that idea might be under different circumstances, what I was thinking was, that there's more than one way to strip."

Terry's breath caught as she felt his fingers splay across her ribs in a questing sort of way. "What do you mean?"

"Well . . . there are things you want to know about me, right? And there sure as hell are things I'd like to know about you. And neither one of us is real anxious to talk. So how about this? The winner gets to ask one question, the loser has to answer it—the truth, no cheating."

His lips were close to her ear, almost touching it. She held herself very still, listening, listening not just to his words but to the hum of tension inside herself. "I don't know," she ventured finally, "the stakes might be too high for me."

Oh, but the idea was as irresistible as it was terrifying. To ask Jack questions and get straightforward answers. . . .

His lips touched words to the outer edge of her ear. "How about it, Doc? Are you game?"

She couldn't hold back a shiver. "Okay," she whispered, "you're on."

Chapter 9

"Right," Wolf said, "you know the rules, and no cheating. I'll feel it if you do." A little thrill of elation rippled through him. Briefly, he wondered what had become of Wolf the gambler, Wolf the man with nerves of steel and ice water running through his veins.

But then, he'd never gambled for stakes like these. Not even with Juan Navarro, the night he'd won his chance for revenge. The risks were terrifying. If he lost, he'd be losing his privacy, pieces of himself, and that was bad enough. But if he won . . . God help him, if he won, the risks were even greater.

"I never cheat," she informed him in a light, airless voice, squirming a little with anticipation.

"All right then, you call it." Loose wisps of her hair tickled his nose and lips; he used his chin to push them out of his way, resisting an urge to nuzzle.

"Match. One . . . two . . ." He put down three fingers and she put down two. She gave a small yelp of vexation.

"That's right, Doc, you lose," he drawled smugly. "My question. Tell you what—I'll make it easy for you. Something simple to start with. You're not married, are you?"

She gave a surprised, and somewhat relieved, laugh, as if she'd been expecting a whole lot worse. "I'd think you'd have figured that out on your own. I don't wear rings, do I?"

"Doesn't mean anything," Jack grunted. "Ever been?"

"That's two questions." But she relented and said lightly, "Okay, call it a freebie. Comes under the category of vital statistics. Yeah, I was—for almost eight years. Divorced, no children. Now you—it's only fair."

"Never married, no kids."

"But you wear rings."

There was a long pause. Then Wolf said flatly, "I've answered your question." He gave her a nudge. "Go on—it's your turn again."

"Oh. Mine... okay. Match." He could feel the tension building inside her, as it was in him. He could feel the nerve-tremors vibrating through her body.

"One... two..."

It was a toss-up whether she'd repeat her evens or not. Guessing she would, he put down his three fingers again.

"Damn," she said softly.

"Don't be so scared, Doc," Wolf said, chuckling to hide his own tension. "I'll be gentle with you. I just want to know one thing. How come you thought it was funny, my saying you were a 'good girl'? If there was ever a classic case of goody-two-shoes—"

She cut him off with a snort. "Goody-two-shoes? You want to know the truth?"

"That's the idea, yeah."

"I was a hellion, Jack. A classic juvenile delinquent."

"I don't believe it."

"It's the truth." He felt her squirm, as if the memories made her uncomfortable, and when she spoke again her

voice seemed faraway. "I think the only reason I wound up
in college instead of prison was because I met Robert."

"Robert? That the man you married?"

He'd thought maybe he could slip that one in, but she
wasn't going to let him get away with it twice. "No more
freebies, Jack. Your turn."

It was easy to outguess her, almost too easy. He wondered again how he could know her so well without knowing her at all. Figuring her stubbornness would make her go
with the evens again, he matched her with a closed fist.

"Shh," he said, cutting off her soft howl of protest, "*now*
tell me about Robert."

"It's too long a story." She sounded grumpy; the lady
really did hate to lose. "I wouldn't know where to start."

"Come on, Doc. You know the rules of the game. He was
your husband, right?"

"Yes."

"And you loved him?"

"Yes, I did. Very much."

He felt her chin come up a notch. So, he thought, she's
defensive about that—I wonder why? "What happened?"

Her head moved restively against his shoulder. He felt her
shift the sleeping baby, cuddling her closer. "You're cheating, Jack! That's too many questions. And it's my turn.
Match."

The odds caught up with him on the next round—either
that or he just underestimated that stubbornness of hers.
She stuck with her evens and matched him.

"*Now.*" He could tell by the note of grim triumph in her
voice that she was going to make him pay in spades for his
hot streak. He wondered whether she'd ask about the rings
or the gun. Whichever it was, he knew she was thinking
about just how to put it so he'd have to give her the whole
answer, not another evasion. Smart lady. His heart began to
pound with the suspense.

"Okay," she said finally, taking a deep breath, "here's my question. What did those two men do that makes you want to kill them? That's what I want to know, Jack."

Terry could feel the recoil in him, the sudden stillness. "Sorry, Doc," he said in the cold flat voice she dreaded. "Any question but that one."

"But you said—"

His hand moved on her ribs, gently, caressingly, a direct and unnerving contrast to the harshness in his voice. "Maybe I'll tell you," he rasped, holding her now as if it was he who needed warming. "But some other time, some other place. You don't want me to answer that question now, Doc. Trust me. Not tonight."

Trust me. She tried to swallow, but a new tightness in her throat wouldn't let her. She was so close to the pain. She'd never been so close to a grown man's pain—not this kind. She could feel it pulsing and writhing like a living thing, just beyond the paper-thin shell of his defenses. And it terrified her. She'd ventured so far beyond her own barricades—farther than she ever had before in her life—but now she gave in to the fear and went scuttling for cover.

She cleared her throat and forced a lightness into her voice. "All right, then, if you're going to be that way about it, I guess I'll have to think of another question. Okay. I know. Just tell me what you're thinking about...right now."

"Right now?" His laugh surprised her after those brief and frightening glimpses of darkness. It was a new one, one she'd never heard before, warm and sensual, rife with erotic suggestion, wicked as sex on a sultry afternoon. "Right now, Doc, if you want to know the truth, all I can think about is making love to you."

She felt herself, and him, grow still. Then something strange happened. There was an explosion of liquid heat inside her; parts of her seemed to swell and develop pulse-beats of their own. The focus of her attention narrowed, became a beam of concentration as intense and concentrated as a laser. From somewhere outside it she heard a voice—her own, but husky and unfamiliar. "But you told me—"

His voice was a rusty purr, just above her ear. "I said I wasn't going to *do* anything. Never said I wouldn't think about it."

He paused to let her think about it, too, and while he did, his hand went roving underneath the poncho, down her side and across her waist below the nestled baby to the gentle hollow of her stomach. It sought and found a place there, inside the waistband of her slacks, flattened palm and splaying fingers spreading a pool of melting warmth, spreading it downward to where the swollen, throbbing places waited.

"Jack—" Her voice was faint and a little frightened.

"Come on, Doc..." He chuckled softly. "Don't tell me you haven't thought about it. You've been thinking about it all day, just like I have, ever since I kissed you."

His hand was motionless, now, riding the swell of her belly, the heat from it soaking through the fabric of her underpants. Beneath it her skin quivered and grew moist.

"Yeah...and it's been driving you crazy, hasn't it? Because you've been wondering how in the hell you could."

How could she? His touch—the intimacy, the gentleness of it—was a torment to her, but his words were worse. This was *Jack*. Jack, whom she detested, who had *used* her, and worse, had stooped so low as to use a child. A man who, even now, was bent on killing. How could she?

She couldn't bear it, his touching her with such intimacy. Her skin shivered in anticipation; her muscles clenched, her thighs drew together in unconscious protection of the tender, throbbing places. The thought of their violation by so hard and ruthless a man made her stomach writhe. She couldn't bear it, she wanted to push his hand away.

And yet, even less bearable was the thought that he might abandon her. The gentleness of his hand, its very stillness, instead of being a reassurance, became an intense frustration. She wanted to move beneath it with catlike abandon, encouraging new intimacies, begging wordlessly for the thing she both needed and dreaded so. Her breasts grew taut and tender, the featherweight of the sleeping baby became excruciating. Oh God, she thought. *How can I?*

She fought it, with all the strength and willpower she had, and trembled with the strain.

"You just can't figure it out, can you, Doc?" He almost crooned the words, teasing the sensitive shell of her ear with his breath. "Can't figure out how a bastard like me can make you feel like this. And you're too proud and stubborn to admit it. You're fighting it—I can feel it. I can feel everything, you know, holding you like this. You can't hide it from me, so you might as well give up."

"Is that so important to you—to make me give up?" Terry whispered, turning her face away from him in an effort to escape that insidious, shiver-inducing whisper.

It was a mistake. She felt the rasp of his beard as he nudged her hair out of his way. Too late, she realized what she'd offered him. She tried to take it back. *Too late.* With a soft chuckle he pressed her head against his shoulder and held it there with his chin, leaving the side of her neck naked and unprotected.

"Ah Doc, don't you know that's the last thing I want? Your pride's one of the things I like best about you. Hell, I even like your stubbornness. I always did like a challenge. . . ."

The shivers began even before his lips touched her. They began in ripples, became cascades, then torrents. She tried to keep them inside but they spiraled away into uncontrollable shudders when his mouth finally came down, hot and open, brushed slowly back and forth, and then closed on the sensitive cords of her neck. She gave a high, helpless cry that ended in a gasp as she felt the gentle pressure of teeth and a different, drawing pressure that seemed to pull at the deepest part of her, the throbbing places. She fought it. Fought the throbbing and the pressure and the terrible compulsion to move in primitive, unconscious rhythms. But she couldn't, she just *couldn't*. She tried so hard, knowing it would be her undoing, but her body was beyond listening to her will. Her spine contracted and her hips lifted.

Jack raised his head and said something, an inarticulate growl of masculine triumph. His hand moved lower, pressed harder. Pinned between his hand and his hard, unyielding body, she could only whimper, "Damn you, Jack...."

His hand moved lower still, fingertips burrowing through damp curls, palm curving, molding to her body's contours, long fingers lying warm and gentle between her thighs.

"Do you want me to stop?" he asked, his words a gruff resonance below her ear. "I will if you want me to."

Stop? She was breathing in gasps, her breasts ached, her arms were nerveless—only *his* left arm supported the sleeping baby now. And her pulse—dear God, it was throbbing like a drum against his hand. She knew he could *feel* it.

"Damn you, *no*," she groaned, furious with him, furious with herself. "You know I don't... want you to stop. Why are you asking? You said you could feel it."

He chuckled. "I don't know, I guess I wanted to see if you'd lie."

His beard was rough on her skin. Not a sandpaper roughness to burn and abrade, but something softer, a caressing, stimulating, tantalizing roughness.

"Damm you, Jack," she whispered, even as her body was squirming against the confining warmth of his hand. "I'll never forgive you for this."

"Just tell me what you want me to do." His voice was hoarse, urgent. "Say the word and I'll stop."

"Just tell me one thing—" Her breath caught and emerged in a whimper. "*Why?* Why are you doing this?"

"Why?" She gasped once when his arm tightened, and again when she felt the rock-hardness of him against her back. She felt his body shake with wry, painful laughter. "That answer your question? I told you if I wanted you to know how I felt, you'd know."

"But," she whispered, "you don't even like me."

He laughed again, this time a deep, rich laugh, sultry with amusement. "You don't like me, either, and look where that's got you. Go figure, huh? But like I said, Doc, it's got nothing to do with liking. The truth is..." One finger slipped between her swollen folds, penetrated the tender, throbbing place and slowly, slowly withdrew. "The truth is, I've wanted to do this since the first time I kissed you. Although... I've gotta say, I never meant it to be quite like this."

She held back a sobbing breath until she couldn't hold it anymore, until it burst from her in an anguished wail. Her chest was heaving with overwhelming need and helpless fury. "That wasn't—don't tell me that! You were just on the make—I know you were. And the second time you were angry. You *hurt* me."

"You know, you're right," he said in a musing growl. His unoccupied hand came from under the poncho to capture her chin. "So let's do it right this time."

She hadn't thought it could get any worse... and then it did. She resisted him, but only a little, turning her head slowly, in obedience to his gentle urging, his softly whispered, "Come on Doc..."

His mouth hovered over hers, bathing her lips with his breath, his words. Her lips trembled, she swallowed painfully and whimpered a little. Once more he slid his finger between her soft folds, a delicate insinuation, in and out again, rubbing silkily over the sensitive place where pain and pleasure met in bright, exquisite agony.

With a desperate, hungry cry she reached for him, opening her mouth in full surrender and greedy anticipation, taking the full penetration of his tongue, all he could give her, begging wordlessly until he gave her more. He deepened the other penetration, too, slowly, slowly, until she felt as if he would touch the very center of her being.

I can't take this, she thought. *I can't.* It had been so long, so long. But had she ever felt like this? She couldn't remember. Oh God . . . Jack, please.

"Let it go," he rasped, crushing the words against her open mouth. "It's all right . . . it's all right."

But it wasn't all right. And she didn't let it go easily. She fought it to the last, struggling against the spiraling sensations and quickening rhythms, trying desperately to hang on to her reason and her sanity. Then he took her mouth again, sealed and claimed it, and she couldn't think at all. He owned her, controlled her, body and mind.

With a cry of anguish and fear she tumbled at last into the vortex, spun with it, right to the edge of oblivion, while her body clenched and shuddered and her pride shattered into a million tiny pieces.

Normal sensation returned bit by bit. She felt her own heartbeat, her own cooling sweat, Jack's heart beating a tattoo against her back, her body, still pulsing in small, residual spasms around his fingers, her ragged breathing and a growing ache inside her chest.

"Hey . . . Doc—" He withdrew his hand slowly and with exquisite care, pressing kisses of reassurance against her temple. *Incredibly gentle, understanding kisses.* "Come on, now it's all right." His voice sounded raw, as if it hurt his throat, but there was something else in it, too, something Terry couldn't define.

But she didn't care. She didn't *want* to define it. She didn't want to think about what might be going on inside him, or how he felt about what had just happened. She didn't want to think about what had happened inside her. She just knew she was never going to forgive him for it. Never.

"Ah, Terry—" Jack said on a ragged sigh.

Terry. Not Doc, or Doña Teresa, but . . . Terry.

"Let me go," she whispered brokenly, even though she wanted nothing more in the world than to crawl into warm, loving arms and be stroked and soothed and petted, to fall asleep listening to the rhythm of a strong man's heartbeat.

Impatient snuffling noises began to come from under the poncho. The baby's head was bobbing against Terry's chest, her tiny body squirming inside its blanket wrappings.

"She's waking up," Terry said woodenly, struggling to sit up. "I need to feed and change her."

"I can't believe she slept through that," Jack said dryly.

Terry didn't say anything at all. She moved away from him and reached for the pack with the formula and disposable diapers in it, her movements jerky and uncoordinated. Her body felt chilled and weak, and oddly disconnected, as if she were suffering from some kind of shock. Strange, Terry thought, we never covered this in medical school.

Behind her she could hear Jack muttering as he unfolded himself, heard the scrape of his boots on the rocks as he got to his feet. There was a rueful groan and then some mild swearing as he gingerly stretched himself, then went crunching to the edge of the shelter and eased himself down onto the ledge. She heard his footsteps fade into the other nighttime sounds.

What's the matter with me? Two desolate tears slipped between her lashes and ran down her cheeks as she sat listening to the baby's hungry, sucking sounds, the squeaky little gulps that must be music to any mother's ears.

What's happening to me? She wasn't a mother, and probably never would be, and the baby was drinking soy milk from a disposable bottle. But her breasts felt swollen and tight, and her nipples ached and chafed against the fabric that confined them. Her whole body, from the throbbing between her thighs to the tingling in her breasts, suddenly felt heated and overripe. She was burgeoning with sensations, positively bursting with life and energy, humming like a flower bed on a hot spring morning.

Who am I? she wondered, weeping angry, bewildered tears. What is this Earth Mother stuff all of a sudden? She was a pediatrician with a thriving practice and a condo in Woodland Hills, for God's sake! Her life was helping other people's children—lots of children. She didn't need children of her own in order to be fulfilled—or, for that matter, a man in her life. She didn't *want* them, either one of them. Children were messy and noisy, and having them was messy and painful and you couldn't even have them without a man around, and men, with the exception of Robert, were worse—messy and egotistical and just plain aggravating!

And loving either one was terrifying.

"I don't want this," she whispered to the baby, who was making the squeaky sounds that meant she was full to the gills and probably had a bubble in her stomach besides. She lifted the now-somnolent infant to her shoulder and began the firm, methodical patting that would bring the bubble up—and hopefully nothing else along with it. "I don't need a sweet little thing like you complicating my life." She kissed the top of the silky head, which had somehow found its way into the hollow of her neck. "You understand? I don't need this. What are you and that awful man doing to me?"

The baby's only response was an enormous burp. Terry laughed tearfully, rewrapped her blankets and settled her once more under the poncho, in the warm hollow just below her breasts. She curled her body protectively around that precious little bundle and tried to fill her ears with the soft infant snores so she wouldn't listen for the sound of Jack's footsteps.

Oh, damn you, Jack.

Wolf sat on a rock near the shelter's entrance, smoking and watching Terry sleep. She was lying on the ground, curled on her side, with her head pillowed on one arm; the other arm was under the poncho, wrapped around the baby.

The flickering light of a small fire he'd built with some branches of a dead scrub juniper danced across her face and struck coppery lights into her hair.

He'd found the juniper on his moonlight ramble. He'd had second thoughts about the fire, partly because it was late enough he figured the Cruz brothers were probably holed up for the night somewhere, and partly because the doc and the little one needed the warmth.

Funny, Wolf thought, she didn't look anything like a statue or a duchess when she was asleep like this, and not much like a doctor, either. She didn't look proud, or stubborn, or aloof. There was something almost childlike about her mouth, the softness of her skin, the way her pale lashes threw spiky shadows across her cheeks in the firelight. Something . . . vulnerable.

He hadn't meant it to go so far. He still wasn't sure how he'd let it happen, or why. He'd never intended to break that proud spirit of hers, but if he had, he was sorry for it now. He knew he'd hurt her. Oh, not physically—she'd wanted him, he was certain of that, and she'd asked him, begged him not to stop when he'd given her the chance to call it off. But that was feeble justification, and he knew it. In a strange way, he still felt as if he'd forced her. Because he knew very well that, while her body had surrendered to him, it had done so completely against her will. Her will had fought him every step of the way, and lost. And the lady did hate to lose! He wondered if she'd ever forgive him.

Doc . . . I'm sorry.

He took a drag on his cigarette, made a face and threw it into the fire. *Remorse.* He'd never felt it before, and didn't care for the taste of it. He'd always taken care to avoid entanglements that might lead to recriminations and hurt feelings, his or anyone else's. Now he knew why. It felt lousy, just plain *bad*.

He felt lonely, too, sitting there watching the doc sleep and remembering how it had felt to hold her, feel her body heat, feel her tremble and grow liquid in his hands, taste her skin, her mouth. And if he didn't squelch those thoughts in a hurry he was going to have to take another cold walk in the moonlight!

Lonely. That was something else he hadn't felt in a long, long time. He'd had his obsession to keep him company, and that had been enough; there hadn't been room for anything else. Now all of a sudden here he was, feeling things like fear and anger, remorse and loneliness, when he'd thought he was immune to those things. What was happening to him? It was a hell of a time for his emotions to start showing signs of resurrection. In fact, the timing couldn't have been worse. With the Cruz brothers loose and on the alert, he needed his focus sharp and his commitment strong. Emotions were a weakness, and in this case, possibly a fatal one. He just couldn't let himself feel anything, not right now. Most of all, he couldn't let himself care.

The smallest of sounds brought him instantly alert, but it was only the doc, stirring a little, trying to get comfortable on the hard ground. After a moment, Wolf got up and got his sports bag, took his cigarettes out of it—he already had the gun, safely tucked away in his waistband—and slipped it under her head. She mumbled something and snuggled down on it with one hand curled under her cheek.

He stayed there for a minute or two longer, balanced on the balls of his feet, fingers tangling in her hair, feeling the texture of it, the soft-crisp texture of curls. He couldn't resist touching her, smoothing a few coppery wisps back from her temple, fingering a tendril behind her ear. Up close like this, he could see the unmistakable evidence of tears.

Something twisted painfully inside him. He withdrew his hand, but stayed where he was for a long time, looking out across the bleak moonscape of the Baja sierras.

Ah, Doc... what in the hell have you done to me?

* * *

Terry woke to the baby's impatient snufflings, a prelude to more insistent, and noisier, demands. Before she even opened her eyes, she smelled the fire and simultaneously realized that she was warm.

Jack had built a fire. He'd built it for the baby and for her, in spite of his worry about killers lurking in the night. That realization collided violently with memories of the night and her vow never, ever to forgive him, producing a bewildering turbulence in her emotions: lightning-quick flashes of insight quickly overriden by rumblings of residual anger, new ideas and unfamiliar feelings like fitful gusts of wind, spurts of cooling rain and, over all, heavy black storm clouds of sultry awareness and indefinable tension.

Terry eased herself away from the baby and sat up, one hand raking back her hair, which had come loose from its fastenings sometime in the night. With her heart beating much too fast for an early dawn, she looked around for Jack.

He was sitting on a rock near the front of the shelter, smoking, as usual, one arm wrapped around a drawn-up knee. When he heard her stirring, he looked around with a wide-eyed, guilty look on his face, crushing out the cigarette with a furtive movement that made her smile deep down inside. It reminded her so much of herself, a rebellious twelve-year-old trying in vain to hide a stolen Camel from the junior high principal.

The notion was short-lived; it evaporated along with the fragile bud of tenderness it had evoked when he turned completely and croaked, "Good mornin'."

Oh Lord, she'd forgotten how rough and wild he looked—hair Indian-long, beard blacker than ever and eyes that terrible, burning blue. In the night it had been different—there'd been only his voice and hands. Now, try as she would to keep them out, the memories came tumbling in, graphic, sensual memories—the soft growl of his voice, the compelling gentleness of his hands. *Rough and gentle.* What was it about that particular contrast that was so devastating, anyway? How could it have such power, that it could take a strong and thoroughly capable woman and turn her into so much quivering jelly?

"'Morning," she mumbled, as her stomach performed another medical miracle. She fidgeted nervously, combing back her hair with her fingers and looking around for the plain but practical band she'd tied it with. Giving up on it, she frowned and cleared her throat. "Did you sleep?"

"Nah." Jack slid down off his rock, stopped to pick up something from the ground and crunched over to her. "Here—hold still."

Her breath caught; she bit down on her lower lip as he gathered her hair into his hands and deftly wrapped the band around it. That accomplished, he didn't move away from her right away but just for a moment let his hands rest on her shoulders—lightly, tentatively, like birds lighting in a swaying branch.

Then he straightened abruptly, paused to scowl at the baby, who was voicing her displeasure at being so long ignored, and snarled, "For God's sake, shut her up before she brings the Cruz brothers right down on top of us." He gave a distracted wave and muttered, "Feed her, or something . . ." as he stomped back to his rock.

The fact that she didn't snap right back at him confused Terry as much as anything that had happened recently. But then, she thought as she took a disposable diaper and a bottle of soy formula from her backpack, maybe it wasn't so remarkable after all. Her anger had always been of short duration, and she could feel it evaporating before her natural curiosity and compassion like dew in the sunshine.

What is it that drives him? She watched him covertly as she changed, fed and burped the hungry baby, gazing at him sideways through the curtain of her lashes. In spite of the intimacies of the night before he was still a mystery to her—more than ever, in fact. In spite of his rough and hard-edged manner and appearance, there was an innate gentleness in him—something in her knew it and had responded to it. And yet he had been driven to kill—not in the heat of the moment, but coldly and methodically, like a wolf, relentlessly tracking his quarry. *Like a wolf*.

She wanted to know. Terry acknowledged that fact with a little thrill that was more excitement than fear. It was true. She wanted to know all about Jack Wolf—where he'd come from, what kind of home and what kind of childhood he'd had—what had happened to cause him such pain and bring him to this—what was the significance of the rings he wore around his neck, a man's ring and a child's? What had happened to her barricades? Where was her professional detachment? More important, where was the deep-rooted fear of emotional involvement that Robert had accused her of, and that he claimed had destroyed their marriage? What was it about this *particular* man?

Curiosity, she told herself staunchly. What else could it possibly be? She'd always had a healthy dose of it, it had gotten her in trouble more than once. That's really all it was, just plain old curiosity. Inquiring minds want to know. . . .

By the time the baby had been filled up and properly deflated, Terry had convinced herself of that and was feeling much better about things. She was also hungry and thirsty, but that could wait until after she'd seen to a more urgent need. She placed the baby on her stomach in the middle of her blanket, wrapped it loosely over her and got to her feet, stifling a groan as circulation surged into cramped limbs.

"Where are you going?" Jack barked at her as she slipped over the rocks at the entrance to the shelter and landed with a thump on the ledge.

She dusted her hands and said pointedly, "I'm going for a *walk*. Is that all right with you?"

He gave a reluctant grunt, then sat up straight as realization struck him. "Hey—what about the kid? You're not leaving her here."

Terry almost laughed out loud at the look on his face. "Don't panic, Jack," she said blithely as she straightened her poncho and set off to find a private spot. Suddenly, and for reasons she couldn't begin to figure out, she was in a much better mood.

It was her favorite time of day, that cool, lavender time just before sunrise. The air was sharp and fresh and smelled of pine and juniper and new grass. An inch or so of rain, about half of Baja's annual winter quota, had fallen in early November, and the grass was making the most of it. A thin film of green was just visible on the slopes, and in the sheltered places around the bases of shrubs and trees there was already an inch or two of fragile new growth. In some of the more sheltered places, such as the crevices between rocks, she was surprised to see that there were even a few wildflowers.

She was surprised, too, to discover that she was facing east. Off in the distance a thin sliver of fire was just burning through the haze, flooding the sky with pink and mauve and fragile, eggshell blue. So the Pacific Ocean and Santa Luisa lay behind her, on the other side of the spine of volcanic rock that had sheltered them through the night. And somewhere over there, beyond the layers and layers of purple and blue and brown, the sun would be rising out of the sparkling, gilded waters of the Sea of Cortez.

As Terry approached the shelter she couldn't see Jack anywhere. She stopped dead-still, missing heartbeats, listening. And then she heard his voice, a low-pitched murmur of sound, and wonder flooded through her, warm as the newly risen sun on her back.

She came the rest of the way on tiptoe and eased herself onto the ledge, trying not to make any noise. Oh so carefully she climbed up the rocks and peered over them, into the shadowy protected place beneath the overhang.

What she saw there stopped her breath and turned her bones to mush.

Chapter 10

Jack was sitting cross-legged beside the dying fire, holding the baby in front of him the way a choirboy might hold a hymnal. And he had the strangest look on his face—as if he couldn't quite decide whether to be puzzled or awed.

"What are you doing, Jack?" Terry asked with a shaken, breathless laugh.

He jerked his head up, looking startled and a little guilty—the choirboy with a comic book in his hymnal. That look on such rugged features, and a certain duskiness creeping up under beard stubble and tan made for a contrast that was both poignant and irresistible.

"Doc! Uh..." He coughed and harrumphed, but it didn't seem to help much, so he lifted one shoulder and growled, "Well, she was starting to make some noise, so I figured I'd better...aw, hell." He coughed some more, threw her an intense blue glare, then motioned her over to him with a jerk of his head. "Hey, listen, Doc, you wanna come tell me what this is? I can't figure out what she's doing. I mean, I know what it *looks* like—"

Terry slid down off the rocks and went to look over his shoulder. "That's a smile, Jack." Her heart fluttered.

"Well, I thought that's what it looked like, but isn't she too young? I thought at this age it was just supposed to be nerve twitches, or gas or something."

"No..." Terry reached across his shoulder to tickle the baby's delicate chin. When the tiny, heart-shaped mouth popped open, a gust of laughter escaped her like a soap bubble on a breeze. "That is most definitely a smile. See how her eyes are crinkled up, and focused right on your face? She's smiling at you, Jack. What in the world did you do?"

The look he threw Terry was quizzical. "I don't know, I was just kind of talkin' to her, I guess. Well, hell," he said, becoming brusque, "she *was* wide-awake. Shouldn't she be asleep, or something?"

"Oh, all babies have wakeful periods," Terry murmured absently. She couldn't seem to tear her eyes away from that round little face, nestled in the cradle of those hard, rough hands. "She's just feeling good for a change... aren't you, angel? Yeah...it's probably the first time in your life you've had a full tummy...."

Then, for a time, there was only silence, while they both looked and looked and looked some more. It was a process Terry had seen repeated again and again—the awestruck silence, the enraptured, searching gaze. A process unchanged since the dawn of time, when the first human parents beheld their firstborn child. The gentle ritual of marking, accepting, validating and welcoming another newcomer to the world.

Something settled in the cooling ashes—the smallest of sounds, but Wolf jumped as if it had been a gunshot. As it might have been, he thought grimly, and they'd have been dead ducks right now, all three of them, for all the attention he'd been paying. A cold, bleak feeling settled over his heart, a feeling he recognized as *fear*.

I'm in trouble, he thought. Serious trouble.

It wasn't just that he'd been so busy playing with a baby—a *baby,* for God's sake!—that he'd let his guard down so far even the doc had managed to sneak up on him. The worst of it was that he could feel things changing inside him, feel his resolve slipping, his priorities changing. Getting Doc and the kid back to civilization safe and sound—that was his number one priority now. He'd accepted that, even though he didn't like the crimp it was putting in his own plans. But now, for the first time, he was beginning to get this idea, just a glimmer every now and then, that maybe he ought to give it up... let the whole thing go. Let the DEA and the drug lords take care of the Cruz brothers.

No. No way. Coldly and deliberately he called up his nightmare, tuned it in and brought it to sharp, hideous focus, let it wash over him, the sights, the sounds and the smell.

He heard a sound, a soft cry, and realized that the doc had called out to him. Called his name. She was kneeling beside him, looking at him, those telltale eyes of hers shining with compassion and concern. He wondered what in the world she'd seen in his face, and how he could have forgotten to shield it from her.

"I'll take her now, if you want.... Jack?" The doc's voice seemed to come from the end of a long tunnel.

He frowned at her and said, "What?" Then looked down at the baby in his hands and muttered, "Oh—yeah. Time to get this show on the road." He thrust the kid in Terry's direction and lurched to his feet.

"Have you eaten?" She asked it calmly, quietly, but she was shaken up, he could hear it in her voice, no matter how much she tried to hide it.

He was shaken up. He shouldn't have let her see so much. God help him, he hadn't meant to. If he ever lost the ability to keep his thoughts and feelings out of his face, he was in big trouble.

Jack, he thought grimly, you are in big trouble.

"Not hungry," he muttered, sticking a cigarette between his stiff, cold lips. He couldn't have eaten right then if his life had depended on it. "I'm not big on breakfast—never have been. I'll catch something later. You go ahead." He waved a hand vaguely in the direction of the packs. "Why don't you . . . do whatever you need to do here to get things packed up and ready to go. I'm gonna go take a look around, check things out. Okay? Back in a few minutes."

She cleared her throat and murmured something he didn't hear. He could feel her eyes on him as he climbed over the rocks and let himself down onto the ledge, and he could still feel them when he'd put pine trees, juniper clumps and solid lava rock between himself and her. He could see her eyes, too, soft, slate-blue, creased a little bit with worry. And no matter how hard he tried, he couldn't seem to shake them.

He made a sweep around the shelter, three hundred and sixty degrees, but didn't find any sign of the Cruz brothers. He hadn't expected to—just figured it was better to be on the safe side.

Wolf was pretty sure his first guess was right, they'd make straight for the coast and try to pick up transportation south. The only thing he didn't know was whether they'd taken advantage of their initial head start, or waited around until dark to pick up supplies in El Refugio. Neither scenario made him happy. On the one hand, there was the possibility of ambush. On the other, figuring two unencumbered men could move a lot faster than a woman carrying a baby, there was the very real likelihood of being overtaken. Both were the reasons why he'd refused Señor Lopez's offers of various modes of wheeled transportation. Wheels required roads, and there was only one that led back to Santa Luisa. On the road, even in a car, he and the doc would be sitting ducks.

No, he was convinced he'd done the right thing. Eighteen miles or so of Baja desert wasn't a cakewalk, but the doc was strong and they had plenty of water. They'd stay off the road but keep close enough to it to keep from getting lost, which was easy to do in the desert, and with any luck, they'd be in Santa Luisa by sundown.

She was packed up and ready when he got back to the shelter, sitting on the ledge, waiting for him. When she saw him coming her eyes lit up, just as if someone had flipped a switch. He wondered what it meant, and whether she was even aware of it or not. He thought probably not; she looked too damn happy for a woman who was starting to have warm feelings for a cold-blooded killer.

"Doc," he said, "you look like an Indian."

She'd been busy in his absence. Since the sun was going to warm things up pretty quickly and she wasn't going to need the poncho, she'd used safety pins and bandages from her medical supplies to make it into a baby carrier, a kind of a sling that held the kid snug against her chest and left her arms free. He could see that little head with its shock of straight black hair tucked in right below the doc's throat.

"Yeah, right," she said dryly, holding out his pack and his sports bag. "A redheaded, freckle-faced Indian."

He took the packs from her, hooked his arm through both sets of straps. Something made him pause and draw his thumb lightly across the bridge of her nose. "Don't see any freckles," he murmured over the soft hiss of her indrawn breath.

Her hand fluttered nervously to the brim of her hat. Her voice was an airless ripple. "Oh well . . . you will by tonight, I'm sure."

"You got something against freckles?"

She laughed and moved away from him, shrugging into her backpack. "Not freckles per se—just the sun damage they represent. That's the doctor talking, of course—I planned to be a dermatologist, at one point. That was when I thought it might make me feel better about having to run around in a 30 SPF sunscreen while all my friends were frying their bodies in coconut oil. It's not easy growing up in Southern California without a tan."

"You seem to have adjusted," Wolf remarked, falling in with her long-legged, buoyant stride while he stole sideways glances at her. He hadn't thought much about it before, but now he looked at her fine, flower-petal skin, the healthy pink in her cheeks, and wondered what was so damn special about a tan.

And then he remembered that Frank's wife, Barbara, had had a great one, and blond hair, too—a classic California girl...from Houston, Texas.

She threw him a look, shading her eyes with her hand and squinting a little against the sun. "Oh, there was a time when I wanted to be a tanned, sexy blonde—doesn't every woman?" She laughed serenely. "It helps when I think that all those people who told me I looked like something that had crawled out from under a rock will be wrinkled and old before their time. I expect to have my revenge in the end."

Wolf didn't reply. His mind was filled with a vision of a sunset sky, red curls tumbling down a slender back, small, firm breasts sculpted in white cotton, face uplifted in secret rapture. And he was thinking that women sure did have a damned peculiar idea about what was sexy.

It was somewhere around mid-morning when they came across the footprints.

"Do you think they belong to the men you're looking for?" Terry asked him as he dropped to one knee to examine the fresh depressions in the soft ground. There was a tight, frozen look to her jaws.

"I'm no tracker," Wolf grunted, squinting around him at the rolling hills, clumps of brush and cactus and boojum trees. "But who else is gonna be on foot out here, huh, Doc? You tell me."

The shiver that rippled down his spine wasn't all dread—there was something else in it, too. Something like exultation, excitement. Maybe, he thought, maybe it wasn't too late after all. He was still on their trail, he knew where they were headed. If he played his cards right, he might still be able to catch them. *God ... just give me one more shot.*

He stood up and dusted off his hands. "Look at it this way. At least now all we have to worry about is what's in front of us. Uh ... how's the little one? You doin' okay?"

"She's fine," Terry said with a smile. "Still sleeping. I think she likes this thing."

"Yeah," Wolf muttered under his breath, "I don't blame her."

"What?"

"Nothing," he grunted. "Just keep your eyes open."

But along about noon he lost the trail. They'd had to circle wide to go around a big patch of cholla cactus, and he figured he must have lost it while he was busy trying to avoid those infernal spines. It bothered him, a lot more than he wanted to admit, and not just because his quarry had given him the slip again. He just had a bad feeling about it.

The midday sun was hot—not the lethal, mind-numbing, body-sapping heat of summer, but the kind that burned between the shoulder blades and on the back of the neck and made Wolf wish he had a hat. He'd never laugh at the doc's hat again, that was for sure.

He kept sneaking glances at her to make sure she and the kid were doing okay, because he had a feeling she'd drop in her tracks before she'd say anything. She really was magnificent, he thought, looking at that haughty profile of hers in bold relief against a delft blue sky. But he wasn't thinking now of marble statues, and probably never would again. More along the lines of a pioneer woman slogging along the Santa Fe Trail in the dust of a covered wagon. Strong woman, the doc....

Without breaking stride she took off her floppy brimmed hat and wiped sweat from her forehead with her shirt-sleeve, squinting hard against the glare. Wolf knew she was missing her sunglasses—so was he, for that matter. The light was fierce, so intense it stripped the colors from the landscape and gave it a milky, undefined look, like an overexposed photograph. There was an odd tension in the air, too. Wolf didn't know what it was, but he could hear it—kind of a high-pitched hum, just barely within the range of human senses. Maybe there was a logical explanation for it, something to do with the heat and light, static electricity—hell, maybe even insects. Or maybe it was just him. Just his instincts, telling him something wasn't right.

"You okay?" he asked the doc. "Need to stop and rest a minute . . . feed the kid?"

She lifted the edge of the disposable diaper she'd put over the baby to keep the sun off of her. "She's still asleep," she said, "but yeah, it would probably be a good idea to stop, if we can find some shade. I'm getting kind of hungry, myself. Aren't you?"

Now that she mentioned it, he did have some rumblings in his belly. Much as he hated to take the time, he knew he'd better eat something, just to keep his strength and stamina up.

He shaded his eyes with his hand and scanned the eroded hills and rain-cut gullies dotted with brush and cholla and the twisted spires the natives called "candles"—the boojum trees. Nothing was moving; there was no sound except for the screaming of his own nerves.

"How about that arroyo over there?" Terry said, pointing. "There should be some shade down in the bottom of it."

Jack gave his backpack a hitch. "Okay, let's check it out." Then he shot out a hand and caught Terry's arm and pulled her back behind him. "Better let me go first," he mumbled. "Check for rattlers . . ."

That was fine with Terry, even though she knew it wasn't snakes he was worried about. She could feel the tension in him again, so thick you could almost reach out and touch

it, the same kind that had filled all the space in the pickup
truck on the drive to El Refugio. No, not quite the same.
Sitting beside him in the pickup, she'd felt completely cut off
from him, as if the tension had created its own force field,
isolating him inside it with only his pain for company. That
morning, she remembered, she'd felt as if he'd forgotten her
existence.

This was different. This time the tension included her, was
somehow even connected to her. She didn't know what it
meant, but it frightened her almost as much as the other.

"Stay here," Jack grunted as he dropped his backpack
and slipped over the edge of the ravine. Terry could see him
reach behind him and take the gun out of the waistband of
his Levi's.

"Jack, you're scaring me," she muttered uneasily, dropping into a crouch. She waited there, listening to her heartbeat, the baby's snores, the emptiness, feeling the tension.
Listening for Jack. The relief that flooded her when she finally heard the crunch of his boots made her knees weak.

"Looks okay—come on down," he rasped, tucking the
gun away and reaching up to help her. "Here—give me your
hand."

As she took it, for one moment she found herself looking down into his eyes, into that burning, terrifying blue.
The tension engulfed her. She felt smothered, panic-
stricken.

"Come on, Doc, don't be afraid. Just sit down there on
the edge and swing your legs over. I've got you."

Numbly, she did as he told her, grateful that Jack had
found his own explanation for her panic, hoping he'd never
know the real reason for it. But her mind was scurrying
around in futile flight, crying, Oh God, I'm falling for him!
I don't want to. I can't believe it. I can't.

"Easy does it. . . ." His hands were firm and warm on her
elbows. "It looks okay—no snakes or scorpions, not that I
could see, anyway. You stay here—feed the kid, take a

siesta, whatever you want. I'm gonna go take a look around, see if I can pick up that trail.''

"Okay," Terry said through locked jaws.

Jack's hands tightened on her elbows. "Hey," he said roughly, giving her a little shake and a searching look. "You gonna be okay?"

"Of course, I'm fine," she heard herself say, in a firm, slightly insulted tone. "You go on—do what you need to do." *But I don't want you to go!*

"You just stay low, keep quiet. Keep the kid quiet." He hesitated, then briefly touched the baby's head, which was beginning to bob around and emit snuffling noises. "I'll be right back."

"We'll be here," Terry said with elaborate unconcern. *Please don't leave me!*

For a moment it seemed as if he'd heard her innermost, unspoken thoughts. His hands shifted, his fingers moved restlessly on her arms. He looked into her eyes, a frown forming, deepening the longer he looked. Tension whined in her ears.

He cleared his throat, coughed and began, "Look, Doc—"

"Weren't you going to eat something?" Terry cut him off, falsely and desperately bossy, pulling away from him to dump the packs onto the ground. "Why don't you take some of these granola bars with you—and don't forget to drink plenty of water, or you'll dehydrate in this heat. Go on—get out of here. I could use the privacy."

"Oh," he said. "Right." He coughed again, rubbed a hand over the back of his neck in wholly uncharacteristic confusion, then dropped to one knee and zipped open one of the packs.

Terry stood straight and tall, much like a post, watching Jack take nutrition bars and a bottle of water out of the pack. She soothed the baby's growing impatience with mechanical pats and prerecorded croons and promises while he

stashed the bars in his pockets, took out his cigarettes and
his lighter. She even waved to him as he went walking off
down the arroyo.

After a moment she took a deep breath and turned with
jerky movements to spread Jack's poncho on the ground in
the meager strip of shade provided by the steep dirt walls of
the arroyo. "Well, little angel," she whispered, "I guess
we'd better see about you, huh?" She sat down, untied the
sling and eased the warm little body away from hers. Instant coolness defined the wet spot on her chest. "Oh, my
goodness—what a mess you've made. Sorry, sweetheart,
we're going to have to take care of this first. I know you
think you're going to starve to death, but you are going to
survive, trust me."

But Angelita was already expressing her extreme displeasure with that decision; having discovered the joy and
comfort of a full stomach, she wasn't about to put up with
anything less.

"My, that's quite a temper you've got," Terry remarked,
laughing uneasily as she dealt efficiently with tape tabs and
plastic bottle covers, remembering what Jack had said about
keeping quiet. She did her best, but the little rascal had built
up a pretty good head of steam and it was some time before
the frantic wails were finally replaced by gentler sounds,
gulps and snuffles and contented little groans.

"Now I know who Julio was imitating when he put on
that show for us in Santa Luisa," she whispered, chuckling
ruefully. "You are going to be a real handful someday, angel, you know that?"

After all that racket, the quiet seemed strangely electric.
Terry sat listening to it, rocking the baby with her body,
trying not to think about the heat, her own hunger, the
trickle of sweat between her breasts and the dryness of her
mouth and skin. She found herself counting the passage of
time with her own heartbeats.

There—at last—she'd heard a noise. The scrape of a shoe on gravel. She straightened, heart hammering, listening so hard her body ached with the tension. Yes—there it was again.

"Jack?" she called, weak with relief. "I'm over here." Then she pulled the baby closer and said his name once more, in a dry soundless whisper, almost like a prayer. "Jack..."

Wolf made a wide sweep around the arroyo without finding any sign of the Cruz brothers. All he'd done was disturb the midday siestas of one rattler—a small one—a couple of lizards and a roadruner, and eat two of those damned nutrition bars, and he was about ready to say to hell with it and get back on the road. He was going to be glad to get back to Santa Luisa, for more reasons than the two he'd left back in that ravine. For one, he was almost out of cigarettes. And he was beginning to daydream about cold beer and hot showers. Damn it, he was starting to itch.

He was on his way back to where he'd left Doc and the baby, smoking his next-to-last cigarette, when he stumbled over the footprints. He stopped dead in his tracks; all the warmth and strength ran right out of his body. He dropped to one knee and traced the impressions with his fingers, hoping and praying they might be his and the doc's, that he'd somehow got his directions twisted. But he knew the doc was wearing some kind of athletic shoe with treads on the soles, and these prints were smooth—both sets of them.

Besides, he knew his directions weren't twisted. And he knew exactly which way those tracks were headed. He sat there looking at them while the sun beat down on his back, hot as ever, hot as fire. And he felt *cold*. Cold clear through to his bones. Because those tracks pointed straight toward the ravine, right toward the place where he'd left the doc.

He wasn't sure what snapped him out of it—the cigarette dropping from his nerveless fingers and burning a hole in his

Levi's and the bejeezus out of his leg might have had something to do with it. In any case, once he'd got the fire out, his mind was clear again, and his body seemed likely to obey his comands.

The first one he gave it was to take his gun out of his waistband, check the chamber and take off the safety. So far so good—his hands were steady as a rock. The next thing he did was veer off those tracks at an angle, so he'd come up on the ravine and the place he'd left the doc from the other direction. With any luck, he thought, he might be able to get behind them.

He moved as fast as he dared, low to the ground, trying not to make a sound. Until he got close to the ravine. Then he dropped and crawled the rest of the way on his belly. He could feel the heat pressing down on him, feel the tension keening in his ears and creeping over his skin, as if he were standing too close to a high voltage power line. He could feel the hair rise along his arms and the back of his neck.

There. He'd heard voices, men's voices. A little to his left. Raising his head a fraction of an inch at a time, he looked over the edge, down into the ravine. His hand curled on the grip of the Smith & Wesson. He held his breath, measuring the distance, calculating his chances.

Damn. His hand went limp; he lowered his head and wiped cold sweat from his face with his forearm. He couldn't risk it—the distances weren't good enough. He was too far from them and they were too close to the doc. He might get one of them, but the other would get her for sure, and probably the little one, too. *He had to get closer.*

He made himself go slowly, covering the ground a few inches at a time, stopping to listen to the voices, the sound of his own breathing. He couldn't let himself rush it, didn't dare let himself think about Terry and what she must be going through down in that ravine. He was a machine now. Cold, efficient, lethal.

When he'd reached a spot he figured was right above the Cruz brothers and the doc he took another look. But it was still no good—they were too close together, and one of them was holding the doc by the arms. He knew they were ready for him, watching for him, just waiting.

He didn't look at Terry's face—he didn't dare. Instead, he shifted the gun to his left hand, picked up a rock and chucked it across the ravine. It hit the far bank with a little *thunk* and dislodged a few pebbles, which trickled down onto the sandy floor.

For an instant the Cruz brothers froze. Then the one holding Terry stuck a gun up under her jaw, while the other one took a few steps in the direction of the noise. By that time Wolf had the gun back in his right hand and was crouched on the edge of the ravine like a panther getting ready to spring.

He watched and waited, timed it to the exact second. The second the Cruz brother who'd gone to investigate decided it was probably just a lizard and started to relax and lower his gun hand. The second just before he turned around.

Chapter 11

When Wolf made that jump he had only one thought in his mind: go for the gun arm.

The way he had it figured, if he could get his hands on the one brother—alive—he had a chance of making the other one let go of the doc and the little one. It would be a stand-off—one life for two.

That was if everything went his way. That was if the one holding a gun to Terry's throat didn't lose his head and pull the trigger at the first sound. And if he cared more for his brother than killing for the sake of killing.

When he came down off that bank his mind was clear. He knew exactly what he had to do and how he was going to do it—but every nerve in his body was braced for the sound of that gunshot. The single shot that would end Terry's life. And even though he'd calculated those odds, even though he'd told himself a quick, painless death would be the kindest thing he could do for her if he failed, still every nerve, every fiber, every cell in his body was screaming in suspense and total rejection of the possiility. *God, if they kill her, too...*

His aim was right on the money. As he landed, he struck the gunman's forearm with the barrel of the Smith & Wesson and felt, with exultant satisfaction, the dull crunch of metal on bone, heard startled shouts and the sound of a gun skittering away across gravelly ground. An instant later he had the arm twisted up and back.

There were shouts, screams, terrifying flurries of violence.

"Drop it!"

"Hey, man—"

"Drop it, Cruz, or I'll blow his head off!"

"I'll kill her...."

"Jack—"

"I said drop it—*now!*"

It was the standoff he'd wanted, but so perilous, so fragile. The other brother had Terry pinned to him, the barrel of the gun shoved right up under her jaw. Wolf's chest heaved, his muscles creaked with strain, his breath whistled through clenched teeth. *At last.* He had his hands on the man who'd killed Frank. Had his arm across the throat of the man who'd raped and tortured Barbara before finally, mercifully cutting her throat. Had his gun pressed against the skull of the man who'd blown Carrie Elizabeth's head off. A blood-red fog obscured his vision; the stench of violence and death crawled in his throat, choking him. His muscles clenched. He'd waited so long for this....

"Jack—please...."

"I'll kill her, man, I'll blow her away, I swear it!"

Wolf shook his head, trying desperately to clear the miasma of nightmare. "Tell him to let her go," he snarled in his prisoner's ear, jamming the muzzle of his gun savagely against the man's neck. *"Tell him*—or you're dead, you hear me?"

There was a nod, a stifled hiccup of pain, a gasp. "Do it, Billy. Do what he says, man!"

Billy. So Wolf had the older brother, the one named Bernardo. The one who called the shots, apparently. The one who must have called the shots that night.

"Come on, Bernie, I can take him!"

"Are you *crazy?* Let her go!"

I can take them both, Wolf thought. When he lowers his gun, when he moves away from her....

"No, man, *you're* crazy!" Billy shouted. "Look at him—look at his face! He's gonna kill us both. I ain't lettin' go of her. No way, man!"

"Jack—no...*please*—"

It was barely a whisper, but he heard it even through the scream of tension, the thunder of his heartbeat, all the ragged sounds of fear and violence. The red mist thinned a little. He saw a face, pale and luminous, shining like a beacon. Doc's face.

"Jack."

He saw a pair of eyes, Doc's eyes, not blue now, but almost black with pain and terror, pleading, beseeching.

The red mist swirled and lifted. He smelled sweat and fear, onions and tobacco. He saw the little one's head bobbing against the doc's chest, that crazy tuft of black hair standing straight up, almost tickling the doc's chin. He saw the gun there, too, and the nervous fingers, opening and closing on the grip.

"All right—all right!" Wolf heard his own voice crack like a bullwhip across the arroyo. "Listen up! I want the woman and the baby. You let 'em go, I let your brother go. That's the deal. Now—put the gun down, Billy—slowly."

"No way, man! Soon as I do, you'll kill me." The fingers twitched restlessly, dangerously near the trigger.

"Okay! Okay—here's what we're gonna do." Wolf paused for a moment, breathing hard. Salt-sweat stung his eyes; he shook his head, blinking it away. "You start her walking toward me. I do the same with Bernie here. One step at a time...one wrong move and you're both dead, you got that? Come on, now—do it!''

"For crissake, Billy, do what he says!"

"Okay, okay, I'm doin' it!"

Come on, Doc. Slowly, slowly, Wolf eased up on his grip a little and took a step back. He felt cold, dead cold. Everything in him protested, but he concentrated on the doc's pale, frozen face, shoved the Smith & Wesson between Bernardo Cruz's shoulder blades and croaked, "Go on—*move.*"

A thousand miles away from him, he could see the doc take one step, then another, wobbling a little bit, looking terrified, like she was walking a tightrope across a canyon. *Come on, Doc.*

One step, and then another, Frank's killer was walking away from him. He'd had him in his hands, the animal who'd brutalized and murdered Barb and Carrie, sweet little Carrie. *And he was letting him walk away.* The agony was almost more than he could take—it was as if his body were being ripped apart.

One step... and another. He could see the doc looking at him like she was drowning and his hand was just out of reach.

Another step and Doc and Bernie would be opposite each other. That would be the moment of truth. If Bernie tried anything, or if Billy lost his head and did something stupid, or if he did.... For one moment he thought about it. Thought about hollering at Terry to hit the deck and then opening fire. It would be his last chance.

And then, just as she came up even with Bernie Cruz, Wolf saw Terry's hand move slightly, move to cover the baby's head in an instinctive gesture of maternal protectiveness, as if her hand alone could stop bullets. And maybe, he thought, in a way, they could. Because something about it—the sight of that slender white hand cradling that little

black head—blew the last remnants of the nightmare out of
Wolf's brain and left him really clearheaded, maybe for the
first time in months.

"Come on, Doc," he said gently, "you're almost home.
Keep on coming."

Bernie was about two steps from his brother; Doc was almost close enough to reach out and touch. One more step
and they'd be home, but not free. All hell was going to
break loose in another second, Wolf knew it. With his pe-
ripheral vision he was already measuring the distance to
cover.

One last step.

Wolf's hand shot out and closed on Terry's arm. "Get
down!" he yelled as he pulled her behind him and shoved
her roughly to the ground. He was already firing, but the
Cruz brothers had broken for cover, too. Billy even managed to get off a few wild shots himself as they ducked
around a bend in the ravine.

Wolf took off after them, mostly to make sure the bas-
tards weren't going to come back and maybe pin him down
in the ravine. He doubted it—the Cruz brothers were cow-
ards at heart. Frontal attacks against an armed man weren't
their style. So once he was certain they were gone, he put the
safety on the Smith & Wesson, stuck it in his waistband and
went back to where he'd left Doc and the baby.

She was still right where he'd thrown her—on her knees,
sitting back on her heels, holding the baby against her chest
with both arms and kind of rocking her back and forth with
her body. She'd lost her hat, and her hair was streaming
down both sides of her neck and sticking to her face in damp
curls.

Something inside Wolf turned over. He covered the rest
of the distance in a couple of strides, reached down to her
and put his hands under her elbows. She came up into his
arms in a blind, sobbing rush.

He didn't say anything, just held her oh, so carefully, with the baby between them, while she hid her face in the hollow of his neck and cried. It wasn't the way he wanted to hold her; his arms ached, his body ached, his heart and soul ached with the need to be closer to her. He was cold, drenched with sweat and shaking like a leaf, and so was she. What he really wanted to do was hold her body against him until they both warmed up and the shaking stopped. And maybe a lot longer than that.

But right now the little one was squirming and complaining between their bodies, waving her fists around and making awful faces to protest the confinement. After one particularly outraged squeal, Terry pulled back in the circle of Wolf's arms, half laughing, sniffling and wiping her eyes. He let his arms drop away from her.

"I can't believe they're gone." She was mopping at her face with her shirtsleeves, an exercise in futility since a new flood of tears was already beginning. "Oh, God. I can't believe ... any of this."

"Come on, Doc." Wolf didn't know how to handle her tears; he reached out and sort of brushed her cheek with his fingers, wondering when he'd ever felt at such a loss. "What's all this for? It's over—you're safe. Don't cry now, for God's sake."

"Don't you dare tell me not to cry!" she yelled, furious with him all of a sudden, and crying all the harder. "This is healthy. It's to relieve tension, you...you jackass! My God, all I seem to do around you is cry, have you noticed that? If I couldn't cry you'd give me ulcers, Jack."

The last word was punctuated with a doubled-up fist, right in the middle of his chest. It hit squarely in the part of him that ached the worst, but the funny thing was, it seemed to make it feel better.

"*Ulcers?*" he said, fighting an urge to laugh, knowing it would only make her madder. "Come on, Doc, you'll never have an ulcer—you don't keep anything inside!"

"And what's *that* supposed to mean, Dr. Wolf?"

"Just what I said." Feeling on more familiar ground with her now that she was furious with him, he touched her cheek again, this time stroking it with the backs of his fingers. When she looked at him with startled, tear-drowned eyes he laughed softly. "You can't keep your feelings out of your eyes, don't you know that? I can read you like a book, Doc."

"Like hell you can..." But her voice had grown faint, her eyes confused.

"Oh yes, I can." He brushed his fingers across her cheek, pushed damp curls away from her face, combed his fingers through her hair. And then he whispered, "Come here, Doc."

He heard the sharp intake of her breath. Her lips quivered; he tasted the cool saltiness of tears. Then suddenly she was laughing and crying and kissing him, and trying to talk to him, all at the same time. And he wasn't in much better shape, himself. He kept touching her face, trying to hold her still and wipe away moisture at the same time, kissing her in light, wondering sips, now on her mouth to cut off gusts of breathless words, then on her eyelids to stem the flood, mixing his whispers with her tears, his breath with her words.

"I can't believe—"

"Shh...it's all right."

"I thought—"

"I know..."

"They were going to kill—"

"Shh...no way, I wasn't gonna let 'em hurt you."

"They told me—I was so scared—"

"Shh...it's okay. It's okay. They're gone now."

"I didn't think—" Suddenly she pulled away from him, jerked her head back and stared at him with wide, wondering eyes. "They're *gone,*" she croaked, looking as mussed and fragile as a wildflower in the rain. "They're gone, you let them go."

"Yeah," Wolf drawled, "looks that way." A tremor rocketed through him; he felt cold again.

Terry shifted the baby to one arm and wiped her face with her shirtsleeve, this time in a businesslike way that let him know there wouldn't be any more tears, at least not for a while.

"Yeah, but—you had a chance to kill them. Why didn't you? I mean, I thought that's what you wanted. Isn't that what you're here for? Isn't that what this is all about?"

Wolf threw up his arms; he was shaking badly now—some kind of shock reaction, he supposed. The doc would probably have a name for it. "Yeah, right!" he shouted. "And get you and what's-her-name there killed for sure. Sure, that's what I want. Geez..." He turned his back on her, rubbing the back of his neck and swearing. He felt lightheaded, a little sick.

"So...you didn't kill them because of me—and Angelita?" Her voice sounded light, breathy. He heard her suck in a little bit more air. "Wow, that's twice now I've gotten in your way, isn't it, Jack?"

He whipped around, glaring, all set to yell at her some more, pour out his rage and frustration. But then a funny thing happened. When he opened his mouth, nothing came out; there was nothing there. The rage was gone. And he discovered that without it he felt empty, weak. And, for some reason, hungry. Tired. God, he was tired. He just wanted to crawl into a hole like a wounded animal and sleep and sleep.

So instead of yelling, he smiled, a bleak, half smile that hurt his face. "Yeah, well...don't worry about it, Doc. There's not going to be a third time."

She didn't say anything for the longest time, just stood there, looking at him with that quiet, blue gaze of hers. He decided there was something sort of *ageless* about her, the way she stood so straight and tall, holding the baby in her arms, her hair streaming down over her shoulders. She seemed invincible; Indian-proud, pioneer-strong.

Well, except for that fair, fragile skin of hers, which wasn't used to the noonday sun. It was already getting pink across the bridge of her nose and the tops of her cheeks.

It did something to him when he saw that. It hurt. He switched his gaze downward and found the baby's bright, black shoe-button eyes, a solemn, infant stare. And that hurt, too.

He could feel something building inside him like a tsunami, rushing in to take the place of the rage. He could feel it filling him up, filling him to bursting. It was pain. And a lot of other things, too. It was too big for him to handle. It was terrifying. He wanted the rage back. He didn't know if he could survive without it.

"Does that mean you've finished?" Terry asked finally. "Is it . . . all over?"

Wolf looked up at the sky, closed his eyes and drew a deep breath. "Yeah," he said on a long exhalation. "It's over."

He bent over and picked up Bernie Cruz's gun. "Get your hat, Doc. We've got a long way to go."

They made it to Santa Luisa just after sundown, the last seven or eight miles on the back of an ancient flatbed Ford loaded with oranges.

This must be how refugees feel, Terry thought blearily— pushed to the limits of endurance, numbed by a bombardment of catastrophes too vast to comprehend.

She did feel numb, but not nearly numb enough. Not so numb that she couldn't feel hunger, blisters or aching muscles, or recognize the symptoms of sunburn and dehydration. There was also a kind of numbness in her mind, but again it wasn't quite enough. It protected her from thinking about how close she'd come to a violent, wasted death, or grappling with the problem of the baby sleeping soundly in her arms. But it didn't keep her from thinking about Jack. Wondering about Jack. Worrying about Jack.

Since the standoff in the arroyo he'd been very quiet—unnaturally quiet, the way the world gets just before a storm. He'd told her it was over, and she thought perhaps he even believed it was. But whatever was going on inside Jack Wolf was far from over—she knew it. She didn't know how, but she did. She could feel it.

Oh, that terrible tension she'd sensed in him was gone now, but something else was happening. She wondered if perhaps the tension was all that had been holding him together. Whatever had been, it was coming unraveled now. He was falling apart before her eyes, and she didn't know what to do about it. She'd never been in a situation like this before. How ironic, that she was a doctor and didn't know how to help him. She'd never felt so helpless, or, in a way that had nothing to do with physical danger, so scared.

The driver of the truck, who happened to be Pepe's brother-in-law, dropped them off at the clinic and rattled off to deliver his load of oranges to the cantina.

"Too late to fly out of here tonight," Jack said, squinting critically at the dying light as he dropped his pack and sports bag onto the clinic's doorstep. "What do you want to do, stay here?"

"Sure," Terry said, taking a fortifying breath. "We usually do. There are folding cots, blankets. No running water, though, I'm afraid. Or room service." It was a feeble enough attempt at humor; she'd just wanted to do something—anything—to ease the strain in his face. He seemed so stiff, as if it were taking all his strength and concentration just to maintain a modicum of control.

"We can go and get something to eat at Pepe's. But first I have to go get the key from Mr. Ortiz next door, so we can put this stuff inside. And I guess I'll have to break the news to him about his truck getting shot."

"Ah hell, I can fix the truck," Jack muttered. "Either that or get him another one, which would probably be cheaper." He frowned suddenly, scratching his chest in an absentminded sort of way. "You don't suppose Mr. Ortiz would have any water, do you? Right now I'd trade a new Chevy 4X4 for a bath."

"They have a hand pump, but I imagine they'd let us have a couple of bucketsful. It's not a hot shower, but it's better than nothing." Terry looked at him and swallowed a gulp of laughter. "God, I hope so. I just realized, Jack—you look like a bum."

But she recognized a new softness in her voice when she said it. Though he was probably about as dirty and disreputable as any human being she'd ever seen, she really didn't see the beard and long hair and scruffy jeans when she looked at him now. As dirty as he was, she just wanted to put her arms around him and hold him, wanted to touch his face with her hands and smooth away the strain lines with her fingers.

"A bum, huh?" Jack said with a crooked little travesty of a smile. "Funny, that's just what my dad used to say."

Terry laughed shakily and said, "Hey, I must look just as bad."

"Doc." He stopped, frowned and took a flattened cigarette pack out of his shirt pocket. He carefully shook the last cigarette out of it, hesitated, then put it between his lips. After a moment he took it out again, stuck it in the pack and put it back in his pocket. "You couldn't look like a bum if you tried. In fact—" The frown deepened.

He snaked out an arm and plucked her hat off, brushed his knuckles down the side of her face and pushed a few loose strands of hair back from her temple. He never did finish what he'd started to say, just left it hanging and went on touching her like that, staring at her with a fierce and wondering look on his face.

"Got a little sunburned," he said finally, drawing his thumb across the bridge of her nose.

Unexpected tears rushed, stinging to the back of her eyes, tears of exhaustion, and too much emotion. But instead of crying, she began to laugh. "Are you kidding me? Everything that's happened, and all I have to show for it is a *sunburn?*"

Jack suddenly slipped his fingers into her hair and gave her head a tense little shake. *"Damn it, Doc, I'm sorry."* His voice was a harsh and guttural whisper. "I never meant to get you into this. Never meant to hurt you."

She shook her head, fighting the tears in earnest, now. "You didn't hurt me, Jack. I don't even know what you got me into, but you didn't hurt me. Besides—" She looked down through a shimmering blur and saw a thatch of inky black hair, a fragile, seashell ear and tiny fingers splayed against a rose-petal cheek. "Maybe," she heard herself say in a choked voice, "it was meant to happen."

"What do you mean?"

She lifted her head and drew a tremulous, almost frightened breath. "I don't know what I mean."

And then, with a defiant sniff, she contradicted herself. "Maybe I'll tell you someday. Right now, I don't know about you, but I'm starving. I'm going to get the keys."

Mr. Ortiz owned several properties in Santa Luisa, including the building that housed the Flying Sams's clinic. How he'd acquired so much real estate Terry didn't know, but he also owned two fishing boats, managing to go out to sea with his older sons every day except Sunday.

The Ortiz house was one of the biggest in Santa Luisa— it had to be, to accommodate the family's large and lively brood. Like the clinic, it had started out a compact, sturdy structure with thick walls of cinder block, stone and adobe, and a roof of plywood and composition shingles. Unlike the clinic, it had subsequently been expanded in several directions, with whatever materials happened to be on hand—

scrap plywood, salvaged wood planks and corrugated tin—
even cactus stalks.

At this hour on a Sunday evening it was deliciously over-
heated from cooking and filled to overflowing with the unmistakable odors of fish, frijoles and green chili peppers, as
well as young Ortizes of all sizes and genders.

While Mr. Ortiz went to get the key to unlock the clinic,
the children gathered around with bright eyes and big, shy
smiles, quietly shuffling and pushing for a chance to look at
and touch the baby, as if they'd never seen one before. Mrs.
Ortiz, a comfortably overweight woman with a pretty, un-
lined face, came to cluck and fuss over her like a mother
hen, and somehow—Terry never knew quite how—in the
midst of all the fussing and cooing and Spanish baby talk,
wound up with the baby cradled on her own more-than-
ample maternal bosom.

Firing orders in a rapid-fire, and to Terry's ears, totally
unintelligible stream of Spanish, Mrs. Ortiz deposited
Angelita in the arms of one of her two female offspring, a
girl of about nine or ten. Before Terry could say a word, the
delighted child had whisked Angelita off to be changed,
cuddling her with the casual confidence and expertise that
spoke of experience beyond her years.

With mixed feelings Terry watched the baby disappear
into the warm inner reaches of the house. It was a relief, of
course, to be able to put down the burden she'd carried for
so many hours, no matter how tiny. But it was strange, how
lonely it seemed, how empty her arms felt.

Mrs. Ortiz wouldn't hear of them eating at Pepe's. Another staccato burst of Spanish directed at two more of her
children resulted in the immediate clearing of two places at
the long, wood plank table. Small, earnest hands clutched
hers and Jack's, towing and urging them until they gave in
and sat down on the rough wooden benches.

Heavy crockery bowls filled with steaming fish stew sea-
soned with tomatoes and onions were immediately set in

front of them, followed by plates heaped with frijoles, rice mixed with vegetables, and a sweet-tasting dish made with cornmeal and fresh corn kernels. Nothing in Terry's memory had ever smelled or tasted so good.

Mr. Ortiz brought in a six-pack of Mexican beer—not ice-cold, but pleasantly cool. After opening three bottles, one for each of them and one for himself, he sat down to listen with stoic acceptance while Jack filled him in on the fate of his pickup truck.

While the men were talking, Terry, who usually preferred tequila, made the discovery that nothing tastes quite as good as beer does when you're really thirsty. She downed the first bottle as if it were water, and then the second one, too. Mr. Ortiz instantly offered her a third, which, after only a polite hesitation, she accepted—perhaps unwisely.

If she hadn't drunk that third beer, maybe she wouldn't have let herself sink so deeply into that warm, noisy atmosphere full of children and the smells of cooking. Maybe she wouldn't have let herself slip back, for a few sweet moments, to another time, another house, another family a lot like this one, an Irish family named Duncan.

And maybe she wouldn't have found herself suddenly remembering how it had felt to be a proud, angry teenager coming to live in that house for the first time, remembering the confusion of loud, boisterous voices, the sea of bright, curious eyes. Robert, the oldest son, already in college but still living at home, had smiled at her. They'd given her soup, she recalled—Campbell's chicken noodle. Then, as now, small hands had taken hers and led her to the table. Then, as now, she'd felt a vast loneliness, an inexpressible yearning. Then, as now, she'd felt perilously close to crying.

She hadn't, though—she'd been too proud and angry. It had been a long time before she'd learned to trust them and let them love her, and even longer before she'd learned to trust and love herself. And maybe, as Robert said, she still hadn't learned to love.

She wasn't going to cry now, either, she told herself. No sir. It was just tiredness and too much beer. Nothing like fatigue and alcohol to loosen up the ol' waterworks. A little fresh air, a good wash and some rest and she'd be fine—her old self again.

Then she looked up and met Jack's eyes across the table, and she wondered if she was ever going to be herself again.

His eyes were different, somehow. Blue, but a *different* blue. They were as intent and unnerving as ever, but the old, burning, too-bright look was gone. Instead, there was something haunted about his eyes. They seemed transparent but shadowed, as if something inside him were calling out to her through a closed window. And looking into them made her feel as if she were standing knee-deep in quicksand.

"Ready to go?" he asked her when she abruptly pushed back the bench and stood up.

She nodded a bit desperately. "I need some air, I think. Will you please thank them for me? I'll go get Angelita."

But Mrs. Ortiz intercepted her, making scolding noises and shooing motions with her hands.

"She says she's sleeping," Jack said in a low voice behind her. "She says not to disturb her. You can leave her here tonight. The children will look after her." He paused and snorted softly.

"What?" Terry whispered.

"She says we look like we need a good night's sleep, too."

"No kidding!" Jack hadn't slept at all last night, she remembered, wondering how long it had been since he'd had a good night's sleep. She turned to him, uncharacteristically anxious and unsure. "I don't know...what do you think? Do you think we should leave her here?"

He looked surprised that she'd asked him, and as uncertain as she. "Well...yeah, I guess so," he said, rubbing at the back of his neck. "I think it'd be okay, don't you?"

My God, Terry thought suddenly, look at us! We're like a couple of brand-new parents suffering separation anxiety! She burst into giggles, but when Jack asked her what was funny, she couldn't tell him—she was too embarrassed. It was just too ridiculous, too absurd. If ever two people were less likely to be parents, or less suited for it, it was them.

"All right, just tell her to be sure to give her the bottled formula—no milk. Tell her milk makes Angelita sick. And to be sure to burp her every ounce or so, because she's not used to—"

"Relax, Doc," Jack said dryly. "I think she probably knows how to burp a kid—she's had enough practice." He took her by the shoulders and turned her around. "Come on, let's get out of here."

They made their escape on the crest of a wave of children, all waving and chattering and calling good-night. Two of the older Ortiz sons, each with a large bucket of water, met them at the bottom of the steps. After escorting them back to the clinic and carrying the water inside, they said their polite good-nights and left.

While Terry found and turned on one of the battery-operated lanterns, Jack brought the packs in and shut the door behind him. He stood for a moment with the packs slung over one arm, sort of fiddling with the key while he studied her with a long, brooding look, then dropped both the packs and key onto the wooden table near the door.

"Well," Terry said brightly after a curiously electric silence. "I guess the first thing is to get cleaned up. We have the folding screens we use to divide examining areas, and I think I have a towel in my bag—we can share, if you—"

"Forget it."

She caught a sharp, nervous sip of air. "What?"

"I said, forget it," Jack growled. "I'm too damn dirty for a bucket." He prowled toward her, restless and wired as a caged wolf. "Come on—" He jerked his head toward the door. "Let's get out of here—go for a swim."

"Right now?" It came out on a gust of breathless laughter.

"Sure, why not? It's not too cold—the water seems warmer at night. There's going to be a bright moon again. Nobody but us on the beach, that's for sure."

Bright moon...dark water. His words called to her, like something wild in the night. She bit down on her lip, clamping down on a surge of recklessness and pure exhilaration. It was the sort of thing she'd done so often in her youth, and had not done in so very, very long. She looked at Jack and saw the same recklessness in him, and her heart took flight like a bird just released from long captivity. We're two of a kind, she thought, exulting in the discovery. *Two of a kind.*

Then she looked closer, looked into his eyes, and a shiver rocked her from head to toe. Because she knew in that moment that *he* was the wild thing calling to her in the night. And that she was going to go to him, recklessly, foolishly, willingly.

Chapter 12

"Come on," Wolf said, scowling impatiently, "get your towel, or a blanket, or whatever you want and let's go."

He never doubted she'd come with him; he'd already seen the answer in her eyes—the flare of excitement, the spark of wildness to match his own. He knew her so well, what she was thinking, what she was feeling, not in any way he could put into words, but with an empathy so deep it seemed as if, for that moment, at least, they were parts of the same whole. He had to remind himself that he still didn't know much about her, or what made her tick. Yet it didn't seem important to him anymore. Regardless of where she'd come from and where he'd come from, they were riding the same wave now, and that was all that mattered.

They walked side by side down the dirt road that led past Pepe's Cantina to the beach in a hurrying silence, as if they were on the way to someplace important and were afraid of being late. They'd both put on Señor Lopez's serapes over their clothes again, and Terry carried a towel and Wolf a blanket. Neither of them had felt the need to bring a flashlight along, although the moon hadn't yet risen above the mountains; the wildness in them felt at home in the dark.

When they had left the music and lights of Pepe's behind them and the sand was soft underfoot, Terry turned her head toward him without slackening her pace and said breathlessly, "What's the matter? You seem...I don't know, sort of wired."

"Wired?"

"Yeah. Like a time bomb with the seconds ticking down."

Wolf grinned in the darkness. It didn't surprise him at all that she'd describe so exactly what he felt. "Ah, hell," he said. "I just needed some air. That house kind of got to me, I guess."

"I know," Terry said. "Me, too. It was hot in there."

"Crowded."

"Too many kids!"

Wolf snorted. "That's something I'd think you'd be used to."

"I see a lot of kids," Terry admitted dryly. "Usually one at a time."

Wolf chuckled softly. They walked a little in silence again, listening to the muted rhythm of waves. "You must be an only child."

"Yes... No—" She paused for a step or two, gave a short laugh and then continued. "Well . . . not exactly."

Wolf glanced toward her. "Which is it, yes or no?"

He felt the slight stiffening in her, the defensiveness. She wasn't used to this. "I was in a lot of foster homes," she explained with an offhanded shrug. "Most of them had kids."

"Foster homes..." he murmured in soft irony, and added unspoken, *I sure did a good job pegging you, didn't I?* He cleared his throat and asked, "So—no blood siblings?"

For a while he thought she wouldn't answer. Her footsteps plodded beside his through the soft sand...two...

three...four...five...before he heard her take a deep breath. He had a sense of a rusty key turning in a very old lock.

"I had a brother. A baby brother...." Her voice was soft and remote.

"What happened?" Wolf asked, his voice as soft as hers. "Did he die?"

"No, he didn't die. My mother gave him up."

"Gave him up?"

"For adoption. When I was five."

Wolf didn't say anything because there was suddenly too much going on inside him. He couldn't bring himself to ask a question because there were too many he wanted to ask. So he walked along beside her and after a while heard her take another deep breath, the way people do when they have an ache they can't reach.

"It's funny...." He could feel her shake her head, shake her hair free so that the breeze from the ocean blew it against his shoulder. Almost, he thought, as if she were trying to shake herself free of the memories. "I was so young," she said almost dreamily, "and he was there for such a short time, and yet I still remember so vividly what he looked like, and how devastated I was when he went away. I swear to God not a day goes by that I don't think about him, wonder where he is now, what he's become. Whether he's happy—" Her voice ended abruptly.

"My God," Wolf whispered.

Suddenly he understood some things he hadn't before. Like why the doc had gotten so emotional about the episode in El Refugio, the baby, that whole thing. Why she'd said that maybe getting stranded there was meant to happen. His mind filled with the image of a brokenhearted little boy running back to kiss his baby sister one more time, and then the image blurred, and the time, place and genders changed.

Without any shadow of doubt he knew that Doc was thinking of it, too.

He felt buffeted and off balance, like he'd just missed getting hit by a truck. He wanted to tell her he understood, but couldn't find the right words. He didn't know what to say to her, so he reached for her hand instead, captured it and brought it impulsively to his mouth.

"Why—" he began before his voice cracked and choked him. He cleared his throat and tried again. *"Why?"*

She gave his hand a little squeeze, rearranging her hand in his so they fit more closely palm to palm, the way lovers hold hands when they walk together. It gave Wolf an odd feeling; he couldn't remember whether he'd ever done such a thing before. He wondered why she'd done it—to comfort herself, or him?

"Why did she give him up?" Doc's voice was gentle now, with less pain in it than compassion. She gave a sad little laugh. "The same reason she kept me with her—because she loved us very much. She couldn't afford to keep us both, and she thought she was doing the best for us. I didn't know that then, of course. I was extremely angry with her in those days. Even more so when she died of an accidental drug overdose four years later. They said it was suicide—now I know she'd never have deliberatley killed herself and left me alone like that, but for a long time I hated her for abandoning both of her children so cruelly. Which is probably why I was such a rotten kid—anger and hatred are ultimately self-destructive."

He felt her look at him, heard her soft, wondering laugh. "I haven't told this stuff to anyone in years, Jack, do you know that? Why am I telling you?"

He shrugged and said hoarsely, "You don't have to."

She squeezed his hand and murmured, "I know. Maybe that's why." She stopped walking and faced him, her face pale in the light of the newly risen moon. "My mother wasn't a bad person, Jack. Just a weak one. Plus—" She shrugged. "She had lousy luck with men. That's why I decided a long, long time ago that I wasn't going to be like her. I made up my mind I was going to be strong, and have better judgment."

"Well," Wolf drawled, "at least you're strong."

He'd meant it as a reference to the fact that she was divorced, but she gave kind of a startled laugh that made him wonder if she thought he was talking about something else. Hell, maybe he had been.

The truth was, he hadn't let himself think too much about what was happening between the doc and him, and he was fairly sure she hadn't, either. The whole thing had come pretty much as a surprise, and with everything else going on, he hadn't really had a chance to figure out what he was going to do about it.

He knew he probably *should* think about it, before it had a chance to go any further. Maybe someday when he stopped bouncing off walls and started thinking again he'd look back on this as one of those times he wished he'd done things differently. Maybe. But right now he didn't have it in him to do much more than just go with the tide, and if the doc happened to be on the same wave he was...so be it.

In any case, she let go of the subject like it was a hot rock. Wolf found that he was sorry. Although he didn't have that itchy curiosity about her anymore, he *was* interested, and besides, tuning in to her had kept him, for a few minutes at least, from thinking about what was happening inside himself. Now she'd let go of his hand, too, and walking beside her in silence with only the cool, salt wind between them he could feel it building up in him again, that cold gray wave without a name, like a tsunami on the horizon.

Ordinarily on a night like this he'd run—hard, fast and alone. But tonight he didn't feel like running, and he didn't feel like being alone. He didn't have to look at the doc, walking there beside him, keeping pace with him step for step, to know exactly what he did want. It was all there in his mind—the taste of her mouth, the smell of her hair, the feel of her body against him. But he did look at her, and she looked back at him, and he knew that she wanted the same thing he did. Damned if he knew why, when he'd lied to her, put her through hell, almost got her killed and most unforgivably of all, humiliated her. She probably didn't know why, either.

Their steps slowed. They didn't touch, just went on looking at each other, searching each other's faces in the moonlight. Trying to make sense of it, Wolf thought. Looking for reasons and justifications when there weren't any, except maybe mutual need. It was simply that the wildness was in them both, and that special kind of loneliness that only comes when the moon drowns the stars and washes the night with silver and fills the heart with nameless yearnings. On nights like this hearts ached to share, and bodies to touch.

Neither of them spoke, although there was still so much that needed to be said between them, questions to be asked and stories to be told. But not now. Not tonight. Tonight they understood each other best without words.

Wolf let the blanket slide from his fingers. Without taking his eyes from the doc's face he pulled his arms in under his poncho, slowly lifted it up and back, shook his head free of it and let it fall. Somewhere behind Terry a wave crashed softly onto the sand. On the hiss of its retreat, or perhaps her indrawn breath, she pulled her own poncho over her head and dropped it at his feet.

Wolf's hands moved down the buttons of his shirt. She watched him avidly, not his hands, but his eyes. The shirt joined the ponchos on the sand. Then for a few minutes they stood motionless, facing each other like strangers at a dance. Strangers, dancing in the moonlight.

Wolf lifted his arms, hesitated, then quickly gathered his T-shirt up and in one swift motion, pulled it off and tossed it away. And then he waited, watching her, neither asking nor urging, feeling fairly sure of her, but needing that final reassurance.

There. He caught her smile—a quick, unexpected smile on a small sip of breath. Her eyes, filled with moonlight, dipped to his naked chest and back up again.

Strip poker in the dark.

A strange excitement filled him. He knew what she was thinking. He could hear it as plainly as if she'd said the words out loud.

She laughed so softly only the wind carried it to his ears. Slowly, taunting him a little, she tugged her shirt loose from the waistband of her slacks and unbuttoned it, pulling the two halves apart.

Wolf's belly knotted; his hands ached with the urge to touch her. One of the hardest things he'd ever done was stand there motionless and keep his hands at his sides.

Another wave crashed onto the shore. Her shirt hit the sand without a sound. Her hand hovered in reflexive shyness at the center clasp of her bra, then dropped.

In the moonlight her body was a luminous, alabaster white, the scrap of a bra not much darker. He knew she was waiting for him, inviting him to take it off, maybe even wanting him to. But he wasn't going to do that. As hard as it was for him to keep from touching her, and as hard as it might be for her, she was going to have to finish the job on her own. Last night he'd taken something from her against her will; tonight she was going to come to him of her own free will, and with that pride of hers intact. Because he'd discovered he never ever wanted to take her again without it.

He saw her chest swell and her stomach tighten.

Come on, Doc . . . come on. Don't be afraid.

It was as if she'd heard him. He saw her bite down on her lower lip, catching back a smile. Slowly, slowly, she reached up with both hands and unhooked the clasp, pulling the two halves of the bra back and letting it slide down her arms.

Then, very deliberately, she lifted her head and shook back her hair.

Wolf's breath caught. Desire skewered him from chest to groin; his body shuddered, buffeted by storms of emotion and a strange, wild exultation. If he lived a hundred years more, he was never going to forget the way she looked, standing there with the moonlight stark and cold on her face and body. He'd never seen anything more beautiful, or more exciting. The proud thrust of jaw and chin, her slender throat, delicate as porcelain, the windblown hair licking the tops of small, perfect breasts and her dark nipples, exquisite as flowers, already budding in the cold night wind.

He was jealous of the wind. He wanted it to be *his* fingers tangling her hair, *his* tongue licking those tender buds erect, *his* mouth sucking them back to honeyed softness, making her shiver and tremble. He wanted it so badly his own body trembled, and his jaws cramped with the strain. And still he didn't touch her.

Instead, he lifted up one foot, bent over and grabbed hold of his boot and pulled it off. It wasn't a graceful maneuver; he could hear the doc's laughter soaring like sea gulls above the crashing of waves. He straightened up, still holding his boot, and gave her a grin of warning and challenge. Her answer was to flick off her shoes, then pull her socks off one at a time and toss them blithely over her shoulder. Laughing at him. Taunting him. He gave her a look that said, "Okay, Doc, you're askin' for it!" and went after his other boot.

By the time he had it off, she was already stepping out of her slacks and skimming down her underpants. Then, while he was still yanking on his belt buckle and cursing his button-fly jeans, she kicked off the last scrap of pale nylon and ran laughing to the water.

Moon madness. That's what it was, she thought—a kind of madness. It must be—she'd never behaved like this before! Frolicking naked in the moonlight before the eyes of a dangerous stranger, laughing, exhilarated, uninhibited as a child, or the child she'd never been.

Except that there was nothing even remotely childish about this night, or the emotions that drove her. In spite of the laughter, this was no innocent child's game. The wildness in her was as elemental as a thunderstorm and as impossible to control. The exhilaration was primitive and centred in the deepest part of her being, the part most essentially female. It was that part which governed her now. The part that knew instinctively her most fundamental purpose and greatest strength, and accepted both with a fierce, primeval joy.

She knew with a thrill of heart-pounding suspense that he was gaining on her as she splashed through the shallows of a receding wave. She felt him right behind her as she dived, arrow-straight, into a cresting swell. Excitement surged through her, pumping adrenaline into her system so that she barely felt the cold. Primed with that same adrenaline, her muscles propelled her through the moon-gilded water, and she felt him there beside her, keeping pace with her, matching her stroke for stroke.

Then she felt him touch her, and obeying his silent signal, turned toward him, treading water and undulating gently with the swell.

God, it's cold! But instead of saying it out loud, she shivered and laughed.

Come on, Doc, keep moving! She heard him loud and clear, even though he only laughed with her and dived into the waves, arching like a dolphin.

She felt the cold glide of his body as it slid past her, and gave a little yelp of surprise when he surfaced behind her, blowing spray. She plunged beneath the surface, reaching for him. He laughed and kicked away from her, teasing her, staying just beyond her reach. Then all at once he disappeared and for a moment she was frightened; but he resurfaced beside her almost immediately, and this time when she reached for him he didn't move away.

Her arms slid around his neck; their legs, still treading water, were a cold, slippery tangle. His hands skimmed the water just below the surface and came up to capture her head, draped in the seaweed curtain of her hair.

For a few seconds they held on to each other, looking into each other's faces, laughing, gasping, streaming water. Then their mouths came together, open and greedy. She felt the rasp of his beard, the clash of teeth; she tasted salt, she tasted *him*.

Oh, but she was hungry—starved for him! Her nails raked his shoulders, her fingers tangled in his hair; her hair wrapped around his arms, imprisoning him in a skein of mermaid silk. And still she couldn't get enough of him—nor he of her.

They separated briefly, only long enough to forestall drowning, then came back again, more ravenous than before. There was a kind of frenzy to the way they kissed, each one frantically trying to find a joining that would appease the bottomless hunger, satisfy the nameless craving. When she couldn't achieve that union, Terry's frenzy became panic. Her chest tightened; finally she tore her mouth away from his and threw back her head, sobbing and gasping for air.

Instantly, Jack's arms slid down and wrapped around her, pulling her hard against him, holding her together. She felt his face against her throat, his lips moving on her skin, saying the words she couldn't hear above the tumult in her ears.

It's all right, Doc . . . I've got you.

He held her and let the waves carry them, and in a strange way the sea seemed part of their dance. A mutual lover, wrapping them in its cold, erotic embrace, rocking their bodies together in sinuous rhythms.

It carried them to the place where the waves troughed. There the sand rose up under their feet, and they could stand in the heaving swell, braced against the current while the water rose to their chests, then fell away again, leaving them naked to the hips, shivering in the chilly caress of the wind.

Terry gave a sharp, startled cry when Jack turned her, caught her roughly against him and raked her hair away from her nape. She felt the cold slipperiness of his body along the length of her back and his mouth, hot and hungry on her neck.

She gasped when she felt the exquisite bites, the strong, sucking pressure, and wriggled in his embrace, rubbing her bottom against him in slow, circling motions. She felt his maleness like cold, silky steel, and caressed it with her softness, caressed and tormented him with her buttocks as he was tormenting her with his mouth and hands.

His hands—oh God, his hands! They were on her breasts, covering them, his fingers manipulating nipples already rock-hard and sensitized beyond bearing. And his hands weren't gentle now; they were rough, insistent, demanding. He chafed her tender nipples, rolled them between his thumbs and forefingers, tugged on them with a hard, rhythmic pressure that wrung from her high, frantic cries. It was the edge of pain, but she didn't know it. The tugging and the pressure were pulling on something deep, deep inside of her, something terrifying in its intensity, something so primitive and powerful she thought she could die from it and not care.

She moaned and arched her body, pushing into his hands, grinding her buttocks against him, seeking, seeking. And then she gave a deep, shuddering gasp as he pushed his knee between her legs and shoved them roughly apart. His hands, his fingers and his mouth increased their terrible, exquisite torture as he brought his leg up between her thighs—*hard* between them, pressing into that most sensitive part of her.

She wanted, she needed to gasp, to cry out, but she had no air left. She couldn't breathe. She was panting, her chest straining, her mouth opened in a shocked, silent scream. He was riding her on that hard ridge of muscle, touching her in all of her most nerve-rich places, including some she hadn't known about until then.

It was too much, too much! And yet, not nearly enough. Something was missing. There was an emptiness inside her, an unbearable, intolerable emptiness. She knew what she wanted, what she *had* to have, it was no longer a question of whether or not, or even of when. She wanted him filling that emptiness, wanted his cold-steel hardness inside her, warming and strengthening in the furnace of her body. And she wanted, needed, him now, or she would die. The only question left to resolve was how.

This is crazy, Wolf thought with an inward groan. I can't do this here—we'll drown!

But he could feel the urgency in her—no greater than his own—so with the next rising swell he hooked an arm behind her knees and lifted her, carrying her through the breaking waves. Although the surf was gentle and there was no undertow, they were both panting by the time he had them standing on firm sand again. Panting, shivering and clinging to each other like survivors of a shipwreck, each afraid that if they lost physical contact, even for a moment, the other would somehow be swept away and lost forever.

She grasped his hand and hung on to it as if it were a life preserver when he left her standing, racked with shudders, and leaned down to pick up her towel. He gave it a cursory shake, then with the same swift, jerky motion, carried it around her shoulders and pulled her right back against him. He sighed as he brought the ends of the towel to her face and sought her mouth again, like a starving man denied food for too long.

He'd never felt such a need, not even in his sexually preoccupied youth, when all he'd thought about was girls, and getting them to bed—or any substitute for a bed—had been his top priority. Something was driving him, right on his heels, driving him fast and hard so he wouldn't have time to think. On some primitive level he sensed that the doc was with him all the way; beyond that, he knew that the time and place were right. And that was all that mattered.

Without breaking off the kiss, he lowered them both to the pile of blankets and clothing they'd dropped in the sand. For a time they hovered there, betwixt and between, kneeling, facing each other, hungrily kissing, raking backs and gripping buttocks with eager, greedy hands, laughing and shivering and making sporadic and clumsy attempts to rearrange the pile into a bed. They gave it up, finally; their movements were too awkward, the urgency too great. She made little whimpering sounds of feminine need; he answered with a deep-throated masculine growl.

Suddenly he gripped her shoulders and tore his mouth away from hers. For a long moment he stared at her, a strange, fierce look that should have frightened her, but didn't. Their chests heaved and strained; she could hear the tortured sounds of their breathing. Then at last his hands bore her down, his hard, cold body followed, coming easily, naturally between her drawn-up knees. She felt the silky length of him, warm now, and gently cradled against her. Braced there on his arms, poised above her, his body trembled with the strain of self-control.

Oh, but she didn't want gentleness now, or self-control. There was that place inside her that craved him, and she'd waited far too long already! With a savage little cry she wrapped her legs around him and arched her back, angling her body so that the way was open to him. She felt him sigh and shudder. She took his face between her hands, and lifting herself up to meet him, swirled her tongue over his lips and into his mouth, opening to him, pulling him in, deeper and deeper.

His muscles clenched and tightened, she felt the pressure, the first stinging shock of penetration, the minute breaking and the giving way. His fingers pushed into her hair as he pushed into her body; his hands encompassed her face as her body closed around him. His thumbs tenderly caressed her cheeks, her rapt breath bathed his lips.

And then, warmly but not deeply housed, he paused. His body relaxed and he merged his breath with hers in gentle, relieved laughter. Laughter just because it felt so good. Relief because it seemed as though they'd waited for it so long. A lifetime.

In a guttural voice, still shaking with wonder and laughter, Wolf said, "Hey, Doc, what's happening here? We don't even like each other."

In a fierce whisper she countered, "Liking's got nothing to do with it!" And lifting her hips, she rocked against him, further enfolding him.

He groaned, "Ah, Doc..." The wildness exploded inside him. He pulled back from her a little and grasped her thighs just above and behind the knees. He gathered himself and drove into her, deep and deeper, as deep as he could, deep as he dared, forcing her breath from her in a long, shuddering gasp.

When he heard it something inside him cried out, fearful of hurting her, yet more terrified of what was happening to him. His body was being wrenched from his control. He could feel it happening and couldn't stop it. Every muscle in his body clenched and trembled, clenched and trembled as he surged into her and then withdrew, again and again and again. Driving toward that release he needed so desperately. But the release seemed just out of reach, while the need kept building and building, like that tidal wave on the horizon. It kept building and growing, becoming more and more powerful, beyond anything he'd ever known or imagined. He knew that inevitably it had to break, but he feared the breaking so much he tried desperately to forestall it, knowing when it did the devastation would be total.

He couldn't lose control. He *couldn't*. Self-control was all that held him together. If he lost that, *he* was lost.

And then—God help him!—she cried out once more, a raw, primitive sound wrenched from her by the throes of her own cataclysm. He felt her writhe and tense, and then her body was rippling and surging around him, clenching and tightening in rapid spasms that stripped away the last ounce of his self-control. His own cry merged with hers as he felt himself falling, felt his body convulsing, every muscle in his body—belly and back, buttocks and thighs. He plunged into her, crushing her against the sand while the violence of their combined contractions emptied him and left him utterly and completely drained.

Lying dazed with Jack's weight pressing down on her, his head cradled on her chest and their bodies still pulsing together in the sweet aftermath of dying, Terry thought, I know what just happened. *It's all right. I know what this is. It's all right.*

She felt him tremble and held him tighter, unable to fight her own wracking shivers, or the tears that trickled from the corners of her eyes and ran down into her hair. It's okay, I understand this, she repeated to herself, staring into the milky sky. It's just release, that's all, from all the danger and tension. We faced death today, Jack. This is an affirmation of life.

But what in the world was this ache inside her, this pressure in her throat, the sobs she didn't dare let go? Why did she hold him so tightly, certain that when he separated from her she would feel agony, as if a part of her were being ripped away?

She was cold, suddenly, dazed and frightened, like a survivor of a holocaust still wandering in circles mumbling, I'm all right, I'm all right.

Jack's lips moved against her throat. He raised his head, shifted his weight a little, then propped himself on one elbow and brought his hand to her face. "Are you okay?" he asked, his voice raw and guttural, touching the moisture at the corner of her eye. "I didn't . . . hurt you—"

"No," Terry whispered, "I'm fine."

He nodded distractedly and eased himself away from her. She made one small, involuntary movement of protest, then let him go. He sat for a moment with his arms resting on his knees, then began to search through his clothes, swearing under his breath. He found what he was looking for, the crumpled cigarette pack in his shirt pocket. His last cigarette. Then the lighter in his pants pocket. He flicked it on, and the flame filled the hollows in his face with shadows.

Terry watched him in silence, trying not to feel rejected. She thought he seemed preoccupied, his movements jerky and uncoordinated, as if he were still shivering inside.

"Are you cold?" she asked softly, putting her hand on the smooth ridge of muscle along his spine.

He flinched when she touched him, then tried to cover it by turning awkwardly and catching her hand. "Nah," he said in a rasping travesty of his drawl, "I'm fine . . . but you better cover up. Here—put this on." He shook his shirt out and draped it haphazardly around her shoulders. Then he mumbled something under his breath and lurched to his feet.

Hurt, aching with abandonment, she watched him walk away from her, not the long, graceful canine stride she'd come to associate with him, but something almost drunken. At the edge of the water he stopped and stood with his back to her, shoulders slightly hunched, mechanically smoking, his lean body like sculpted pewter in the moonlight. He seemed so cold, she thought; so far away, and so unutterably *lonely*.

The lone wolf. Once again in her mind's eye she saw him, loping along the beach in the moonlight.

All at once the picture tilted, swam out of focus and snapped back in again. And suddenly she really did understand.

Chapter 13

Terry sat up slowly, pulling Jack's shirt around her and searching clumsily for the sleeves. She managed to stand, but found that her legs were still wobbly and staggered a bit as she made her way through the soft sand. Just behind him she stopped and wrapped her arms and the two halves of his shirt around her. She was shivering uncontrollably, partly with cold, partly from the aftershock of lovemaking, and partly from dread.

God help me, she thought with a tiny whimper of helpless laughter. How *did* one comfort a Wolf?

He heard the sound she made and spoke without turning, in a gentle, ragged voice. "You're cold, Doc. Go on back, keep warm."

"Jack—" When she touched him he stiffened, hardening himself against her. "Jack, what's wrong?"

He lifted the cigarette to his mouth, pulled hard on it, then lowered it again, moving like a broken marionette. She heard the sharp hiss of his exhalation.

"Jack, please talk to me. Tell me what's wrong."

He looked up at the sky for a moment, then shook his head and in an oddly furred voice, mumbled, "Doc...I can't."

"Yes you can, damn it!" She put her hands on his cold, rigid body and tried to turn him. It was like tugging on a truck. Tears were rising in her eyes and in her voice, her heart pounding so hard it hurt. "You *have* to!"

He gave a heartrending little hiccup of laughter, then took one last, quick drag on his cigarette and dropped it onto the damp sand. As he turned to her, she felt shudders careening through his body.

"Doc," he said in a broken whisper, "I think what I have to do right now is hold you. Will you do that? Just let me hold you?"

"Jack." His name was a cry, which became a sob as she lifted her arms to his neck. His arms came around her in a rush, wrapping her so tightly it hurt. She felt the rings he wore on the chain around his neck biting into her own flesh.

But he was stiff at first, still trying desperately to hold his emotions back. She felt him take several deep, uneven breaths, his body quaking with each one, like a steel spring coming unwound.

"I don't want to do this," he gasped, shaking his head violently. "I can't do this."

"I know, I know. But I think you have to."

"Ah...God."

"Come on, Jack, let it go. Please, you've been holding it in too long."

She wove her fingers through his hair, gently kneaded the taut muscles in his neck and shoulders until she felt them begin to loosen, until she felt the bony ridge of his jaw rest against her ear. *"Let it go."*

His hands lifted, opened and closed again almost spasmodically, gripping her shoulders, her hair. She felt his body begin to shake, and held him even more tightly, bracing herself for the sound she thought must be one of the most gut-wrenching in all the world. The raw, throat-tearing sound of a strong man's grief.

So this is it, she thought wonderingly as she held him, staring out at the rippling water through a fog of tears. The thing I've been afraid of all these years, the thing I've been hiding from behind my barricades. Caring for someone so much it hurts.

She'd been right to be afraid. It hurt, deep down inside, so deep she felt that something fundamental in her very being had been touched, and irrevocably changed. And, oh God, her barricades were gone! Without them she felt vulnerable and insecure, she could get hurt, even more than she already was. Her heart was left wide open and unprotected. She had no defenses at all.

Oh God, I'm scared. *I'm scared.*

She began to rub his back, patiently stroking and soothing him with her strong, gentle hands. Gradually the shaking subsided, and he turned his face into her hair.

"Ah, damn," he whispered, holding her even more tightly. "Damn it, Doc, I'm sorry."

"It's all right, it's all right." She was shaking now, too, as she lifted one hand to his head and smoothed his hair, gently massaging his neck muscles. "Tell me about it, Jack. Talk to me. It had something to do with those men, didn't it? Those men you wanted to kill—"

"Ah, God—" He lifted his head; she felt him writhe with pain and rejection, and the words come in agony, as if ripped from his body. "I let them go. *I let them go.* I let him down . . . I'm sorry, Frank."

"You let *who* down, Jack?" She was holding him so tightly, holding him together. "Who is Frank?"

"My brother. Frank was my brother. They killed him—" Shudders wracked him. His body was like a ship, buffeted by storms of grief beyond imagining, and all Terry could do was hang on to him and pray he wouldn't break apart. "Oh God—they killed him. And Barb, too—his wife—and their little girl, Carrie. They killed them, Doc—I don't want to tell you what they did to them. I don't want to. I can't—''

"It's all right, you don't have to. It's all right...."

"I found them. I went because they hadn't answered the phone—and I found them. Frank was still alive—just barely. I promised him—I promised I'd find them. I promised...ah, God! I let you down again, Frank. I'm sorry...I'm sorry."

She held him. It was all she could do. Numb and cold with horror, weeping herself, she held him and stroked him and cradled his head in the warm hollow of her neck. And she remembered the pain she'd sensed in him, the feverish brightness of his eyes, and the unbearable tension. No wonder, she thought. *No wonder.* He hadn't cried for them before, she was sure of it. He hadn't cried at all, until now.

Eventually, when the worst of the storm had spent itself, she managed to get him back to the pile of clothing and the blanket. She spread the ponchos on the sand, lay down with him and pulled the blanket and the ponchos around them. He was cold, so cold, naked in every sense of the word. Within the blankets, she wrapped herself around him, shutting out the cold, pouring her own warmth into him, cradling and comforting him with gentle hands and loving words until he slept.

Is this what it means to be a woman? she thought, just before exhaustion and the strong, steady rhythm of Jack's heartbeat carried her into oblivion. To nurture, comfort, protect. To love.

She thought of the man asleep in her arms, the man she'd judged a cold-blooded killer. She thought of little Angelita, peacefully sleeping now in a warm, crowded, loving house, and of the way she'd felt when a real killer put a gun to her throat and told her with obscene pleasure the things he would do to her and to that baby. And she knew, beyond any doubt, even though she had been trained and sworn to save lives, that to protect this man and that baby, she, too, would kill.

Wolf woke up with a confusing sense of unreality, as if he were only dreaming he was awake, and was somehow a kid again, sleeping in his old bed in his parents' house in Orange Grove, California. Then he opened his eyes and saw the moon still high overhead, and knew that he was on a Baja beach and a long, long way from being a kid. And he felt as if for the first time in six months he was truly awake. The nightmare was over.

He raised himself on one elbow and looked down at the woman sleeping beside him, her hair a dark pool on the sand-colored ponchos, robbed of its color by the moonlight. Even though he knew it might wake her, he couldn't resist touching her, trailing his fingertips along her forehead, down the side of her face, stroking a stray curl behind her ear. God, he thought, she's so beautiful.

And then he stopped, confused, because suddenly he didn't know whether she was beautiful or not. It struck him that he'd completely lost his objectivity where she was concerned; that he didn't really know what she looked like anymore, or care. She was just Doc to him now. Unutterably beautiful.

He touched her soft lips with his fingers, then, moved by impulse, leaned down and kissed her. And after the first moment, felt them grow firm and vibrant with awareness. Her body stirred against him; her hand came from the blankets to touch his face.

"'Mornin', Doc," he whispered.

"Is it morning?" Her voice was husky.

"Sometime in the morning. Still a couple of hours before the fishermen come out. Hmm." He licked his lips. "You taste salty."

She stretched, which he found a delightful exercise. "You know, too much salt's bad for you."

"Too bad." He licked *her* lips. "I've developed an insatiable craving." She opened her mouth in instantaneous response and he swirled his tongue into it, then deeper, an intoxicated kiss, languid and slow. "I think," he murmured thickly when he finally withdrew, "that I'm going to have to make love to you again. Do you mind?"

His hand lay on her forehead, gently stroking. Hers lay along the side of his face; her thumb slid across his lips and he captured it and drew it into the warmth of his mouth.

"No," she whispered, "I don't mind."

For a while, neither of them moved, just looked at each other. Wolf's throat tightened. He swallowed, laughed a little and wondered how in the world he could feel so weak and emotional and not be worried about the consequences. Instead, he felt light, ridiculously carefree, and oh, so tender. He was assailed with tenderness—overcome with it. He felt that there must be words to tell her how he felt, and that if he couldn't tell her he would burst. But since he didn't know what the words were, he finally just whispered, "Come 'ere, Doc..." and leaned down and kissed her again.

He poured all the tenderness he felt into that kiss, letting himself go, thinking of nothing but her. And then, still kissing her, he rolled onto his back and pulled her with him, because he wanted her close to him, all-over close, and didn't want to have to worry about keeping his weight off her. With a little encouragement from him she brought her knees up along his sides. He slipped his hand between them, found her soft and moist and ready, opened her with his fingers and eased himself inside her, so gently, so tenderly.

Warmly sheathed in her body, he drew his knees up against her bottom, wrapped his arms around her and pulled her down onto his chest. In that way he touched her everywhere he could, so that it felt as if she were a part of him, as if he couldn't separate the parts of him from the parts of her. He'd never known such closeness.

He began to move, then, but so slowly, so gently, that it didn't disturb the closeness. Their bodies moved to one rhythm, gradually heated and swelled together, merged and melted in one sweet, shimmering peace. It was a joining as simple and warm as sunshine, as nurturing as a soft spring rain, miraculous and joyful as every new life.

For a long time afterward, neither of them moved, or spoke. But because Wolf knew that some of her shivering were sobs, and that the warmth he felt in the hollow of his neck was partly her tears, and because he couldn't bear not knowing, he finally stroked the hair back from her face, kissed the top of her head and murmured, "Doc? Why are you crying?"

She sniffed and in a blurred, liquid voice said, "I'm not sure I can explain."

"Try."

"I think—" She raised herself to look down at him and said in a teary little rush, "I think I'm scared."

The tenderness billowed inside him, until he thought he'd explode with it. "Hey," he said huskily, "you got nothing to be scared of. Not anymore." He took her face between his hands and stroked away her tears with his thumbs. "It's all over—you're safe."

"No—that's not—" She caught back the words along with her breath and looked at him searchingly, tracing the bony ridges and whiskery hollows of his face with her fingers. "*Is* it over, Jack? For you, I mean." She touched the rings that lay nestled in the hollow of his throat. "Is it really over?"

His hand moved reflexively, and closed around the rings. Frank's wedding ring, the one he'd held in his sweaty palm as his brother's best man. The tiny heart ring he'd given Carrie for her birthday—her third, if he remembered it right. Then his fingers relaxed, and he slowly drew the chain off over his head, carefully dropped it into one of the shoes that lay on the sand beside him. He'd keep the rings, but not next to his skin, a constant, burning reminder of his loss. He put them away, along with his memories.

Wolf closed his eyes, wrapped his arms around the doc and pulled her back down where she belonged. "Yeah," he said on a long exhausted sigh, feeling the last of the cold and the horror drain out of him. "It's really over."

Just outside the motel-room door, Terry paused with her arms full of packages. I can't believe it, she thought, as her heart performed the now-familiar miracle. Just look at the *change* in him.

Through the open, uncurtained window she could see Jack clearly. He was sitting on the foot of the bed holding Angelita on his knees, the way she'd seen him hold her once before—like a choirboy holding a hymn book. It was obvious he didn't know Terry was there, because the look on his face was utterly besotted, and the sounds she heard coming through the screen were—well, there was only one way to describe them: they were *croons*.

"Baby talk, Jack?" she said on a ripple of teasing laughter as she let herself into the room with her key, wistfully longing to share that precious moment, knowing her presence would shatter it.

"Hey!" Looking indignant, Jack lifted Angelita to his shoulder and began to pat her vigorously and jiggle her up and down. "I was just...singing to her. Yeah, that's right. I was tryin' to convince the little rascal she should go to sleep. I don't know what's the matter with her, Doc. I did what you told me to—changed her diaper, fed her, burped her—but she doesn't seem to want to go back to sleep. See? Look at her—she's just lookin' around, like this little black-eyed periscope...didn't you?" He started to add something to Angelita in what was most certainly a croon, then caught himself and gave a blustery cough to cover it up.

Terry dropped her packages onto the bed and sat down beside him. "Hi, angel—feel like playing, huh?" she whispered as she reached over to lift a feather of Jack's hair away from the two bright shoe-button eyes that were peering solemnly over his shoulder. His hair felt slippery-clean and smelled of an unfamiliar brand of shampoo, something vaguely herbal. She had to fight an impulse to weave her fingers through it.

"Oops," he said suddenly, addressing the baby, whose fragile neck muscles had just given up the task of holding her head erect. "Here, what are you doin, darlin'?"

Angelita's head wobbled, then clunked down onto his shoulder. Murmuring soothing nonsense, Jack cradled her head in his big, rough hand and pressed it against his smooth, clean-shaven jaw.

Terry's heart gave a queer little flutter.

It wasn't just that he looked so different, she thought, or even that he seemed so much younger, so much more relaxed. But every now and then she caught him in an attitude almost of wonder, like a man just awakened from a long, long sleep.

"Did you get through to your office?" he asked in a low murmur, unconsciously beginning to joggle Angelita on his shoulder.

"Yeah, I did, finally. Everything's fine. Carl had already told them I'd been held up, so they've been frantically rescheduling patients. I told them to reschedule tomorrow, too, and refer any emergencies to Dr. Pauling— he and I back each other up occasionally—so we don't have to rush back tonight...."

She gave a self-conscious little cough and bounced up off of the bed. In a voice just a bit too loud she said, "I talked to Carl, too. I told him about Angelita."

"Yeah?" Jack sounded curiously wary. "What did he have to say?"

Terry laughed. "About the same thing we did, at first. 'You're kidding!' He's never run into a situation like this, either. But...he said he'd look into it, and hopefully get started on the legalities. I know it's going to be incredibly complicated, and involve God knows how many agencies...." Her voice trailed off. She looked at the baby, who had dropped off to sleep with her head tucked in the hollow under Jack's chin, mouth open, softly snoring.

She took a deep breath and turned abruptly away. "Anyway, for now he thinks I should keep her with me—says we'll declare her a medical emergency, if we have to. And he says not to worry, that we'll probably just end up handling it like a private adoption. He knows a lawyer who specializes in foreign adoptions, and I guess there are an awful lot of people eagerly waiting...."

There was a little silence. Jack muttered, "Yeah, I imagine..." then frowned and cleared his throat. "Hey, it feels like she's asleep. You want to take her?"

"What? Oh...sure." She moved close to him, but instead of handing over his burden, Jack seemed to be waiting for her to take it. She hesitated, then carefully eased her hands under the sleeping baby. But no matter how careful she was, she couldn't avoid touching *him*. Feeling the soaking warmth of his chest against the backs of her hands, the hard resilience of muscle, the pulsing of his heartbeat. Touching him for the first time since that morning, remembering waking up naked in his arms.

Heat enveloped her. She felt clumsy, tongue-tied.

"You going to put her right there, in the middle of the bed?"

"Yes, sure—why not?" All her confidence deserted her. Suddenly she couldn't even bring herself to look at him. "She should be all right there—she's too young to creep or turn over, but I guess we could put pillows around her, just in case."

"Here," Jack said, "I have a better idea." He pulled a drawer out of the dresser and turned triumphantly. "*Voilà*— instant crib."

Terry gave a breathy gasp of laughter. "That's funny," she said faintly, momentarily caught in a little eddy of déjà vu. "I think I remember...my brother used to sleep in a dresser drawer."

"Yeah?" Jack's eyes flared at her for an instant, a brief but vivid reminder of the wolf. "Well, then we know it works. Here—we put a towel in the bottom, see—like this."

Terry stood silently while she watched him turn the drawer into a cosy bed, holding Angelita and slowly rotating her upper body back and forth. Rocking the baby, soothing herself.

I don't understand myself today, she thought, suddenly and inexplicably miserable. She didn't understand what this feeling was inside her or why she should feel so awkward and strange, so distanced from Jack, when last night, just a few hours ago, she'd never felt closer to anyone in her life. She wanted that closeness again—*longed* for it. But—and this was the crux of her misery—she didn't have any idea what *Jack* wanted. She couldn't read him today, that was the problem—couldn't read him at all! The only thing she knew for certain was that last night he'd needed her; beyond that she was blind, uncertain, as frightened as a child lost in a strange city. She wasn't going to presume anything, that was for sure! She wasn't going to be like her mother, mistaking sex for affection and mutual need for love.

If only they could have talked about some of this! But the morning had been so rushed and busy—they'd had to get up and be dressed before the fishermen came, get the plane ready to go, get everything packed and the clinic locked up. Then they'd gone to pick up Angelita at the Ortiz house, which had taken longer than expected because Mrs. Ortiz had insisted they eat breakfast, and no one in the family had seemed able to understand why Angelita couldn't just stay there with them. Because of that, leave-taking had been a prolonged and tearful process, with each of the Ortiz chil-

dren insisting on holding the baby one more time, hugging
and kissing her goodbye.

Then there had been the matter of deciding where to go.
Jack had been all business about that, as if the only thing on
his mind was getting her back where she belonged. As if the
responsibility for her safety were weighing heavily on him.
As if, she thought miserably, he couldn't wait to get rid of
it—and her.

The plane needed fuel—that was top priority—so Jack
had decided first to make the relatively short hop across the
peninsula to Mulege, which also had the advantage of having a hotel right next to the airstrip where they could rest and
freshen up. But beyond that, there'd been no chance to talk
on the flight—Angelita hadn't taken to air tavel at all well
and had screamed the whole time.

In Mulege, while Jack was seeing to the needs of the
plane, Terry had taken care of checking in, getting Angelita fed and settled down, and had indulged herself in the
luxuries of hot running water and soap. When Jack had returned she'd turned both the bathroom and the baby-sitting
over to him and had taken a cab, driven by a very fat woman
wearing an orange-and-pink muumuu, into town to shop for
some necessities.

Now she was back, and here was Jack looking scrubbed
and clean-shaven and barely recognizable. And instead of
handling the situation like a responsible adult, just one look,
one touch, and she was behaving like a gawky teenager, not
knowing what to do with her eyes or her hands, wondering
about every word, worrying over hidden meanings, afraid
to expect or reveal too much.

For instance, even as she watched Angelita settle into her
snug nest with her knees pulled under her and her bottom in
the air, even as she noted, with another of those queer little
heart flutters, that Jack had managed to put the diaper on
backward, even then she was wondering *why*. What did it
mean, his making a bed for the baby? Did he have a partic-

ular reason for not wanting a baby sleeping in the middle of the bed, or was she presuming he'd want to make love to her again so soon, or for that matter, ever again?

The self-doubts tumbled in on her like an avalanche. She'd only gotten one room, should she have gotten two? Would he think she was presuming something that wasn't going to happen? She should have at least gotten two beds!

The bed. There it was, right smack in the middle of the room, impossible to avoid looking at or bumping into. What did he expect would happen now? What did she *want* to happen now? What had happened between them last night?

Maybe after all it was just one of those crazy things that happen sometimes in a crisis, where afterward everyone sort of fidgets and looks vaguely embarrassed, and finally all concerned agree it never really happened, shake hands and go their separate ways.

I hate this, she thought in bitter self-disgust. I'm a thirty-five-year-old doctor and I haven't exactly led a sheltered life. You'd think I'd know how to handle this better!

Oh, but she didn't...she didn't! She was discovering that falling in love was every bit as terrifying at thirty-five as it was at fifteen, and all the education in the world couldn't have helped her.

"Doc? Hey—come back!"

She shook her head and laughed to disguise the tremor in her voice. "I'm sorry—what did you say?"

"I said, what did you buy?" Jack gave the box of disposable diapers he was holding a toss, caught it and grinned. "Besides Pampers."

Draped across the bedspread, casually propped on one elbow, shirt half-unbuttoned, he didn't seem to be suffering any of her self-doubt. Gone was that canine itchiness, the feverish tension, the brittleness and cynicism that had once kept her so edgy and troubled. Now he seemed all languid grace and masculine confidence, with a gleam of little-boy curiosity in his blue eyes that she found incredibly appealing. And she was more edgy and troubled than ever.

"Uh...clothes and things for Angelita, mostly," she said, feeling out of breath, as if she'd run all the way back from Mulege. "And...uh—"

"What's this?" He'd already picked up one of the larger bags. Terry made an involuntary movement toward the bed.

"Oh—that. That's just...something I bought. For me. I've pretty much exhausted my supply of clean clothes, so I thought I'd better pick up something. You know—a T-shirt, and, uh... It's nothing, really—"

"Yeah? Can I see?"

"Oh—" She made another uncoordinated little motion toward him, but it was too late—the bright, gaudy material was tumbling onto the bedspread. Her fist clenched and unclenched. Heat pumped into her cheeks as she lifted her shoulders in a helpless shrug. "What can I say—it was one of those street stalls—you know the tourist traps. I guess I fell right in...."

She didn't know why in the world she'd bought it, it was nothing she'd ever wear—one of those Mexican-style sundresses with a full skirt and sleeves, and elastic around the neck so it could be worn off-the-shoulders. It wasn't her style and the color—lavender with splashes of poppy and yellow to clash wondrously with her hair—wasn't her color, either.

"Put it on," Wolf said.

Her breath caught. "What?"

He gave the dress a little shake, flicked it so it fanned across the foot of the bed and settled in sinuous billows on a cushion of air. "Come on, I'm serious. I want to see you in it."

She covered her mouth with her fingertips and looked at him as if he'd just set fire to the mattress. The pink in her cheeks wasn't sunburn. A curious warmth poured through him, warmth to match the sunshine flowers in that dress, warmth to rival the heat of embarrassment he could feel coming from her in waves.

It hadn't occurred to him the doc might be shy or self-conscious about her body, but now that he thought about it... There'd been that one incredible moment, of course, when she'd offered her body to the setting sun, but then she hadn't known he was watching. He tried to remember—she did always seem to cover herself from throat to wrists, but he'd thought that was just because of her sensitivity to the sun. Then there was last night, but that had been last night, and the wildness had been in them both. And this morning she'd been awake and dressed before him.

"Doc?" he said wonderingly, and got up off the bed, taking the dress with him.

A small cardboard package fell out of its folds onto the floor. He heard a faint gasp as he bent to pick it up.

Wolf didn't think he'd ever known a moment quite like that one. If ever a situation called for a poker face this was it, but God help him, he just didn't know if he had it in him. The tenderness he felt for her was indescribable; the joy, like an explosion inside him. He wanted to laugh out loud, but he didn't dare; he could feel her embarrassment in almost palpable waves. Please, God, he thought, just let me do this right.

He turned the little packet over in his fingers, frowned at the enraptured couple silhouetted against a gaudy sunset on the front of it, then cleared his throat and drawled, "I don't know, Doc, don't you think this is kind of like lockin' up the barn after the horse has already been stolen? Or in this case, I guess it would be lockin' up the horse...."

It wasn't much, but it did the trick; she burst out laughing. She was still suffering, but at least she had a way to let off some of the tension. While she was doing that, Wolf reached into his shirt pocket and took out the cigarettes he'd picked up in the hotel gift shop earlier, and the other little package he'd bought there along with it. The one almost identical to hers.

"Here," he said handing it to her. "Great minds think alike. At least now we've got a nice selection to choose from."

She gave a few more gulps of laughter, then stopped and looked at him, her eyes going wide with wonder. "You mean, you thought of it, too?" She shook her head, trying hard to regain her composure. "Listen, Jack, I don't want you to think—"

"Hell, yes." Wolf shouted, angry at himself suddenly, remembering that he'd sworn never to rob her of her pride again and wishing he'd somehow handled things better. "Of course I thought about it! I'm not completely irresponsible, even if I acted like it last night—"

"Jack, I don't want you to think—"

"Dammit, Doc, the last thing I want to do—"

"—that just because of last night I expect—"

"Doc, for once, just shut up, give me those damn things and go put on the dress!"

Chapter 14

It surprised him when she did as he told her without a word of argument. And it didn't make him happy. He hated the uncertainty in her eyes, the vulnerable look to her mouth and chin. He knew he'd done something to give her that look, and was sorry for it, just as two nights ago he'd felt sorry about taking her pride. Damn it, he didn't want her meek acquiescence! He wanted her yelling back at him, proud and haughty—and yes, a little bit bossy, too. He felt an angry helplessness inside, as if he'd accidentally broken something beautiful, and didn't know how to put it back together again.

He took out his cigarettes and lit one without thinking, then looked over at the little one asleep in the dresser drawer and went and blew the smoke out through the window screen. He smoked the cigarette standing outside the door, watching the play of sunlight through trailing vines on the adobe paving stones and thinking about how quickly and irrevocably people's lives could change.

The trouble was, those changes had hit him so hard and so fast he was still reeling from the blows. He figured he was missing some pieces himself, and before he could even think about the doc, or what he was going to do with the rest of his life, and where she fit into it, he had to figure out how to put himself back together. He needed to crawl into a cave somewhere and let himself heal. The one thing he knew for sure was that when he crawled out of that cave he wanted Doc there waiting for him. He just didn't know what to do about her in the meantime.

Damn it, he didn't want to hurt her. And he was finding out that she was a whole lot more fragile than he'd first thought. Tough, but fragile. In a way she reminded him of wildflowers. The basic plant could survive just about anything, but the blossoming, ah, the blossoming, so rare, so lovely, so easily crushed. He wanted to cup her in his hands and shield her from the buffeting of the wind and rain, shelter her from the burning sun. He wanted her blossoming for him, and him alone, over and over again.

It was a new experience for him, this concern for someone else's well-being, this desire to nurture and protect—one of the changes that had him so off stride and out of balance—one of the most frightening changes. He didn't have much practice caring for someone, and wasn't sure he knew how to go about it. He just knew that thinking about the doc's vulnerability and worrying about hurting her was making his stomach flutter and his palms sweat.

He threw down his cigarette and crushed it with his boot, then frowned at his watch. He wondered what was taking Doc so long with that dress.

Who am I kidding? Terry thought, surveying her reflection in the bathroom mirror. *This isn't me.*

She closed her eyes and groaned inwardly. But it *was* her, and that was the problem. Putting on this ridiculous dress hadn't magically transformed her, it only made her, well, her *deficiencies* all the more obvious. To illustrate her own point she stuck out her tongue at her reflection in self-mockery, threw out her chest and put her hands on the puffed bodice of the dress, right over the two bright red hibiscus flowers where her breasts should have been. The dress and the flowers promptly deflated.

And that was only the beginning. Her shoulders were too broad, her collarbones too prominent, her skin too white. Except, of course, for the lovely bright pink sunburned patches on her cheeks and nose. *Her nose*—oh God yes, she couldn't forget her nose! When she was being kind to herself she usually thought of it as high-bridged, but who was she kidding? That was a bump—no two ways about it. All her features were like that—angular and bony—except for her lips, which were much too full and didn't match the rest of her face. Her hair was way too curly, and had a tendency to get frizzy around her face. And she had pale eyelashes.

For the first time since the painful, angry years of her youth she closed her eyes and prayed the familiar teenager's prayer: Oh please, God, just this one time, couldn't you *please* make me pretty?

When she opened her eyes and found no discernible changes in her reflection, she stared intently at it and tried to think why it should suddenly matter so much to her what she looked like. She'd accepted her looks long ago; she was comfortable with herself. She *was*. Her appearance had never seemed to matter to Robert, one way or the other, and last night—and the night before that—it apparently hadn't bothered Jack much, either.

Last night. She closed her eyes again as a tingling pink wash crept under her skin—that was another negative, blushing—and she thought, Oh, but that was last night! Last night had been . . . night, and the things that happened had just . . . happened. This was different, planning to make love, preparing for it. Even if it was what she wanted, even if her body was tingling with wanting, and parts of her were already swelling and pulsing in anticipation of his touch, it was different.

Oh, God, please make me prettier!

Wolf was leaning against the doorjamb thinking about lighting up another cigarette when she finally came out of the bathroom. For a minute or two he didn't say anything, just looked at her.

She'd twisted most of her hair into a knot on top of her head, leaving her neck bare save for some loose curls around her ears and on her nape. She had a long, slender neck, Wolf discovered. With her hair up like that, and along with her aristocratic nose and naturally regal bearing, she made him think of ballet dancers and Egyptian princesses. He was enjoying the new image so much it took him a minute or two to notice that she looked scared to death.

He straightened slowly, came in and closed the door behind him. With his hand still on the doorknob he paused and drawled softly, "Well, hello there, Little Red Riding Hood."

She looked startled, then gave a little gulp of laughter and looked away. After a moment she lifted chagrined eyes to his and murmured, "Is it that obvious?"

"Mm-hmm, it is to me. I told you Doc, you can't keep anything from me, I can read you like a book."

She gave another spurt of that distressed laughter. Her voice trembled slightly. "That's not fair, Jack. I can't read you at all."

He prowled toward her, every nerve in him suddenly hungry and eager to touch, conscious of even the press of his feet against the floor, the rub of his skin against the fabric of his jeans. His palms tingled, already speeding pleasure-impulses to his nerve centers in anticipation of that first sweet contact with her naked shoulders, making his body swell and his voice grow rich and husky. "I don't know, Doc...you read me pretty well last night."

"That was . . . different." Her breath sighed between her lips as his hands just brushed the satin-smooth curve of her shoulders. He felt the tiny upward lift of her chest, the delicate ripple of her swallow.

He bent to touch his smile to the rose-petal edge of her ear, letting his warm breath pour into it and overflow down the side of her neck. "How different?" he whispered, taking a tiny sip of her earlobe.

"You weren't—" She gasped softly as he took a bigger sip. He felt her sway, and cupped his hands around her shoulders in gentle support. His thumbs found the silky ridges, the down-filled hollows of her collarbones. She sighed. "You weren't . . . hiding from me last night."

"And I'm hiding from you now?" he murmured, moving his lips along the side of her neck.

She managed to nod, but her head was wilting. He slid his hand along the top of her shoulder and up the side of her neck, gently encouraging her head to nest in his palm.

"I don't know . . . I didn't know—" she whispered, and had to swallow. "Um . . . how you feel about . . . this." *This* was his mouth, traveling up and down the virginal white column of her throat. Sharp furrows in her forehead betrayed the effort even the simplest of words cost her. "I, um . . . didn't know what you wanted . . . if you wanted . . ." With a gallant surge of will, she lifted her head and focused an accusing frown on him. "I didn't know you were going to buy condoms!"

Laughing, he pushed his fingers into her hair and gave her head a shake. "Well, hell, I didn't know you were, either!"

They laughed together gently, softly, looking into each other's eyes. Hers were shining with laughter's tears; fascinated, still cradling her head in one hand, he fanned the fingers of the other across her face, touching the beads of moisture in the corners of her eyes, smoothing them down the sides of her face in a glimmering trail.

"So," she whispered huskily, lifting her face, moving with his touch, "I guess you can't read me as well as you thought."

He looked deeply and intently into her eyes; then, still looking, leaned over and tasted her. "I said I could read your *feelings*, Doc...." He tasted again, and again, then brushed back her hair and held it out of his way, as if it might help him to see inside her. "There's still an awful lot I don't know about what makes you tick. An awful lot I'd like to know."

A tear trickled from the corner of her eye—not laughter, just emotion. More emotion than she could hold. She sniffed and said shakily, "Well, there's a lot I'd like to know about you, too."

He looked at her for a while longer, then kissed her again, slowly this time. Deeply. Her eyes closed and so did his. With a sigh he sank into her warmth and she tangled her tongue with his. "Hmm..." he said a long time later, his voice thickened and soft, "it seems neither one of us is big on talking. This could take awhile...."

"Mmm...maybe—" She swayed drunkenly back into his kiss, and when she came up for air, gasped, "Maybe we should play match for answers ... like we did before."

"Uh-uh." He held her face captive between his hands, stroking moisture across her lips with his thumb. "Not this time, Doc." There was a harshness in his voice she didn't understand, and then a gentle little smile, as if he were sorry for it. "Anything you tell me I want you to tell me of your own free will."

"But I do want to tell you," she whispered, with a rush of emotion that was almost panic, desperately wanting not to disappoint him, wanting to give everything she had to give, finding for the first time in her life that there was nothing she wanted to hold back. "Ask me." She shook her head, catching at his wrists. "Ask me anything. I'll tell you if I can."

"Anything?" His chuckle rippled across the base of her throat as he laid her gently back against the leather-hard sling of his arm. "Maybe later. I don't feel much like talking right now." His fingers dived beneath the elastic top of her dress.

She gasped when she felt the sudden rush of cold air over her skin, and made an involuntary movement with her hand. Jack's hand began a slow glide upward over her ribs and the meager swell of her breast, then stopped. He eased her upright and separated himself from her, leaving her trembly and shell-shocked.

He mumbled, "Hold it right there a minute...." Numb and shaking, she watched him move to the windows and pull the curtains closed, then turn back to her, frowning. "Feel better now?"

She nodded, but it was a lie. She felt ridiculous, forlorn and abandoned, inadequate.

Jack growled softly, "Come 'ere, Doc." But then it was he who moved, coming back to her with that lithe, canine prowl. He caught her wrists and pulled them out, away from her body. "Don't hide yourself."

She shook her head, wanting to crawl into a hole, or better yet, the sanctuary of his arms, and hide herself there. But he held her still and away from him and raked her naked breasts with a hard, hungry glare. "I want to look at you...."

She gave a helpless, humiliated laugh. "Well, there's not much to see...."

"Doc—" His voice was so harsh, his grip on her wrists so hard she thought he was angry. Then he shook his head and pulled her close, gently enfolded her and whispered into her hair. "Ah, Doc...I want to make love to you with all the lights blazing, but I won't, not until you want it, too. I just want to know one thing. How in the hell did you get to be...what, thirty?"

"Thirty-five."

"Hey, really? So am I." Well, almost. It would be a year and a half before he was thirty-five, but he wasn't going to tell her that—not just yet. He found it intriguing that she was a little older than he was, but he had an idea she might not feel the same way about it, not until she'd got some of her confidence back.

So he framed her face with his hand and pulled back again, just enough to look searchingly into her face. "What I want to know is, how did you get to be thirty-five years old without knowing how beautiful you are?"

"Jack," she chided gently, shaking her head, "you don't have to say that. I know what I look like. Honest."

"The hell you do!" He pulled back from her a little farther and watched her shrink reflexively under his gaze. "If you had any idea what you look like, or how sexy you are, you wouldn't be trying to hide yourself like this!"

Puzzled creases appeared between her eyes, as if he'd spoken in a foreign langue. "Sexy? Me?"

Anger swamped him. Dammit, how could she be so smart about some things and so dumb about this? "Geez, Doc! How in the hell were you married—" And then he saw the look in her eyes and knew that he was doing the one thing he'd told himself he'd never do again—hurting her. So he banked his anger and gentled his voice and murmured with a sigh, "Doc...do something for me. Just close your eyes."

"Close my eyes?"

But she didn't, just went on looking at him, looking so confused, so lost, that finally he skimmed his hand lightly over her forehead and down, closing her eyes for her. "Yeah, that's right," he said on a long, slow expiration. "I'm shutting mine, too. Now, pretend it's night. It's dark, and there's just you and me. And I'm touching...."

Her dress was down to her waist already, held there with a sash. He left it for the time being and put his hands on her sides, just under her arms. He felt the sharp, soft sigh of her breath; the outward press of her ribs against his palms.

"Ah . . . Doc," he whispered, not trying to hide the shaking in his voice. "I just wish there was some way you could know what this feels like. Your skin is so soft . . . I can feel your heart beating—so fast it feels like it's trying to jump into my hands."

Very gently, in slow motion, he moved his hands to cover her breasts. "Yeah . . ." he growled as he heard the faint sucking sound of her catching breath, felt the heating, the almost imperceptible swelling. He began gentle, circling motions and almost instantly felt her nipples bead and nudge against the nerve-rich centers of his palms.

"Ah . . . Doc—" His chest felt so full, words almost choked him. "This feels so good, to you *and* to me. Your breasts are so responsive, I just barely touch them and your nipples get hard, and so sensitive they almost hurt, don't they? I know they do. I want to kiss them, Doc. I want to put my mouth here . . . do you want me to do that?"

Her only answer was a whimpering sound. She was already breathing in shallow sips, leaning against him, needing his support, so he guided her to the bed, pushed her down on the edge and laid her gently back. Lying beside her, he encircled her breast with his hand, bent down and laved it—first lightly, then roughly—with his tongue. When he drew it into his mouth she moaned and drew one knee up and in, rubbing her thighs together.

"Where do you feel it?" he whispered, letting the words themselves, his tongue, his breath tease her nipple to unbearable tightness. "Do you feel it all inside you? Deep iside, deep down here. . . ." He skimmed his hand up along the inside of her thigh, pushing under her dress, pushing it impatiently out of the way. Then he cupped her warm, pulsing mound, rubbed the sensitive places through a slippery barrier of nylon, feeling the heat, the moistness, the swelling and the wanting.

He lifted his head and whispered, "Doc, open your eyes. Look at me." She made a fretful sound and moved her body sinuously, rocking against his hand. He leaned over her, pressing his body all along hers, and growled against her ear, "Come on Doc, I want you to see me...us...how good you feel to me...." His fingers pressed deeper into the slick, giving fabric, and he felt her lift against his hand. "Do you know," he breathed, "how sexy that is? The way you respond to my touch... Your whole body is so responsive... I want to touch every part of you."

He raised his head and looked down at her; she looked back at him with drunken and wondering eyes, rose-flushed skin and bee-stung lips. He closed his eyes and groaned aloud. "Oh, Lord. Doc, I can't look at you, or I'm going to have to end this before I want to. Just—" He caught his breath as he felt her hands skim down his sides and back, searching for his belt buckle. "No, baby, don't touch me, or I'm afraid I'll explode. Not yet, I have to kiss you first. I want to kiss you here, Doc, do you mind?"

He chuckled a little, when he asked that, because he knew she was beyond words. Then he put his mouth where his hand had been. He swirled his tongue over the thin-stretched fabric, wetting it, probing the warm tumescence underneath, and felt her rib cage lift in sharp, shallow pants. "Easy," he murmured, soothing her. "It's all right."

But then he wound his fingers in the nylon fabric and pulled it, pulled it taut until it slipped between her folds, rubbing, pressing intolerably on her most sensitive places. He covered her petals with his mouth, followed the line of the fabric with his tongue, probing, teasing, until she arched and moaned, until reaching for something to hold on to, she tangled her fingers in his hair. He lifted his head just for a moment and whispered, "Open for me now, baby, that's right."

With his hands he gently spread her, until there was no part of her that did not lay open to the hungry forays of his fingers, mouth and tongue. For a while he lost himself in the dizzying, intoxicating mysteries of her body, aware of nothing but the heat, scent and textures of her, the small, unconscious sounds she made. He felt her quickening, tightening panic, her shattering release, and still he didn't stop, although she begged him to, only gentling his stroking until he felt her relax and the cycle begin all over again.

This time, though, by the time he'd brought her once more to the edge and tipped her over, her cries had become sobs, and her hands, clutching his shoulders, had real desperation in them. So he gathered her close, wrapped her in his arms and nurtured and comforted her until her sobs and shivers had subsided and she lay peacefully at last, her face buried in the humid curve of his neck.

"I don't understand," she said after a while, with a little gulping sniff.

"What don't you understand?" Wolf murmured, stroking her hair.

"How I could be like this. I never was before. What are you doing to me, Jack?" Her voice was high and wondering, almost like a child's.

He raised his head, tenderly kissed the top of hers, then pulled her over so she lay draped on top of him, her legs sweetly entwined with his. The pressure on the front of his jeans was excruciating, but he didn't want to do anything about it—not yet.

"It's not me," he said huskily, "don't you know that? How come you're a doctor and you don't know that? It's *you*—you have this beautiful, strong, healthy body—it's all there. All I have to do is touch you—the responses are yours. You are one helluva sexy lady, Doc—face it."

"But that's just it." She sighed, and settled uneasily on his chest. "I never was before. I was never able to... respond to Rob—to my husband like that."

"Yeah?" Wolf lifted his head briefly, then lay back and looked at the ceiling. He wouldn't have been human if a part of him hadn't rejoiced in that, but he was curious, too. Curious, and even angry. "Hey—" he said with an edge of roughness in his voice, "If you couldn't respond to your husand in...how many years of marriage—"

"Seven."

"*Seven years?* Geez, Doc. Let me tell you something—it wasn't your fault!"

"Then whose was it?" she asked, answering his anger with quiet logic. "It wasn't Robert's. Robert was kind, and loving, and patient. I just couldn't respond to him like I should have. I don't know why."

"Maybe," Wolf rasped, "you just didn't love him."

Her voice was very soft. "That's what he said. He said I was aloof. I always thought that was just a euphemism for frigid."

Wolf snorted. "Frigid—there's a word you don't hear much anymore. Doc, if you're frigid, *I'm* Little Red Riding Hood!"

She gave a snuffling laugh and turned her face against his chest. After a moment, she raised her head and looked at him with searching, troubled eyes. "I did love him, though, Jack. That's why I didn't understand, and thought there must be something basically wrong with me—maybe scars from my childhood, something to do with my mother, I don't know. Robert was everything to me—the father who abandoned me, the brother I lost, the best friend I never had."

Everything, Wolf thought, but a lover.

"That's why I felt like such a failure when it ended—I felt as if I'd let him down, somehow."

Personally, Wolf was of the opinion that it was the other way around, that pretty much everybody had failed *her*, right from day one. And it had come to him quite suddenly that he couldn't think of anything he'd rather spend the rest of his life doing than making it up to her.

But instead of telling her that, he tightened his arms around her and said into the curls on her temple, "Doc, I don't want to talk about your ex-husband right now, do you? What I'd really like to do is test the resilience of those new responses of yours. Are you game?''

There was a little pause. Then she drew a shaky breath and said, "I don't know. Touch me and let's find out." She gave an experimental little wiggle, rubbing her front on his front until he groaned aloud.

"Doc," he gasped as he rolled her over and pressed her against the mattress, "you keep doin' that and you won't have time to respond ... Doc—''

Incredible, Terry thought. After everything that had happened, the whole emotional roller coaster of a weekend, and it had all come down to this: she'd never felt so happy.

It didn't really make a whole lot of sense, considering she was lying in a Baja motel-room bed, in a tangle of sheets and discarded clothing, intimately entwined with a man she still knew next to nothing about, and that asleep in a dresser drawer next to the bed there was an abandoned baby whose welfare and future had been unexpectedly thrust into her keeping. But in spite of those things—or perhaps because of them?—she was utterly and completely happy.

She lay awake in the waning afternoon, listening to Jack's peaceful breathing, trying to think why it should be so. Trying to think why she should feel so somnolent, so relaxed curled next to his body, when she'd never been much of a cuddler before. But his heartbeat, pumping so strongly against her cheek, seemed as much a part of her as her own, and her hand seemed to fit the hard concavity of his belly like a small wild creature in its own nest. It was hard for her to tell where she left off and he began.

Jack. She said his name silently, trying out the sound of it in her mind. *Jack Wolf.* She felt an odd, effervescent tingling all through her. So this is what it feels like, she thought in awe—falling in love. Not like a bolt of lightning or an explosion of fireworks, but more like a gentle, crystalline rain, soaking into the depths of her being, bringing feelings to life, making her feel as young and fresh and fertile as springtime.

Fertile. Her eyes slid unbidden to the box of condoms on the nightstand. They'd used them, of course, although they'd both have preferred not to, and had spent some giddy time joking and complaining about the inconvenience. They weren't complete idiots. But Terry was suddenly thinking about the night up on the mountain, the heaviness, the nursing ache, that strange, maternal yearning. And she thought about last night, and what Jack had said earlier about locking up the barn after the horse had been stolen. She listened to Angelita's soft snores and stirred restlessly.

"What is it, Doc?" Jack mumbled sleepily. "Are you sore?"

"No," Terry whispered, "not at all." It was true—she didn't hurt anywhere. He'd been so incredibly, devastatingly gentle.

"Then what's wrong? I can feel it—you're tense. Can't you sleep?"

"I was just thinking—" But she couldn't tell him what she'd been thinking. Couldn't tell him she'd been wondering what it might feel like to be pregnant, to have a child of her own. A baby... But who was she kidding? She didn't know how to be a mother. She was a *doctor,* she didn't have time to take care of a baby. It was out of the question. Impossible. So instead she murmured, "I was wondering why you nearly always call me Doc, and not by my name. I asked you once before, but you didn't answer me."

"Hmm..." His voice was furry with fatigue. "I guess it's because I never did think you looked like a Terry. Terry seems like a freckle-faced tomboy to me. I don't know...I thought you should have a queen's name—Katherine, or Elizabeth, or maybe something...softer. Anne, maybe."

"Really?" Terry said wonderingly. "Is that how you see me?"

He chuckled softly and pulled her closer, resting his chin on her curls. "Well, it was, for a while. Not anymore, though. I think maybe I'm beginning to see a little bit of Terry in you—a few more freckles, maybe, and we'll see...." His voice grew thoughtful; one hand traced the length of her back, from her neck to her bottom and back up again. "But I think it's too late, anyway, Doc. I think you're always gonna be just Doc to me."

Always. That sounded an awful lot like a promise to her. She snuggled down into the warmth and security of it and slept.

When Terry woke sometime later, it was to the familiar snorts and snuffles of Angelita waking and wanting to be fed. Jack must have heard it at almost the same moment, because they both sat up together, struggling to untangle themselves, both saying groggily at almost the same moment, "Stay put—I'll get her."

Jack was quicker. He was first to get himself sorted out and upright and mobile, leaving Terry to enjoy the luxury of a good stretch, and the joy of watching him walk across the room, lithe, naked, and completely unself-conscious. Her heart performed the now-familar acrobatics as he bent down to pick up Angelita, thigh muscles flexing, back muscles rippling and pulling in well-defined patterns. And when he turned, and she saw that tiny little baby cuddled against his broad masculine shoulder...

Oh God, she thought as he carefully placed the baby in the middle of the bed and lay back down beside her. That's it—I'm a goner!

They lay facing each other with Angelita between them, watching her stretch and squirm and make faces.

"There," Jack said, "*that* was a smile!"

"Uh-uh," Terry corrected him, "that one was gas."

"Like hell ... I know a smile when I see one."

Very soon, though, Angelita tired of games and began to fuss in earnest. Terry pulled on the Mexican dress and got up to get a disposable diaper and the last bottle of soy formula from her medical pack.

Jack got up, too, and while Terry was feeding Angelita, took a quick shower and dressed.

"I'm starving," he announced when he came out of the bathroom. "You know, what we ought to do is go and have a nice dinner in Mulege—candles on the table, cold margaritas, the whole bit. My treat." He leaned over and kissed her, just lingeringly enough to make her heart rate kick into second gear. "What do you say?"

She smiled at him and nodded toward the greedily sucking baby in her arms. "You're forgetting—we don't have a sitter."

"Oh. Yeah, right." He looked almost comically nonplussed. "Tell you what—you stay here, take care of the little one, and I'll go see if I can find us something to eat—okay?"

"Okay," she whispered. Quivering with tenderness, she watched him tuck in his shirttail, sit down to put on his boots and stand up again to tuck away his wallet and cigarettes, thinking how good it was to watch a man—her man—do those simple things.

Almost to the door, he hesitated and came back. Without saying anything, or even looking her way, he picked up his sports bag and laid it on the bed, zipped it open and took out the gun. She didn't say anything, either, just sat quietly and watched him check the chamber, set the safety, and tuck the gun away in the waistband of his Levi's, out of sight inside his shirt. She understood why he might still feel a need to carry it, and she forgave him for bringing the ugliness and horror back into the room. But she found that she was moving slowly and rhythmically back and forth, back and forth, rocking Angelita, soothing herself.

"What are those for?" she asked in a too-bright voice as, almost in an afterthought, Jack slipped a pack of playing cards into his shirt pocket, along with his cigarettes. "Planning to find a game?"

Jack laughed, a reprise of his old sardonic chuckle. "You never know—might have a chance to pick up a few pesos— just in case the plastic wears thin." His smile slipped awry, and became poignant again. "I gave all my cash to Mr. Ortiz, Doc—for the pickup."

"Oh." She stared at him, all at once intrigued. "Are you a gambler? A professional, I mean?" It had just occurred to her that she didn't really have any idea what he did for a living, when he wasn't hunting down hit men. It would be almost *too* wild, she thought, if she'd managed to fall in love with a gambler after all her vows to avoid her mother's mistakes!

She wasn't really surprised to discover, on further reflection, that it didn't make any difference at all in the way she felt about him. And maybe that was the truth that explained her mother. When it came to feelings, there wasn't really any choice after all.

"I have been, at times," Jack said, watching her with a return of his old intensity. "I've done a lot of things, at times. . . . Rodeoing, trucking, motorcycle racing—hell, believe it or not, I've even been a cop." He paused, one hand on the door frame, thinking about it. "What I'm best at, though—besides poker—I guess, is fixing things."

"Fixing things?"

"Yeah—like customizing and reconditioning cars. Making things new again. My dad had—has—a shop. I guess I picked it up from him. . . ." His voice trailed off. He laughed softly, shaking his head and watching his boot rub a hole in the floor.

"What's so funny?" Terry murmured.

"I was just thinking. It's ironic—I'm the one that had the sitcom childhood. Shoot—my mom was Donna Reed, my dad was Father Knows Best, and my brother and I...I guess we were Wally and the Beave. He was the fair-haired boy and I was always in trouble.'' He looked up at her and shrugged, smiling a sad, crooked little smile. ''I'm the black sheep, Doc. That's what I am, and what I'll always be.''

He gave her a mocking salute, and was gone.

She sat still for several minutes, torn without quite knowing why. Oh, but she did know why. Though her instincts told her it wasn't so, the facts—the man himself—told her she'd gone and done what she'd sworn she'd never do—fallen in love unwisely. With a black sheep, a rogue and a gambler! She was her mother's daughter, after all.

Oh God, she thought, where are my barricades? This hurts!

When she heard the scrape of boots on the paving stones outside the door her heart gave a leap. Jack had come back. He must have forgotten something, and he'd come back. She wouldn't let him leave again until they'd talked about this. She needed to know, once and for all, what she was getting into. Before it was too late.

The doorknob rattled. Terry gave an exasperated little laugh. That was it, then—he'd forgotten his key. She got up off the bed, still carrying Angelita and the bottle, and went to let him in.

''That was quick, Jack—''

The smile congealed on her lips. Something icy crawled down her spine and turned her knees to water. She opened her mouth to scream, but no sound came out. She backed up automatically, but only took one step before stark terror paralyzed her.

Smiling their almost identically cruel, sensual smiles, the Cruz brothers pushed into the room and closed the door behind them.

Chapter 15

Wolf got about as far as the hotel courtyard before he started to miss her. If it had just been a matter of food, he'd have picked up something right there and gotten himself back to her as fast as he could. There were two reasons why he didn't.

First, there was the look on the doc's face when he left her, the doubting look in her eyes when he'd made that remark about being a black sheep. She couldn't keep anything from him—he'd known instantly what she was thinking. He knew she was sitting in that motel room right now, scared to death, wondering if she was making the same mistake her mother'd made. Wondering what in the hell had happened to her resolve to be strong, and have better judgment.

Well, dammit, she was right to be scared. If she was falling for him, it sure as hell wasn't the smartest thing she'd ever done. And he couldn't think of a single reason why she should, other than the fact that he was falling for her, too, and was absolutely convinced that he was the only one in the world who could ever make her happy. But the fact was, he had nothing whatsoever to offer her, not even a house or a steady job. Not that he wasn't capable of getting both—he just hadn't thought in those terms before. He knew his dad had always dreamed he'd come into the shop with him, and take it over when he retired, a prospect he'd rejected out of hand. Now he wondered if maybe he'd been too busy being the black sheep to realize it might be something he'd enjoy doing, after all.

So he had to do some serious thinking about the doc, and where he—and they—were going to go from here. He didn't know if he had the nerve to ask her to share his life, but he did know that for him, the prospect of life without her in it wasn't even worth considering.

The second reason he didn't turn around and go running back to her then and there had to do with the Smith & Wesson tucked inside the waistband of his jeans. It had occurred to him this morning on the flight across the peninsula that Mulege was about the closest town of any size to El Refugio de Los Angeles on the Trans-Baja Highway. He knew if he were the Cruz brothers, he'd either head here, or south to Loreto. So it was probably a fifty-fifty chance they'd show up sooner or later, and a good bit less than that that they were here already. Neither of those odds made Wolf happy. He'd already checked out the airstrip and the hotel on the quiet, so as not to scare Doc. Now he figured on taking a quick look around town, maybe ask a few questions. And while he was at it, do something he should have done a long time ago—put in a call to the DEA. The Cruz brothers were their problem now. He was done with them.

"What's taking him so long?" Billy prowled the room, pausing to trail the barrel of his gun across the tops of Terry's breasts, just for the pleasure of watching her flinch. "Huh, Red? I'm getting tired of waiting."

Other than that involuntary reflex, Terry didn't move or speak. Billy's sadistic threats and comments no longer fazed her; in the last hour she'd grown almost immune to terror, at least on her own behalf. Her eyes were focused almost hypnotically on Angelita, cradled in Bernardo Cruz's lap, the silky tuft of black hair nestled incongruously against blue denim and cold steel. She could see the baby's fists waving, tiny fingers clutching at nothing, and knew that she was centered on Cruz's face, possibly even smiling at him. Smiling at the man who would blow her to pieces as casually as he would swat a fly.

But though Terry's eyes were on Bernardo and Angelita, her mind concentrated solely on Jack. Searching for him, casting about in the darkness and trying to home in on his frequency, sending out images of danger and warning, broadcasting with laserlike intensity, over and over again. He always said he could read her eyes like a book; her only hope was that he could read her mind as well.

That was the worst of it, Terry thought—the utter *powerlessness*. There was nothing she could do. She didn't dare move or make a sound. Bernardo would kill Angelita, she was absolutely certain of it. And after that she could only pray he would kill her, too. Quickly. She could still hear the horror in Jack's voice.

I don't want to tell you what they did to them, Doc. I can't.

Oh God, she thought, don't let this happen to him again. He'd never survive it. *Please God.*

But she had no way to warn him. No way at all. All she could do was sit still and focus her mind with every ounce of her strength and will. *Jack.*

Wolf was uneasy. There'd been no news of the Cruz brothers in Mulege, but for some reason he wasn't satisfied. He'd been able to make a phone call to his contact in the DEA with the tip on Frank Wolf's killers, so it was only a matter of time before either they or the drug lords took care of the problem. It couldn't be soon enough for him. Just because he wasn't bent on doing it himself anymore didn't mean he'd be resting easy until those two were put away for good.

In spite of those worries, he'd picked up a couple of lobsters at a place he knew of and had spent most of the taxi ride back to the motel thinking about the fun he and Doc were going to have eating them, slowly, with all that warm melted butter.

It wasn't so bad after all, he decided, not having a babysitter.

But now, for some reason, the closer he got to the motel, the more uneasy he felt. It reminded him of the way he used to get when a California Santa Ana wind was blowing— itchy skin and crawly scalp and a particular keening tension that set his teeth on edge. Come to think of it, it was the way he'd felt out there on the desert, right after he'd found the Cruz brothers' footprints.

Gambler's instinct? Or something nagging at the back of his mind that he should have noticed?

Whatever it was, it had been right often enough in the past that he knew better than to ignore it. On his way through the courtyard he stopped and sat down on the edge of the fountain and took off his boots. Figuring anybody who happened to see him was going to think he was plain crazy, he tucked the boots and the boxes with the lobster dinners behind some bougainvillea and continued along the outdoor corridor to his room, cat-silent in his stockinged feet.

A couple of doors from his own he flattened against the wall to listen. Nothing. Silence. Too damn quiet, he thought. Something's not right.

And then he thought, Jack, you are plain crazy. The little one was probably just asleep, and Doc, too. God knows, she should have been exhausted.

He probably *was* a little crazy, considering where he'd been the past six months. Living in hell. A man didn't come out of that all ready for a house in the suburbs and Sunday-afternoon softball games for excitement. Another reason why he'd need to go carefully where the doc was concerned. She didn't need his kind of trouble. No, he thought, he'd better straighten himself out first, and then he'd see about Doc.

Right now, though, all he could think about was getting back to her. He covered the rest of the distance in long, silent strides and put his hand on the doorknob. Then he remembered he needed his key. Damn—did he have it with him, or was he going to have to knock and wake her up? He started to go through his pockets.

And then he heard it. A sound that froze him in his tracks. Angelita's impatient hungry cry, cut off in mid-wail. *Cut off.* The hair on the back of Wolf's neck lifted. He went cold, dead cold. The doc wouldn't have done that. Never in a million years. *Doc wouldn't do that.*

"I'm tellin' you," Billy said, "somethin's wrong. He shoulda been back by now. I think we oughta—"

"Shut up," his brother growled. "I heard something."

"Come on, man. Why don't we just—"

"Sssht!"

Terry rose to her feet in alarm, every nerve and muscle jerking and jumping. Under Bernardo's hand, she could see Angelita's face turning purple; her tiny fists were tense and quivering. A wave of horror engulfed her. Dear God, was he going to smother a baby just to keep her silent? She had to do something.

"Maybe he went to the plane," she gasped in desperation. "Maybe—" Both men turned hard, glittering eyes on her. Tension crackled through the room.

"Plane?" Bernie said in a soft, dangerous voice.

"We...we were going to fly home tonight," Terry babbled, rapidly and wildly improvising. "Maybe he went to get it ready. That's probably where he is—at the airstrip. He'll probably be back any minute. Please—if you'll just—"

"A plane..." Bernie said thoughtfully.

"Hey, that's it, man—he could fly us outta here!"

"Please—" Terry said in a high, desperate whimper, her hands reaching, clutching. "Don't— You're smothering her!"

Either unaware or uncaring, Bernie ignored her. His mind was occupied with the new information, chewing over new possibilities. But all of a sudden something happened inside Terry. Her terror vanished. Cold, quiet rage took its place. Completely unmindful of the consequences, she took two steps—and simply plucked the struggling baby out of Bernie's grasp.

Then she turned her back to him, trying to soothe the frantic infant, bracing herself for the bullet she expected to slam into her body, or at the very least, the grip of cruel, hurting hands. Neither came, and she felt a wonderful surge of strength and power. Maybe it was just the simple matter of taking control and *doing* something. And maybe it was something much more primitive, something to do with holding that infant in her arms. She felt utterly fearless, invincible. Anyone daring to harm her child would have to kill her first!

"Shut her up, goddammit," Bernie snarled. "I have to think."

"Her bottle is in my bag," Terry said calmly.

"Get it. Go on."

As she sat rocking Angelita, listening to her snuffles and gulps, listening to the two men discussing their new plans, she felt absolutely calm, quietly determined. She was going to survive this, somehow. She *knew* it. It was going to be all right. She and Jack and Angelita were going to make it through this. Together. Her heart sang its anthem to him, over and over.

Jack…I know you're with me. We're going to be all right.

Wolf leaned against the wall, cold sweat pouring off him in sheets. God help him, when he got his hands on the doc, he might strangle her himself! What was she thinking of? Didn't she realize what kind of men she was dealing with? When he thought about that might have happened, his legs got weak. If anything happened to Doc…

Now they were talking about taking her and the little one to the plane and waiting for him there. Wolf's mind was racing. Possibilities and scenarios played through his head like high-speed videos. They had a chance. A good chance. But he had to let the doc know he was with her. He had to get a message to her somehow.

He knew he only had a few seconds. Any minute now they were going to come through that door, and when they did, he'd better be long gone. His only hope was to get to the airstrip first and pick his spot. And—damn, he was going to have to go without his boots!

First he had to figure out a way to get that message to Doc. Something she'd understand, and they wouldn't.

Inspiration struck. Please Lord, don't let my hands shake, he prayed, as he took his deck of cards out of his shirt pocket. Crouched on one knee, he shuffled through them, searching for the one he wanted.

"One sound, one stupid move and you and the kid are both dead, you understand?" Bernie's fingers dug viciously into Terry's upper arm.

Willing herself not to gasp or cry out, she nodded and said calmly, "I understand."

"Okay—let's go."

Billy Cruz opened the door and held it. Cradling Angelita, Terry focused on the rectangle of dappled sunlight and began to walk toward it. She could feel the gun, like a knuckle pressing against her ribs. *Jack . . . where are you?*

Just outside the door, a tiny splash of color on the paving stones caught at her vision like a snag on a fishing line. Flower petals, her mind said.

And then her heart cried out, no, not flowers—a playing card! A face card. The jack of hearts.

Jack! Her heart took off like a rocket—soared into the stratosphere. He was here—somewhere. Watching over her, biding his time, waiting his chance. She *felt* him. She could see him in her mind, the lone wolf, pacing along in the shadows just beyond the light.

Her mind was calm, focused. She knew Jack was there, and that he'd wait for his best chance. He only needed one. And she would do her best to give it to him.

Outside the motel's shady courtyard, the heat and light were merciless. The sunlight glanced off the hard-packed airstrip and the white sand beach beyond it like hammer blows. Heat waves shimmered and danced, making the squat buildings and the small planes at the far end of the runway look oddly disembodied, like mirages. Squinting in that terrible glare, Terry strained to pick out the little red-and-white Cessna. She didn't see Jack anywhere. She didn't see anyone.

But he's there, she told herself. He's there somewhere, I know he is. His message told me so. He's here with me . . . I just have to trust him.

The walk seemed endless, the red-and-white Cessna no closer. Angelita fussed and Terry soothed her automatically, ignoring the press of Bernie's gun in her ribs. She could hear sea gulls crying, the distant crash of waves, the almost subaudible hum of heat and tension. And still she saw no one.

Jack, where are you? I know you're here somewhere. I know it. Jack.

"Which one?" Bernie growled.

"There—" Terry pointed. "The red-and-white one."

He gave her a vicious jab with the barrel of the gun. "Okay—we wait inside for your friend. You first—open the door. Nice and slow, now, you understand me? Or I kill the little one first."

Terry nodded. Her hand stretched out, reaching for the door handle.

And suddenly, just like that, she knew where Jack was. She *knew*. He was in the plane. He had to be. He had his gun—he'd be waiting for a clear shot. And she was in the way, again right smack in his line of fire!

She had only a split second to make her decision, and she did it in less. She simply dropped—like a stone. As she went down she twisted her body and wrapped her arms around Angelita to shield her from the fall, and as a result fell hard on her side. Half-stunned, she rolled onto her back, under the fuselage of the plane.

As she rolled, all hell broke loose above and all around her. she heard shouts, gunshots—a terrifying barrage of them. Something struck the calf of her leg—she thought someone had kicked her, until she felt a white-hot, stabbing pain. Lying on her back, she frantically kicked backward, trying to scoot herself and Angelita as far under the plane as she could.

It was the last thing she rememered.

What the hell! Wolf thought. The instant the doc hit the ground he'd had the door of the plane open and was all ready to open fire, and then the whole damn world had exploded! Bullets flying everywhere! He'd done the only thing he could—he'd pulled the door shut and hit the deck. He could hear bullets slamming into the plane—he hoped to God the owner had insurance! The side of his face felt hot, as if someone had slapped him hard; he touched it with his fingers, felt a warm stickiness and began to swear. What in the hell was going on?

And where was Doc?

The second the shooting stopped, Wolf had the door of the plane open, scrambling, half falling in his haste to get out, to get to the doc. He didn't even have to glance at what was left of the Cruz brothers to know they weren't going to be anybody's problem anymore. He thought vaguely that he should have some sort of feelings about that, but he didn't. The only thing that mattered—the *only* thing—was finding Doc and the little one. Finding them alive. God help him— God help the idiots who'd opened fire—if anything had happened to the doc.

When he saw her lying on the ground underneath the plane, when he saw the blood, it was as if there'd been an earthquake inside him. The world tilted and grew dark.

Doc. He didn't hear himself call her name—it might only have been in his mind. He was on his belly, crawling to her, reaching for her, thinking that if he ever got his hands on her, and if she was still breathing, he'd never let go of her again. Or the little one, either.

Angelita was screaming her head off, nothing wrong with her, that was for sure! But Terry was so still. And yet he couldn't see any blood, except for her leg, and a little tiny bit on her hair. He felt for her, touched her, then put his head down on his arm, suddenly weak and cold with shock and relief. She was breathing. She must have hit her head on the landing gear and knocked herself out cold, but she was alive. *Alive!*

And then, while he was still lying there shaking like a leaf and trying to get enough strength in his arms and legs to crawl out from under the plane and find out what in the hell was going on, Wolf heard the scrape of leather shoes on hard-packed dirt. An icy trickle of warning crawled down his spine, but he didn't have enough strength left in him to react. Lifting his head slowly, squinting in the glare, he focused his eyes on a pair of immaculate white trouser legs. Followed them upward, blearily registering the silver-white jacket, silver belt buckle, dainty hands... and a sapphire ring, winking in the sunlight.

"Navarro..." Wolf croaked.

The barrel chest shook; the impassive Mayan mask split to reveal small white teeth. There was a sound like blowing sand, and then something clattered onto the ground a few inches from Wolf's nose. A handful of poker chips.

"My game, Mr. Wolf," Juan Navarro said.

He turned. His two bodyguards fell into place behind him, their Uzis slung over their shoulders. All three walked away unhurried down the long shimmering runway, disappearing finally in the heat waves, like a mirage.

The first thing Terry became aware of was the noise. Angelita was yelling her head off. The baby was hungry— needed to be fed. She struggled to sit up, but something, someone, was keeping her back, holding her down. Then she remembered. The Cruz brothers! Bernie had Angelita, he was doing something to her, smothering her. She had to stop him!

"Easy, *easy!*" a voice growled in her ear. "She's okay, I've got her. *Geez,* Doc—calm down!"

"Jack?" It was a startling sound, not at all like her voice, high and quavering. She stopped fighting and let her head fall back, and realized then that it was resting in someone's lap. Jack's lap. Slowly, the rest of him swam into focus. There was Angelita, squirming and wailing in his arms, and his face, dark and bloody. "You're hurt," she said clearly, struggling again.

"Just a scratch." His voice sounded funny, too. Rough and garbled. "You're the one that's hurt, dummy—you've got a bump on your head the size of a golf ball, and you've been shot in the leg. You're bleeding—I've gotta get you out from under there—get you to a doctor. Dammit, Doc—"

"*I'm* the doctor," she said faintly, frowning at him. At least it explained the way she felt, the pain, the nausea. But that didn't seem important. All she could see was Jack's face, his wonderful, dear, rough and rugged face. She reached up with shaking fingers to touch the blood on his cheek. "Don't go away," she said thickly. "Don't you dare leave me . . ."

"I won't, Doc. I'm stayin' right here."

"No, I don't mean here. I mean ever. I don't care if you're a gambler—"

"Doc—"

"—or a black sheep. Just because I love you doesn't mean—"

"Doc, will you for once just shut up and listen to me? I'm not going—" He made a choking sound and stared down at her with a hard, hungry look. "What did you say?"

"I'm not my mother," she said earnestly, trying with a kind of desperation to make him understand.

And miraculously, it seemed that he did. A smile spread across his bloody face, a beautiful smile, the most beautiful smile she'd ever seen. He lifted her and pressed her face into the hollow of his neck. Rocking her a little, laying his cheek against her forehead, he whispered, "I know you're not, Doc. It's going to be okay. I promise it is. Hey—I'm going to tell you something my dad always says, every time his and my mom's anniversary rolls around."

"What?" she gasped, fighting the pain, fighting to stay awake.

She felt something warm and wet soak into her hair like a blessing, and heard Jack's ragged whisper. "Wolves mate for life."

She began to cry, then, and his name became a sob. "Jack—"

"Shh . . . it's okay. I think somebody's coming, finally. It's sure taken them long enough—"

Urgently, she broke into his swearing. "Jack—Angelita!"

"It's okay, she's right here."

"I want her—"

"Shh, she's fine, I've got her."

"No, I mean—I want to *keep* her."

"Okay, Doc, we'll keep her. Don't worry about anything, okay? Just hang on—"

"Jack?" The pain was intense, the blackness closing in. But there was one more thing she had to know. "The Cruz brothers?"

"Dead. Both of them."

"Then it's over? Really over?"

"Yeah," Wolf breathed, "it's really over." Then he pulled her tightly against him, her and the little one. "Hell no, it's not over," he heard himself croak. "It's just beginning, Doc. Just beginning..."

It wasn't a bad little church, Wolf thought, as churches went. Although of course, he couldn't really consider himself an expert on churches; it had been quite a few years since he'd spent much time in one. This particular church had gone a little overboard on gold-painted angels and plaster-of-paris saints, but then, this was Tijuana. Here it looked all right, somehow.

And besides, he'd almost swear that angel right above the baptismal font was winking at him.

"Okay, let's see, who do we have here?" the priest said. He was wearing white robes, and spoke in perfect though heavily accented English. "This is..."

"Angelita," Terry said in a soft, breathless voice. She looked over at Wolf, and he gave her a nod of encouragement. She'd thrown away her crutches only that morning, bound and determined to carry the little one for her christening. "Her name is Angelita Teresa."

"Ah—yes. And you are the godparents?"

"No—the parents," Wolf said firmly, ignoring the doc's elbow in his ribs. After all, it was only a small, temporary lie. The ball was already rolling—or the steamroller was. A steamroller named Dr. Terry Duncan. These last few weeks, while he'd been busy talking to the DEA and various Mexican authorities, closing the book once and for all on the Frank Wolf murder case, she'd been busy, too, filling out forms and signing papers and meeting with lawyers and immigration people. There were still a few things to take care of, but that was just red tape. As far as Wolf was concerned, Angelita was already theirs—his and Doc's.

"Where are the godparents?" the priest said. "Do we have—"

"Right here," Ingrid announced, hauling Carl Wahlberg along by the arm. "We're the godparents."

"Okay..." The priest made a note of that, then looked around and said, "Well, we seem to have everyone. Will you all come closer, please, and we will begin. Oh—I am sorry." He paused and looked down at the small brown hand that was tugging urgently on his robes. "Well," he said somberly, "I seem to have missed someone. And who is this young man?"

Julio shrank back against Wolf's knees, suddenly overcome with shyness.

Wolf put both hands on Julio's shoulders and gave them a reassuring squeeze. "This is Julio," he said. The boy looked up at him and grinned, showing his dimples. Wolf grinned back at him. *"El hermano grande.* The big brother."

Julio proudly nodded confirmation, then turned to wave at the thin, quiet man who stood alone at the back of the church, his Sunday-best shirt buttoned to his chin, a straw hat clutched tightly in work-worn hands. Mr. Yberra had come that morning to attend his daughter's christening, and to sign the final papers that would give her away.

"All right, then," the priest said. "Come forward, please. Godparents here, parents...there. And big brother right here in front—okay?"

Julio nodded enthusiastically. He sidled up next to the doc and reached up to touch Angelita's white christening gown. Wolf moved in closer to her, too, and put his arm around her waist. She looked at him and smiled. He saw her mouth the words he'd been seeing in her eyes for weeks now.

I love you.

Boy, he thought, when Lady Luck—or Somebody Else—decided to smile on him, She really did a good job of it!

He looked at the doc's flame-red head so close to him, and at the one corkscrew curl that was hanging over her shoulder and getting mixed up with Angelita's tuft of straight black hair.

Saints and angels.

He looked up at the plaster-of-paris angel above the baptismal font—the one who was winking at him.

Yeah, he thought, taking a deep, deep breath, letting happiness pour through him like a warm Baja sunshine. It wasn't a bad little church. Might be a nice place for a wedding....

He wondered how Doc would feel about it.

I wonder how he feels about all this, Terry thought.

She smiled to herself and pressed her lips gently to Angelita's downy head, breathing in the clean-baby smell, thinking about the secret she'd been carrying around for several days now. The sweet, wonderful, terrifying secret....

I wonder how he'll feel about becoming a father... what kind of father he'll be?

A little thrill of joy, excitement and fear rippled through her. *What kind of mother will I be?*

She wasn't worried about Jack anymore, or her own judgment, either. Wolves mate for life, wasn't that what he'd said? She'd even read somewhere that wolves are loving parents, too. And now that she'd met the plump, gray-haired couple holding hands there in the front pew, she believed it.

She wondered how Jack would feel about getting married. This little church wouldn't be a bad place for it—just a small wedding, with Jack's parents, Ingrid and Carl, and Angelita, of course.

She looked over at him—and saw the answer in his eyes, shining all over his face, bathing her in warmth and love. She didn't have to ask how he felt about it. She could read him like a book.

*   *   *   *   *

NORA ROBERTS

Love has a language all its own, and for centuries, flowers have symbolized love's finest expression. Discover the language of flowers—and love—in this romantic collection of 48 favorite books by bestselling author Nora Roberts.

Starting in February, two titles will be available each month at your favorite retail outlet.

In February, look for:

Irish Thoroughbred, Volume #1
The Law Is A Lady, Volume #2

In March, look for:

Irish Rose, Volume #3
Storm Warning, Volume #4

Collect all 48 titles and become fluent in

THE LANGUAGE of LOVE

Silhouette Special Edition

is pleased to present

A GOOD MAN WALKS IN
by Ginna Gray

The story of one strong woman's comeback
and the man who was there for her, Travis McCall,
the renegade cousin to those Blaine siblings,
from Ginna Gray's bestselling trio

FOOLS RUSH IN (#416)
WHERE ANGELS FEAR (#468)
ONCE IN A LIFETIME (#661)

Rebecca Quinn sought shelter at the hideaway on Rincon
Island. Finding Travis McCall—the object of all her childhood
crushes—holed up in the same house threatened to ruin the
respite she so desperately needed. Until their first kiss . . .
Then Travis set out to prove to his lovely Rebecca that man
can be good and love, sublime.

You'll want to be there when Rebecca's disillusionment turns
to joy.

A GOOD MAN WALKS IN #722

Available at your favorite retail outlet this February.

Take 4 bestselling love stories FREE

Plus get a FREE surprise gift!

From the popular author of the bestselling title
DUNCAN'S BRIDE (Intimate Moments #349)
comes the

LINDA HOWARD

COLLECTION

Two exquisite collector's editions that contain four of
Linda Howard's early passionate love stories. To add
these special volumes to your own library, be sure
to look for:

VOLUME ONE: *Midnight Rainbow*
Diamond Bay
(Available in March)

VOLUME TWO: *Heartbreaker*
White Lies
(Available in April)

Silhouette Books®

SLH92